25 (3-95)2

THE HOLY INNOCENTS

THE HOLY
INNOCENTS

Kate Sedley

St. Martin's Press
New York

M

Library of Congress Cataloging-in-Publication Data

Sedley, Kate.
The holy innocents / Kate Sedley.
p.   cm.
ISBN 0-312-11823-6
1. Great Britain—History—Wars of the Roses, 1455–1485—
Fiction.   I. Title.
PR6069.E323H65   1995
823′.914—dc20   94-38167   CIP

First published in Great Britain by Headline

First U.S. Edition: February 1995
10 9 8 7 6 5 4 3 2 1

THE HOLY INNOCENTS

Chapter One

I saw them before they saw me, and so was able to step aside into the shadow of the trees which crowded down to the water's edge on either bank of the River Harbourne. It was barely dawn, and a cold, clinging, grey mist, filtering through interlaced branches of oak and alder, ash and beech, helped my presence to remain undetected as the robbers approached.

They walked in single file, their feet making no sound on the thick carpet of last year's leaves, sodden now with the rains of early April. Once, there was a crackle of beechmast and the snap of a twig as someone stepped carelessly, only to be reprimanded instantly by an angry hiss from his companions. By now, I could smell them, the mixed scent of damp and sweat and dirt emanating from their clothes, and I stealthily withdrew yet deeper into the shelter of the bushes, putting a brake of holly and stunted elder between myself and these desperate men; for one glimpse had been enough to assure me that they were outlaws, wolf-heads, living rough in the forests of south Devon.

As the leader drew abreast of my hiding-place, a shaft of watery sunlight pierced the overhanging canopy of trees, illuminating a narrow, weasel-like face and a back bent almost double by the weight of a sack slung across one shoulder. His

1

night's booty plainly included animals from some outlying farm, judging by the blood which dripped from the coarsely woven fabric and spread in a dark stain across the mesh. The next man also carried a bulging sack, although its bumps and protrusions gave no clue in this case as to what it might contain. The third outlaw had not bothered, or had been in too great a hurry, to tie the neck of his bag securely and it had burst open to reveal its contents, a crop of vegetables from plundered gardens and smallholdings. The fourth villain held a live and struggling hen beneath one arm, its beak tied with a strip of filthy cloth in order to muffle its hysterical clucking. At that moment, however, the sunlight faded, and the rest of the ragamuffin procession became nothing more than shadows as they followed each other along the track, carved through the undergrowth by the passage of many feet. I counted ten of them in all, a band of cut-throats who were obviously terrorizing the districts about the township of Totnes. That they were desperate men, prepared to stop at nothing, not even murder, was attested to by the wicked-looking array of knives and daggers which they wore in their belts. I had no doubt that any one of them would kill as much for pleasure as for gain, and would have no compunction whatsoever in despatching any poor soul unfortunate enough to fall in their way. As for myself, a chapman carrying money as well as goods about his person, I should have been a dead man had they chanced to clap eyes upon me.

Long after the final robber had passed from my line of vision, I stood quietly, hardly daring to breathe, lest some straggler should yet be hurrying to catch up his evil brethren. I was conscious of the deep quiet of the woods, of the pillared trees and thickets of bramble stretching down to the river's edge, the sliding sparkle of water showing where the

Harbourne lapped placidly over its stony bed. Satisfied at last that the outlaws must be well out of hailing distance, and offering up thanks to the Virgin for my deliverance, I stepped down once more on to the track and resumed my journey. For, provided he could not call upon the aid of his fellows, the possibility of a man on his own did not trouble me. My height and girth, as readers of my previous chronicles will know, was sufficient in those days to assure me of victory in any hand-to-hand combat.

I had been on the road now for at least two months, making my way south from Bristol, which, after the events of the past year, had become my home. I had spent the winter in the cottage of my mother-in-law, Margaret Walker, venturing out to sell my wares only as far as the surrounding villages during the months of frost and snow, and trying to console her in some measure for the loss of my wife, her only child. In this, I was greatly helped by the existence of Elizabeth, my baby daughter, whose birth had caused her mother's untimely death. My deepest regret, which still remains with me even to this day, when I am an old man of seventy, was that I could feel so little grief for Lillis. But I had known her for less than a year when she died. I had not been looking to settle, but circumstances had forced me into marriage; and had God not decided, in His wisdom, to take her from me, it is possible that we might have been happy together, although somehow I doubt it. Lillis was too possessive, and I too anxious to get back on the open road once the lighter nights and longer days of spring approached, for us to have achieved much domestic harmony.

My mother-in-law was far more willing to accept me for what I was; and although she made no secret of the fact that she would have liked me to stay in Bristol and help with the rearing of the child, she did not attempt to stop me when, well before Easter, I announced my intended departure.

'I shall return before winter is far advanced,' I told her, kissing her weather-beaten cheek and humping my pack on to my shoulders. 'Look after Elizabeth for me.'

She nodded, and I salved my uneasy conscience by leaving her sufficient money to ensure her independence from the spinning which was her trade, did she so wish it. She came to the cottage door and watched me as I set off in the direction of the Redcliffe Gate, but even with her eyes upon me, I was unable to keep the spring from my step which the prospect of freedom gave me.

I walked south, selling my wares in the coastal villages and hamlets of Somerset and Devon, where I did a roaring trade, the inhabitants being starved of visitors and news throughout the long months of winter. I was treated royally, as befitted one of their earliest harbingers of spring, and was offered many a free meal and bed out of gratitude. In return, I gave them such gossip concerning their neighbours as I had managed to glean during my travels, and was able to inform them of the rumours which had reached Bristol just before I left: King Edward was cajoling money from a reluctant Parliament and mustering his forces in order to mount an invasion of France. Finally, I turned inland, across the wastes of Dartmoor and so down into the lush peninsula which lies south and east of Plymouth. The Hams our Saxon forebears called it, a countryside which, with its luminous fairy uplands and mysteriously shadowed dales, must surely be the equal of anything to be found in the whole of Christendom. And so, by slow degrees, I reached the cluster of houses at the mouth of the Dart, then followed the river's southern bank until I reached Bow Creek and the Dart's tributary, the

Harbourne, where I did good business among the wives and daughters of Tuckenhay, an isolated settlement, as anxious for news as everywhere else on my journey.

The next day being Sunday, I had rested, spending an unexpectedly warm night out of doors and rising before dawn to swill my face and hands in the crystal clear water of the Harbourne. Somewhere far above me, glimpsed between the boughs of the trees, the last star burned, blue-white like frost, before it, too, began to fade with the advent of the light. And the first, muted strains of birdsong had just fallen on my ears when I espied the band of outlaws, treading softly, coming along the track towards me.

I was hungry by the time I reached Bow Bridge, so I sat down by the water's edge, lowered my pack to the ground and took out the lump of wheaten bread and slab of goat's-milk cheese given me by one of the Tuckenhay women for the previous day's supper. The portions had been generous, so I had prudently saved some for the morning, knowing how empty my stomach always felt on waking. On the opposite side of the river, the woods rose steeply, promising a hard climb, so, having finished eating, I lay back on the turf and closed my eyes for a few minutes; or, at least, that was all I intended. By the time I opened them again, however, the sun was well above the horizon, its rays spreading outwards in a shallow saucer of light which foretold another warm day, like the one before. A man, crossing the bridge, an axe resting on one shoulder, grinned and gave me 'good-day'. He was shortly followed by others, the first carrying a billhook and the second swinging a spade from one sinewy hand. I was reminded that, it now being April, there was much work to be done in the woods; felling timber before the ground became too soft for the carters to cart it away, stripping bark for the tanyards and replanting saplings.

I scrambled to my feet and hailed the last man, who waited, a trifle impatiently I thought, while I picked up my pack and approached him. Nevertheless, his smile was good-humoured enough until I mentioned the outlaws.

'Oh, aye!' he exclaimed bitterly. 'We know all about them. Been terrorizing these parts for months past, they have. The Sheriff and his *posse* have been searching for 'em since well afore Christmas, but with no success. They hunt by night and go to ground in the daytime. They've bolt-holes impossible to find unless you know every inch of the forests. Which no one does, o' course. Our enclosures are mainly within a mile or two of the edge. I wonder whose farms and holdings they raided last night, then, the devils!'

'Is it impossible to mount guard at night?' I asked, and he shrugged.

'A few foolhardy fellows've tried that, Maister, but there's too many of the outlaws and they're murderin' bastards. One man who challenged 'em was run through with his own pitch-fork and another had an arm lopped off. Worse than that, they killed a couple o' children. Since then, we all bury our heads under the blankets at night and hope that if our property's attacked, we don't hear 'em. Better to be robbed of all you have and live to tell the tale, rather than be a dead hero.'

I nodded agreement and said with forced cheerfulness, 'The law will catch up with them some day.'

The man grunted doubtfully. 'Maybe. More like they'll move on to another part of the county and disappear as suddenly as they arrived. It's understandable, I suppose. No member of the *posse* wants to risk his life unnecessarily, and these rogues have no compunction when it comes to killing.

You were wiser than you knew not to tangle with 'em. They'd've made minced meat even of a great fellow like you. But if you're headed for the town, you can report what you saw to one of the wardens, who'll tell the Mayor, who'll pass the information on to the Sheriff. That way, you'll've done your duty.'

'I'll do that,' I promised and wished him good morning. I was halfway across the bridge, when he called after me.

'Chapman!' I turned enquiringly. The woodsman was grinning. 'Be warned! The women of the villages hereabouts are out in force today.' I must have looked confused, because he added impatiently, 'It's Hock Monday!'

Was it indeed already two weeks since Easter? I seemed to have lost track of time. I raised my hand. 'Thanks for the warning, friend. I'll be careful. Have you been caught already?'

He shook his head. 'I came the long way round, but there won't be any avoiding 'em by now. They all rise early for hocking. Dessay I'll be caught myself by nightfall.' But he spoke cheerfully, as one looking forward to his ordeal.

'Ah well,' I answered, 'you and the rest of the men can get your own back tomorrow.'

The woodsman's eyes gleamed predatorily as he said goodbye. 'Can't stand here talking all day. There's work to be done. I'll wish you good luck at the hands of the women.' He winked. 'They won't let a good-looking young fellow like you go easily once they trap you. I can guess what sort of forfeit they'll demand from you!' And he disappeared amongst the trees, roaring with laughter.

The sun was by now quite hot, presaging one of those April days which can often prove to be warmer than those of high summer, so capricious is the weather of this island. I toiled

7

up the slope ahead of me, the trees gradually thinning and falling away on either side of the track until only one or two bordered the rutted pathway. I had refilled my pack from a cargo ship lying in the roads at Dartmouth, and in consequence was weighed down by my load, head bent forward, not looking where I was going. All my attention was concentrated upon my feet, making sure that I did not trip or twist my ankle. I had the assistance of a stout cudgel, my trusty 'Plymouth cloak', as such weapons were called in this part of the country, so I was able to make the ascent without too much trouble. Nevertheless, I was tired as I crested the rise and off my guard...

Something caught me across my shins and sent me sprawling, face downwards in the dirt. For a moment or two, I lay there, winded, trying to gather my wits and figure out what had happened to me. Before I could do so, however, there were shouts of laughter and I found myself surrounded by three or four women. From my prone position, all I could see at that moment was the hems of their skirts and their shoes. I dragged myself to my knees, painfully aware of cutting a ridiculous figure and, as a result, seething with anger. I had been hocked and must now pay a forfeit. I slipped the pack from my shoulders and rose, drawing myself up to my full height, which in those days, before rheumatic pains caused me to stoop a little, was over six feet. It was a great height, even more so then than it is today, when young people have grown much taller, and few men I ever met could equal me in stature. (One exception, of course, was King Edward, that golden giant, grandfather of our present Henry.)

I heard one of the younger women draw in her breath in wonder, while the eldest of the group, a toothless granny, cackled with laughter.

'God save us! It's Goliath himself come amongst us. Right, Master Chapman, you knows the rules. You've to pay a forfeit.'

The women, some half-dozen of them, had by now formed a circle around me. The rope which had been tied between two trees, one on either side of the track, and used to bring me down, was removed and bound lightly about my wrists.

'There's plenty of stuff in my pack,' I said hurriedly. 'Needles, thread, ribbons, lace and a length of silk brocade from the hold of a Portuguese merchantman, lying off Dartmouth. You may help yourselves.'

The old woman laughed again. 'These fine girls can buy those things, my honey, with the pin-money their goodmen do give them. But a splendid young fellow like you, why you've better things to offer.'

I felt the blood surge into my face, which seemed to afford all the women great amusement. I have often noticed throughout the course of my life, that whereas a single woman, on her own, will be all maidenly blushes and modesty, women hunting in a pack can be cruder and rougher than men. One who looked to be the youngest, an apple-cheeked lass of barely – or so I judged – fourteen or fifteen summers, giggled, 'Let's ask for the laces from his codpiece.'

My colour deepened even further and I took an instinctive step backward in order to protect my person, causing a storm of merriment from my captors.

'He's bashful!' exclaimed a pretty young girl with wide, cornflower-blue eyes and a strand of hair, the colour of ripe wheat, escaping from under her cap. 'A great lum-cock like that, and he's blushing!'

'Anything in my pack!' I offered again in desperation.

The granny wagged an ancient, admonitory finger. 'It's

Hocktide, chapman! You knows the rules as well as anyone. Men's turn to hock tomorrow, ours today. So if Janet here wishes the laces from your codpiece, she's within her rights.' She gave her toothless grin, plainly enjoying my discomfiture.

My tormentors began edging towards me, giggling and nudging one another in the ribs. I struggled to free my hands from the rope which bound my wrists behind my back, but discovered that although my bonds were lightly tied, they were nonetheless knotted fast. If I took to my heels, apart from breaking the rules and traditions of hocktide, I should have to abandon my pack and cudgel, which might then be considered the women's legitimate booty.

Suddenly, one of them, who so far had stood a little apart from the others, smiling but not joining in their more vociferous merriment, came to my rescue. She moved between me and her companions, spreading wide her arms to protect me.

'Enough!' she protested, laughing. 'Claim a forfeit and let the poor lad go! We've had our fun. Now, what's it to be? I think a kiss apiece would suffice, don't you agree? Granny Praule, in deference to your age, you can go first.'

There were cries of, 'Spoil sport, Grizelda!' but in general, the women seemed content with this solution. Granny Praule pressed her withered, dry lips to mine, and, in relief, I gave her a smacking kiss which evoked another cackle and a pat on the arm.

'My! My!' She gave a little skip. 'You're a good lad, Chapman! I haven't been kissed like that these thirty years! You've brought back memories of my youth I thought I'd forgotten. I was a pretty girl, though you might find it hard to believe nowadays. I had the men after me like bees round a honey-pot.'

The rest of the women stepped forward, one by one, to

claim their forfeit, some a little more boldly than the others, standing close to me as they placed the r mouths on mine. My rescuer, the woman they had addressed as Grizelda, was last, and at close range, I could see that she was not as young as most of her companions. I judged her to be some thirty summers; a handsome woman, with strong features and very dark brown eyes. Her complexion, too, was dark, and had she been a man I might have been tempted to think of her as swarthy, but her skin was too soft and delicate for that. In colouring, she reminded me of Lillis, so I knew, without seeing it, that the hair neatly concealed beneath the snow-white coif and blue linen hood was black. But there the resemblance ended. In physique, Grizelda was taller and much stronger than my dead wife. There was also a maturity about her, unmatched in Lillis, who, despite her twenty summers, had been childlike.

Two of the women, having unbound my wrists, proceeded to reset the trap for their next unwary victim, while the rest concealed themselves again amongst the bushes. All, that is, except Grizelda, who took her leave. When her friends protested, she laughed and shook her head.

'I have work to do. Cheese to make and the hen to feed. The poor creature's not been let out of her coop this morning, I was up and about so early.' She turned to me. 'Master Chapman, if you care to accompany me as far as my holding, I'll protect you from any further hockers you might meet, and tell them that you've already paid your forfeit. My name,' she added, 'is Grizelda Harbourne.'

'I'm called Roger,' I answered, 'and I accept your offer very willingly. I shouldn't care to fall into the hands of any of your sister hockers if they are anything like you and your companions.'

There were shrieks of delight at this compliment before they were shushed by the youngest of the group – Janet by name, if I remembered rightly – with the information that another man was ascending the path. Hastily, I shouldered my pack and offered Grizelda Harbourne my arm.

We skirted the tiny village of Ashprington and traversed a belt of trees, arriving finally at a clearing. Here, a low, one-storey cottage was set in the middle of a smallholding which consisted of a plot for growing a little corn and a few vegetables, a hen-coop, a pig-sty and a field where a cow was grazing. The cottage itself was furnished with a table on a pair of trestles, two benches, one covered with a piece of tapestry, which were ranged against the walls, and a central hearth surrounded by all the necessary impedimenta of cooking. At one end of the room, another piece of tapestry, faded and darned, imperfectly concealed a bed, the foot of which protruded some inches beyond the curtain.

I felt a stab of surprise as, invited in by Grizelda, I stepped across the threshold. There was no reason for my astonishment; the cottage was typical of its kind and no more than I should normally have expected to find on any smallholding. But there was something about my hostess, her bearing, her tone of command when speaking to the other women, the slightly disdainful glance she cast around her present home, which suggested to me that she had known better times, been used to more gracious surroundings.

'Have you eaten?' she asked, waving me to one of the benches against the wall.

'I had some bread and cheese an hour or more ago, down by the river. Food left over from last night's supper.'

She smiled understandingly. 'Not enough for a great frame like yours. If you can wait awhile, I'll give you breakfast.

There's ale and bread and some salted bacon, or I can cook you a mess of eggs, if you'd prefer it.'

'The eggs would make a welcome change,' I said. 'Could you also spare me a pot of hot water to shave with?'

She nodded. 'There's water heating in the cauldron over the fire.' She reached down an iron pot with a handle from a shelf. 'Here, use this. And while you shave, I'll collect the eggs and free the poor bird from her coop.'

She went out, and I took the razor from my pack, looking for something with which to sharpen it. Then I noticed a leather strop hanging from a hook behind the door. I wondered who it belonged to, for there was no other sign of a man's presence in the cottage. I dipped the iron pot in the seething water, lathered my chin with a piece of the cheap black soap which I always carried with me, and began to scrape off the night's growth of stubble. I had hardly begun before Grizelda reappeared in the doorway.

She extended both hands. 'Well, here are the eggs,' she said, 'but there's no sign of the hen. The door of the coop has been forced and there are feathers on the ground. I'm afraid she's been stolen.'

Chapter Two

I hurriedly finished shaving, then followed Grizelda outside to the coop, where I knelt down to examine it more closely. She was right: the wooden latch had been forced and there was a drift of white feathers lying close by. I glanced up at the cow, placidly grazing, then at the pig, snorting and rootling in its sty.

'You may count yourself very fortunate, Mistress Harbourne,' I said, 'that only the hen was taken. They must have stumbled upon your holding during the return journey, when time and their capacity to carry anything more was limited. Otherwise, you would have lost your other animals as well.'

'They?' Grizelda frowned. 'Who are "they", Master Chapman?'

'Why, the outlaws who, I understand, have been terrorizing this district for some months past. Surely, living as you do in these parts, you can't be ignorant of their depredations?'

She turned very pale and raised one hand to her heart, as though to still its beating. Her eyes dilated.

'The robbers, you mean! The idea had not occurred to me. I assumed it was some local thief – largely, I suppose, because there is no other damage apart from the theft of Félice. I

15

know of these men, of course, but they slaughter cattle, root up whole plantations.' She drew a long, shuddering breath. 'They even do murder. But none of that has happened here. Only my poor little hen has been stolen. Why should you think them responsible for the theft?'

Briefly, I told her of my encounter with the outlaws earlier that morning. 'And one of them was carrying a hen under his arm, her beak tied to keep her from squawking.'

Grizelda blinked back tears. 'Will they kill her?'

I straightened up, stretching my cramped legs, and smiled reassuringly. 'I shouldn't think so. If that had been their intention, they would have wrung her neck before carrying her off. They would never have gone to the trouble of muffling her. They have taken her as a layer. Outlaws, I presume, enjoy eggs as well as their more law-abiding brothers.' I glanced round me yet again, at the little clearing, bright with spring grass, surrounded by the shadowy trees. 'I repeat, you were extremely lucky. They must have come across your cottage when they were already laden down with booty. They probably heard the hen clucking and decided to take her on the spur of the moment. I'm sorry. You'll miss her.'

Grizelda nodded slowly. 'Félice was not only a companion, but also a source of livelihood. I was able to sell her eggs in Totnes market and the scrapings from the coop to the washerwomen of the town for bleach. Bird droppings help make an excellent lye, as you probably know.' Her worried gaze met mine, and she shivered. 'I can't believe those devils were here, prowling around my cottage, while I slept in ignorance inside. It makes my flesh crawl to think of it.'

I hesitated, unwilling to commit myself, but at the same time racked with guilt at the thought of her sleeping here alone. Having once stumbled upon her holding, it was probable that the outlaws would return to steal the cow and pig they had been forced to leave behind. Reluctantly, I said, 'I propose selling my wares in Totnes today, but I can return at sundown, should you wish it. If you can provide me with bracken and a blanket, I shall be comfortable on the floor. It's what I'm used to.'

A smile lifted the corners of her mouth, and she touched me fleetingly on the arm.

'You're very kind, Master Chapman, but I have no need to impose upon you. I have a friend in Ashprington. She and her goodman will give me and the animals shelter if I ask it.'

I breathed a silent sigh of relief, then caught the mocking look of understanding in those deep brown eyes. Flushing slightly, I urged, 'Let me beg you to do so, for tonight at least, and for some nights to come, if they can shelter you.'

'I shall visit my friend as soon as you have left. Now, let me get you your breakfast. We have the last eggs Félice laid before she was taken.' Her voice trembled, and she turned abruptly on her heel, moving in the direction of the cottage.

I was about to follow her, but suddenly stood rooted to the spot. Had I been a dog, my hackles would have risen. Grizelda, pausing to look over her shoulder, called, 'What's the matter?' When I did not reply, she retraced her steps a little. 'What is it?' she insisted.

For answer, I shook my head, waving her to silence and scanning the encircling trees, but, except for the distant drilling of a woodpecker, all was still and silent. Cautiously, I advanced to the edge of that pillared darkness and padded between the ivy-covered trunks, some with yawning holes wide enough for owls to nest in . . . Then, from the corner of one eye, I detected a flash of movement and spun about to meet it, cursing that I did not have my cudgel with me. It was in the cottage, where I had abandoned it when Grizelda and I went out to inspect the hen-coop.

The scarecrow figure who came at me had a knife. I saw the bright flash of the blade as he raised it, ready to strike. Grizelda, who had come running, screamed at the sight of it, fortunately deflecting my adversary's attention and giving me that necessary moment's grace in which to grab his wrist in a crushing grip, before twisting his arm up behind him. The man yelped with pain and dropped his knife from fingers which suddenly had no feeling. I let him go, stooping quickly to obtain possession of the weapon before he could retrieve it. Then, while he was still nursing his injured wrist, I put one arm in a stranglehold about his neck, pinioning him with the other clasped around his body.

'Run back to the cottage and get something to tie him up with,' I commanded Grizelda.

She did not move, however. 'I know this man,' she said. 'He's not one of the outlaws, if that is what you're thinking. His name is Innes Woodsman, and he's slept rough in the woods around here for a number of years. When my father was alive, he did occasional jobs about the holding for his meals and shelter in the wintertime. Let him go, Chapman. He's harmless.'

'No man is harmless who carries a knife such as this.' And with a jerk of my head, I indicated the wicked-looking blade which I had tucked into my belt.

Grizelda raised a determined chin. 'All the same, I owe him a favour. I should be grateful if you would turn him loose and say nothing to anyone of this incident.' She added a shade defiantly, 'To please me.'

I released my prisoner with great reluctance. 'Very well, to please you,' I agreed. 'But I'm keeping the knife. He's too ready to use it on strangers.'

Innes Woodsman spoke abruptly, in a vicious, rasping voice. 'It's my hunting knife. I need it for killing rabbits and the like.'

I eyed him with abhorrence. The strong sense of evil, which had alerted me to his presence, remained with me and refused to be shaken off.

'If it's a hunting knife, why did you try to kill me with it?'

The narrow, weather-beaten face took on a shifty look and he made no answer. Grizelda said quietly, 'He probably thought it was me. Oh, he wouldn't really have harmed me,' she added swiftly, in explanation. 'He intended giving me a fright, that's all. He bears me a grudge.'

I was appalled. 'And you're willing to let him go? The rogue should be handed over to the Sheriff and clapped in gaol.'

'No,' she answered firmly. 'He has some reason for his resentment. It would be unjust to imprison him.' She looked straitly at the woodsman. 'This is your last chance for clemency, Innes. My patience is wearing thin. If you don't go away from here and leave me alone, I shall take Master Chapman's advice and lay a complaint against you.' She tilted her head to one side and, as a shaft of sunlight struck between the branches of the trees, I saw something which, surprisingly, I had not noticed before; the faint, white puckering of a long-healed scar, running from her right eyebrow halfway down her cheek. She went on, 'I suppose it wasn't you who stole my hen, Félice?'

Innes Woodsman spat viciously. 'I wouldn't touch that scrawny bird if you paid me.'

Grizelda nodded. 'Very well, I believe you. But remember what I've said and go away from here or I'll carry out my threat. I mean it.'

'I'm not going without my knife,' he answered sullenly.

She turned to me. 'Give it to him, please, Chapman. He

needs it to survive.' I complied, but with the greatest misgivings. She smiled her thanks and, when the man had sloped
out of sight amongst the trees, took my arm and squeezed it.
'Now, let's return to the cottage and I'll cook you those eggs.'

I cleared my plate and scraped up the remains with a crust
of black bread. The eggs, beaten and thickened over the fire,
had tasted delicious, flavoured with the fat from a small lump
of bacon. Grizelda, seated beside me on a bench I had dragged up to the table, pushed a plate of oatcakes and a crock
of honey towards me.

'Now that you've blunted the edge of your appetite, let
me ask you a question. How did you know that Innes was
there, in the woods? I'm sure you could neither have heard
nor seen him from where you were standing, alongside the
coop.'

I spread honey, thick and golden, on an oatcake and bit
into it before replying. 'I . . . I had a sensation of evil somewhere close at hand.'

I half expected her to eye me askance, but she didn't. 'You
have the sight?' she asked me.

I took another bite of oatcake, wiping the honey from my
chin with the back of my hand, and glanced furtively towards
the open doorway, as though I were afraid someone might
be outside, listening. I lowered my voice.

'Not truly, no; but now and then, I have dreams, and, on
occasions such as this morning, a sense of being threatened.
You don't find that . . . heretical?'

She shook her head. 'I don't have the gift myself, but my
mother did, a little. She kept it a secret from everyone but
me, for fear that she might be branded a witch.'

There was silence for a moment or two while I munched

my way through yet another oatcake. When I had swallowed the final crumb, I said, 'Now it's my turn to pose a question. What grudge does that villain hold against you?'

I thought for a moment that she might refuse to answer, or tell me that it was none of my business; that breaking bread with her did not give me the right to pry into her affairs. I believe, indeed, that she did momentarily entertain the notion, for she closed her lips tightly and shot me a speculative glance from beneath lowered lids. But almost immediately, she relented, opened her eyes wide and smiled.

'When my father died five years ago, I allowed Innes Woodsman, somewhat against my better judgement, to live here, in return for his work about the holding. As I told you, he had helped my father in his latter years and knew the running of the place. I had not lived here myself since my ninth birthday, shortly after the death of my mother. Understandably, I suppose, Innes thought himself well set up for the rest of his days, and, indeed, I should probably have left him here, undisturbed, if only because I was too lazy to dispose of the property.' She took an oatcake from the dish and began to nibble it, absent-mindedly, her face grown suddenly sombre. 'At least ... Perhaps that was true for a while, but of latter years ...'

Her voice tailed away into silence, and she stared past me, lost in thought, lost to her surroundings.

'Of latter years?' I prompted, when my curiosity could no longer be contained.

Grizelda started. 'I'm sorry, Chapman, my wits were wool-gathering. What was I saying?'

'That you let Innes Woodsman stay here as tenant because you were at first too lazy to get rid of the holding, but that after that ... ?'

'Ah, yes. After that,' she added, deliberately lightening her tone, 'I think I must have experienced one of your premonitions, or something like. It was almost as if I knew that one day I should need to return here again.'

'Which you did.'

'Yes. Some three months since, it became necessary for me to do so.' The smile she gave me was palpably false, and the slight quaver in her voice indicated suppressed emotion. 'I had, therefore, to turn Innes Woodsman out, and I'm afraid that I did not do it very gently. I was not in a . . . a gentle mood at the time. He found himself forced once more to sleep rough, bereft of the shelter he had come to take for granted.'

I could see that she felt guilty about what had happened and hastened to offer what comfort I could. Leaning my elbows on the table, I said, 'But the holding belongs to you, as it belonged to your father? It is not held in fief from some landlord?'

This time, her smile was genuine. 'Do I say yea or nay to that? Yes to your first question, no to your second.'

'Well, then!' I encouraged her. 'You were within your rights. There is nothing to blame yourself for.'

She shook her head, still smiling. 'As I said just now, I could have treated Innes with greater kindness, shown more consideration for his plight.' She rose from the bench to fetch me a mazer of ale from the barrel which stood in one corner.

'You are too severe on yourself,' I answered. 'There was nothing you could have said or done which would have made him less resentful. All in all, it was probably kinder to be blunt with him than try to sweeten the unpalatable.'

She laughed, returning to the table and setting the brimming mazer down in front of me. She did not resume her seat, but stood at the end of the table, watching me while I drank.

I was thirstier than I knew and drained the bowl in one go, wiping my mouth with the back of my hand. 'That's good ale,' I said, when I had finished.

Grizelda took the mazer to refill it. 'Oh, you'll get none of your inferior brews here, and no sallop, either.' She glanced disparagingly around her. 'This place may look what it is, Chapman, a hovel, but I've been used to better things.' Her tone was mocking, but also slightly bitter.

I replied gently: 'This is no hovel, believe me! I know. I've seen plenty on my travels.'

She made no answer, going to the door and looking out while I drank my second cup of ale. Seen in profile, she looked a little older than she did when face to face; but she was a handsome creature, for all that. I experienced the familiar stirring of attraction, but hastily suppressed it. I was too recently a widower to bed another woman, and felt that it would be a betrayal of Lillis's memory to do so too soon. Self-enforced continence was a sop to my conscience, but it did not prevent me from wanting Grizelda Harbourne.

Becoming aware of my scrutiny, she half-turned her head to look at me. After a moment, she came back to the table, smiling faintly, as though she had guessed my thoughts.

'I have to thank you, Chapman,' she said.

I shook my head. 'I've done nothing,' I protested. 'I would have done more, had you allowed me to have my way. I would have had Innes Woodsman in custody by now, in the castle gaol.'

'I didn't mean that.' She fidgeted with the fringed ends of the leather girdle about her waist. 'I know I must have said things which have aroused your curiosity, but you have curbed the desire to ask questions, and it's for that that I'm grateful. Mine has not been an easy life. There have been events . . .' Here, her voice became suspended by emotion, and it was a

23

while before she was able to go on. But at last, she had sufficient command over herself to continue, 'There have been events which I find it too painful to discuss. And recent months have been the blackest of all.'

She had grown extremely pale, and for a moment, I was afraid that she might faint. I rose quickly to my feet, ready to support her if she fell, but my assistance was unnecessary. She recovered herself almost immediately, blushing for her weakness. As the tide of colour surged up beneath her skin, I noticed again the scar on the right side of her face, the thin, white line running from eyebrow to cheek. Conscious of the direction of my gaze, she put up a hand to touch it.

'I fell out of a tree as a child, cutting my face open on a branch as I did so. Such a trivial accident for which to bear so permanent a reminder.'

'You could have broken your neck,' I said. 'I wouldn't call that trivial.'

She shrugged. 'I was young, not above thirteen summers, and you fall easily at that age. Bones are greener. But you're right. I could have suffered more hurt than I did. However, all I have to show for my carelessness is the scar, and that, I flatter myself, is not too noticeable.'

'No, indeed.' I regarded her admiringly. 'You are a handsome woman. You don't need me to tell you that. But, forgive me, why have you never married? I can't believe that the men of these parts are so blind that not one of them has asked you.'

She gave a deep, throaty laugh, not displeased by my temerity. But her tone was astringent as she answered, 'What dower do I have, Master Chapman? Who'd have me?'

'You have this holding, an attraction to many men I should have thought.'

I saw at once that I had offended her, and recollected her contempt for the place – her reference to it as a hovel – and her claim to have known 'better things'. I realized then that her aspirations in marriage would be equally lofty, and that she would be unwilling to settle for any cottar or woodsman; not even, perhaps, for a respectable tradesman. And failing any offer from a higher rank, she preferred dignified spinsterhood.

There were many things about Grizelda Harbourne that I still did not know, and many questions that I should have liked to ask her, but I had neither the time nor the right to do so. I turned and picked up my pack and my cudgel.

'I must be on my way,' I said. 'I've taken up too much of your time already and I want to be in Totnes well before dinner. But before I leave, I want your promise that you'll go to your friends in Ashprington and beg a bed for the next few nights. After what has happened, you shouldn't remain here on your own.'

'You really think me in danger of being robbed again?' When I nodded, she smiled resignedly. 'Very well. And to show my gratitude for your concern, I shall walk with you some of the way towards the town. There could still be hockers about the countryside. You are liable to be caught again.'

I laughed. 'And you don't think a great fellow like me capable of standing up for himself?'

'You did precious little standing up an hour or so ago,' Grizelda responded drily. 'And very uncomfortable you looked, sprawling there on the ground.' She added reflectively, 'Big lads such as you are often shy of women in any numbers. I've hocked many men in my time, and it's always the little fellows who are most at ease, giving as good as they get and enjoying each moment of the forfeit. Mark my words, when it's your turn to hock tomorrow, they'll be in the forefront of the gangs.'

I was disconcerted to discover that she could read me so well. It was true, I was inclined to be shy in the presence of younger women, but had hoped that I concealed the fact. I consoled myself with the thought that very few people were as percipient as Grizelda Harbourne, and that the circumstances under which we had met had been awkward ones for me.

I made one last effort to dissuade her from accompanying me, expressing concern that she must be tired, having risen so early. But she merely laughed and brushed aside my fears.

'I'm like my father,' she said, 'of strong constitution. Moreover, I enjoy walking, so it will be no penance to go with you a little way.'

Finding her so determined, I gave in with a good grace, and we set out together in the direction of Totnes. 'How will you manage without your hen?' I asked her.

'Buy eggs from my neighbours, or spend a few groats of my hard-earned savings to get myself another. But no bird will be able to replace my dear Félice.'

We encountered no more hockers, although once, in the distance, we heard sounds of merriment and women's voices shrieking with delight as some unwary man was caught in their toils. But where we were, the only noise was the rustling of the leaves as a small breeze went whispering amongst them. Grizelda seemed to know the more isolated woodland paths, where the beechmast beneath our feet was rich and golden, and where the green mist of unfolding beech leaves made a shade undisturbed by anyone other than ourselves.

We came out suddenly on to the high, clear ground above Totnes, with the town spread out before us, tumbling down

the hillside and spilling over beyond its walls to the tidal
marshes and busy shipping quays on the River Dart, far below
us. To our right was the castle, raised upon its mound,
and beyond that the town's main buildings, including the
Benedictine Priory of Saint Mary, the guildhall and houses of
the most important burghers, all confined by walls and a ditch
and earthworks, which might once have been topped by a
palisade. And beyond that again, lay more houses, mills and
the meadows and orchards of the Priory. The streets hummed
with life, and my spirits lifted. I could do good business here,
in the market place and by knocking on doors. A thriving
township by the look of it.

Grizelda said, 'I'll leave you here. Go down the hill and in
at the West Gate. It's near the cattle market they call the
Rotherfold. Or you can go by South Street, which will bring
you south of East Gate into the unwalled part of the town.'
She reached up and, unexpectedly, kissed my cheek. 'Good
luck, Chapman.'

Before I had recovered from my surprise, she had swung
on her heel and was gone. As she disappeared once more
into the belt of woodland from which we had just emerged,
I shouted, 'God be with you!' But if she heard me, she gave
no sign, not even a glance over her shoulder. I watched until
I could no longer see the blue of her skirt among the trees,
then, hoisting my pack a little higher on my back, I started
to descend the hill.

Chapter Three

Geoffrey of Monmouth, in his *Historia Britonum*, tells us that Brutus, son of Sylvius, grandson of Aeneas the Trojan, founded Totnes, and gave his name to the whole island of Britain – but there are some things I have always begged leave to doubt. On the other hand, having seen it for myself, I would take anyone's word that Totnes is a rich and thriving town, and that its wealth is founded on wool. All trades connected with that commodity – tucking, fulling, spinning, weaving, dyeing – are well represented both within and without its walls; and while other occupations do of course flourish there, it is the fleece of the Devonshire sheep which is responsible for its general air of prosperity. Or perhaps I should say 'was', for I have not visited the place for many years now.

And one thing at least I know has changed. In that spring of 1475, the castle was still in the possession of the powerful Zouche family, all ardent supporters of the House of York, and therefore the climate of the town was also Yorkist. During the time that I spent there, I never heard a single whisper against King Edward or his younger brother, Prince Richard. Nowadays, however, that freebooting Lancastrian, Sir Richard Edgecombe of Cotehele, is lord of Totnes and appoints the castle's constables.

But I digress . . . I followed Grizelda's direction and went in by the West Gate, close to the cattle market. A drover entered just ahead of me, driving two of his beasts to the shambles for slaughter, and I asked him who in authority I might speak to concerning my sighting of the outlaws. He suggested the names of several Town Wardens, who would pass my information on to the Mayor who, in his turn, would decide if it were of sufficient importance to be retailed to the Sheriff.

'But if you want to catch the early-morning trade,' my informant advised me, nodding at my pack, 'I'd leave all such civic matters until later. The women will be out and about betimes today. Most of 'em have been up since dawn, hocking, and they'll be in the mood to spend money. If you've any blue ribbons in your pack,' he added, 'save some for me. My woman fancies herself in a blue ribbon, though why I don't know! An uglier face it'd be hard to find between here and t'other side o' Dartmoor. If you want a good stand,' he continued charitably, 'take up a position opposite the Priory, near the Guildhall.'

I thanked him and moved away. He called after me, 'As to that other business, try Thomas Cozin. He's a Warden of the Leech Well. He'll give you a sympathetic hearing and not ask too many awkward questions.' The friendly eyes twinkled. 'Such as why you didn't try to capture the entire band of ruffians single-handed.'

I laughed, in recognition of the drover's shrewd appreciation of the pitfalls of dealing with Authority, repeated my thanks and strode out, past the pillory and the shambles, past prosperous looking houses and shops to an open space alongside the Guildhall, near the East Gate. There was already a small crowd of vendors, selling pies and hot pigs' feet, bundles of rushes and earthenware pots. A wandering minstrel was piping a jig and a trio of jugglers entertained those townspeople who had already spent their money, but were not yet prepared to return home to dinner.

By the greatest good fortune, no other chapman had yet arrived to peddle his wares, so I was able to claim the undivided attention of the women once I had opened my pack and displayed its contents. I did a good trade in needles, thread, laces and other such mundane objects among the wives and beldams; but the younger, flightier women vied with each other in the purchase of ribbons and brooches, coloured leather tags for their girdles and kerchiefs of fine white linen, trimmed with Honiton lace.

I had sold more than half my stock when I saw a little knot of women coming towards me, their eager faces plainly expressing interest in my goods. A second look convinced me that they were a mother and three young daughters, so alike were they in their natural vivacity and general glow of good health. All were plump and round, like little robins, and with a delicacy and refinement of manner that raised them above the common ruck. But neither were they noble; there was only one servant girl, who carried the basket, attendant upon them, and their cloaks were made of camlet, trimmed with squirrel, not fur, lined with sarcinet. The family of a rich burgher, I decided, although I could take small credit for such an obvious deduction.

As they gathered around me, laughing and chattering, I could see that there was not much more than sixteen summers between the mother and her eldest child, a girl just entering upon womanhood and very conscious of the fact, judging by the provocative glances she directed towards all the men within range of her sparkling hazel eyes. I myself was the recipient of more than one glance, but steadfastly refused to return them, giving all my attention to the older woman and devoutly thankful that Joan, as her sisters called her, had not been a member of the hocking party I had encountered that morning. The two younger girls, variously addressed as Elizabeth and Ursula, were not as yet interested in the male sex except for their father, who, from their conversation, they regarded as the provider and source of all good things.

'Mother, may I have this brooch? It's so pretty and I'm sure Father would wish me to have it, don't you think so?'

'Oh, Mother, look at this doll. Father won't mind if you buy it for me.'

'Mother, I want a new needle-case and there's an ivory one here which is big enough to hold at least half a dozen needles. If I explain to Father that I really do need it, he won't care if you purchase it for me.'

'Mother, this lawn kerchief will go very well at the neck of my green woollen gown. Father was saying only yesterday that it lacked sufficient adornment.'

Their parent, giving only half an ear to her two younger daughters' requirements, was busy on her own account, making a selection of my wares, her small white hands hovering predatorily above the open pack, fluttering from object to object, touching first one thing and then another, unable to decide what she most wanted to buy. She, too, seemed to have no fear of a husbandly reprimand for her spendthrift ways as she selected ribbons, laces, two beautifully hammered pewter belt-tags and a pair of gloves, made in Spain. But the object of her greatest desire was the length of ivory silk brocade which, like the gloves, had come from the hold of the Portuguese merchantman, lying off Dartmouth. She fingered it longingly, but when I named my price, she did, at last, hesitate, as though such a purchase might stretch even uxorious tolerance too far.

'Buy it, Mother,' urged the middle girl, who was named, like my own child, Elizabeth, after our Queen. 'Father remarked the other day that you need a new gown, didn't he, Joan? And if he should quibble at the expense, I'm sure Uncle Oliver would be delighted to purchase it for you. He was inquiring yesterday how he could repay your hospitality. He has been staying with us for nearly three weeks.'

Her mother still hesitated, however. 'I'm sure you're right, dearling, but I cannot presume on either your uncle's generosity or your father's goodwill. But it is beautiful,' she breathed, smoothing the brocade again. 'See how it shimmers in the light.' She thought for a moment, then seemed to make up her mind. 'Chapman,' she said, 'after dinner, when you have finished here, will you be so kind as to bring this length of silk to my house, so that my husband can inspect it and judge of its quality for himself?'

'I shall be most pleased to do so,' I answered, 'if you'll give me your direction.'

She waved a delicate hand, prismatic with rings. 'A little way up the hill. Ask for Warden Thomas Cozin. Everyone knows where we live.' She spoke with all the certainty of someone of standing in the local community, and I had noted from the first that most passers-by acknowledged her and her daughters with a bow, a curtsey or a respectful word of greeting.

'Thomas Cozin?' I glanced at her sharply. 'Warden of the Leech Well?'

She looked pleased. 'You've heard of him already?'

I explained the circumstances as speedily as I could, and

she frowned, her eyebrows almost meeting across the delicate, tip-tilted nose.

'The outlaws were foraging again last night? Oh dear, oh dear! They are becoming such a menace in these parts.' She lowered her voice so that her daughters should not hear. 'The great fear is that they will grow so daring that they may find some way into the upper part of the town during the hours of darkness. The gates are locked from sundown until the sounding of the Angelus, but as you can see for yourself, we are defended in part by a simple ditch and earthworks. Determined, evil men, could discover a way in, I'm sure.' She shuddered. 'And they have proved themselves capable of murder.'

'Two children, I understand.'

Mistress Cozin nodded, unable for a moment to continue speaking. At last, she whispered, 'Two innocents. Two little holy innocents with less than a dozen summers between the pair of them.' She laid a hand on my arm, such a display of familiarity with a tradesman demonstrating the measure of her distress. 'You must certainly tell my husband all you remember of the outlaws, Chapman. Even the smallest recollection may be of value.'

I doubted this, for the light had been poor and they were, when all was said and done, just men like a hundred others. Not one had had a club foot or a monstrous hump upon his back to distinguish him from his law-abiding fellows. Nevertheless, now that I was committed to visiting the Cozin household, I should do my duty and report what I had seen to the Warden.

'I shall be with you after the dinner hour,' I promised. 'At this rate, my pack will be empty long before then.'

A squeeze of my wrist, and Mistress Cozin released me,

suddenly aware of the impropriety of her conduct.

'I shall tell my husband to expect you. Come girls,' she added, raising her voice, 'we must be off. Put your purchases in Jenny's basket. Ursula! Elizabeth! Hurry along, now. Joan, don't dawdle, please!'

The latter turned slowly from her contemplation of a young man listening to the minstrel, gave me a long, smouldering look from beneath her lashes and reluctantly followed her mother and sisters as they moved away. I blushed and hastily averted my eyes. Mistress Cozin called over her shoulder, 'Don't forget, Chapman!' and, with the faithful Jenny trailing after them, mother and daughters began climbing the hill.

Long before the sun had reached its zenith, I had sold the bulk of my wares and was thinking of my dinner. It seemed many hours since I had eaten breakfast in Grizelda's cottage, and my appetite, always large, told me it was time to go in search of food. So I bought two meat pies, from a pie shop, and a flask of ale and retraced my steps beneath the West Gate. From there, I followed the track which led downhill, past the cattle market, past the town's medicinal spring, the Leech Well, and past the Magdalen Leper Hospital to the meadows about St Peter's Quay, close by the ancient demesne of Cherry Cross. Here, within sight of the placidly flowing Dart and the dam which had tamed the tidal marshes south of the foregate, I assuaged my burning hunger and reflected on the events of the morning.

So much had happened since I had opened my eyes in the lee of a hedge just before daybreak that I was growing suspicious; suspicious that God was once again taking a hand in my affairs and using me as His divine instrument against evil. For ever since I had renounced my novitiate, four and a half years earlier, just after my mother's death and in defiance of her wishes, I had been plunged into a series of adventures which, at the risk to myself of injury and danger, had resulted in villains being brought to justice for their crimes. It had been shown to me that I had a talent for solving puzzles and unravelling mysteries that baffled other people; and I had long ago accepted that this was God's way of exacting retribution for my abandonment of the religious life. Not that my acceptance was meek and wholehearted; far from it! I got angry with God. I told Him plainly that I thought it extremely unfair that He should constantly be interfering in my life like this. I argued that there was no reason why I should obey Him, and that I was entitled to a quiet existence, free from aggravation. He listened sympathetically. He always does. And I always lost.

I drank my ale slowly, staring into the distance on the other side of the river, where horizons were blurred and the contours of hills soft and mellow in the hazy afternoon mist. Perhaps, after all, I was wrong, for nothing had happened so far which could require my special talents. I did not feel that I was expected to go single-handed after a band of dangerous outlaws; that merely required dogged persistence and a great deal of luck on the part of the Sheriff and his *posse*. Yet neither could I throw off the nagging doubt that there was something I had missed; some intimation that God had need of me again.

I scrambled to my feet, exchanged a few pleasantries with the workmen on the quay who were busy loading a ship with bales of woollen cloth, and set off back the way I had come. I was abreast of the leper hospital – a creditably large building, with chapel and hall and accommodation for, I judged, some half-dozen lazars – and was making for the

track between it and the Leech Well when I heard the jingle
of harness and the thud of hooves, heralds of an approaching
horseman. Turning my head, I saw a big chestnut with pale
mane and tail, who flashed me a glance from brilliant, imperi-
ous eyes as he drew within range. The light ran like liquid
bronze across the shining coat and rippling, powerful muscles.
A superb beast, who must have cost his owner a fortune.

I transferred my attention to the rider, a man whose lower
face was concealed by a thick, full, dark brown beard. He
was fashionably and richly dressed, with riding boots of soft
red leather, a short red velvet cloak lined with sable, and a
black velvet cap adorned with a brooch, comprised of pearls
encircling a large, winking ruby. A man of substance, obviously, yet there was a nervousness about him, as though he
were unused to riding such a mettlesome mount. He held the
animal on too short a rein and sat uneasily in the saddle.
I watched his erratic progress down the hill in the direction
of the bridge which crossed the Dart at the bottom of the
foregate. Then I ascended the incline to the West Gate and
re-entered the town.

As Mistress Cozin had predicted, I had no difficulty locating
the home she shared with her husband and daughters. The
first person I asked at once pointed out the house in the
shadow of the Priory, and advised me that the family was
within. Plainly the comings and goings of the Cozins were of
interest to their neighbours, and my first impression of their
importance in the town was strengthened.

The house had a frontage two rooms deep and two storeys
high. As I later discovered, a side passage, from which the
stairs rose steeply to the upper floor, led into a courtyard,
beyond which were the kitchens; and beyond that again, lay

the stables, workshops and storehouses. As there seemed to be no back entrance, I took my courage in both hands and rapped loudly on the front door.

My knock was answered by the little maid, Jenny, whom I had seen that morning, attending her mistress. She led me upstairs to the front parlour, where the lady of the house and her daughters were sitting. This room had been extended out over the street, supported on pillars, a privilege for which householders had to pay a substantial fine. Unprepared for such preferential treatment, I stood awkwardly, just inside the door, stooping a little, as I so often did, to prevent the top of my head from brushing the ceiling. The two younger girls immediately started to giggle but were frowned into silence by their mother.

Mistress Cozin indicated a stool. 'Pray be seated, Chapman. My husband and his brother will be with us very shortly. Meanwhile, you may lay out the brocade.' Her gaze sharpened with anxiety. 'You still have it? You haven't sold it in the meantime?'

'No, no,' I assured her, and produced it from my pack, letting it cascade in a shimmering waterfall across my arm.

She breathed a sigh of relief just as the door behind me opened, and her husband and his brother walked in. I stumbled once more to my feet, trying not to let my astonishment show.

Thomas and Oliver Cozin were twins and as alike as two ears of wheat. But what caused my surprise was not their similarity, but the fact that either should be in any way connected with the four pretty and lively females seated around me. That Thomas Cozin was much older than his wife was immediately apparent, and, as I later learned, he must then have been in his forty-fifth year, he and his brother claiming to have been born around the time that the witch, La Pucelle, was captured by the Burgundians outside Compiègne. My first impression of the pair was one of greyness; grey hair, grey eyes, grey clothes. Both stooped a little and were very lean, the shape of the skull prominent beneath the parchment-like, finely stretched skin. There was something dusty and desiccated about them; and while I could imagine a marriage of convenience between Thomas and his sprightly, attractive wife, in my youthful arrogance I was unable to picture it as a love match.

My ignorance was immediately dispelled, as all four women rose and fluttered towards father and uncle, uttering little cries of pleasure, settling them in the best chairs; even the self-absorbed Joan hastened to pour them wine. The men displayed equal warmth, kissing cheeks and embracing trim waists with their bony arms. And as subsequent conversation led me to understand that they had been parted for no more than an hour since dinner, their show of affection was all the more remarkable. I have rarely in my life met a family so devoted to one another as that one.

'So this is the chapman,' Thomas Cozin observed as he sipped his wine. He smiled encouragingly at me. 'You have something to tell me, I believe, concerning the outlaws. And so you shall, once' – and the grey eyes twinkled with laughter – 'the important part of your business here is concluded.' He turned to his wife. 'Alice, my dear, this, I presume, is the brocade you are so anxious to show me.'

She nodded and caressed the silk with a reverent hand. 'I know it's a great deal of money, Thomas, but nothing like so much as you would have to pay here, in Totnes.'

'Nor in Exeter,' Oliver Cozin put in. 'It is certainly a fine piece of material, and now that I have seen it, I should like to present it as a gift to you, my dearest sister, in gratitude for your hospitality these past three weeks.'

A good-natured argument immediately ensued between him and his brother as to who should pay for the brocade; an altercation finally resolved by my suggestion that they should each contribute half the price.

'The wisdom of Solomon,' smiled Thomas Cozin.

'An old head on young shoulders,' agreed his brother.

The matter being thus amicably settled to everyone's satisfaction, Alice and her daughters bore the brocade away to inspect it more closely in the privacy of her bedchamber, while I was left with the men to tell the story of my morning's adventure. When I had finished, Thomas Cozin thanked me politely, but was of the opinion that it would be pointless to trouble either the Mayor or the Sheriff with it.

'You saw too little, Master Chapman, for your story to be of much help.'

I inclined my head in agreement. 'My own feelings, your honour, so I'll trouble you no longer.' I gathered up my pack and stowed away the two gold angels in the purse at my belt, buckling it securely. 'I'll wish you good-day and delay you no further.'

But as I rose to my feet, I was detained by Oliver Cozin.

'A moment, Chapman.' He regarded me speculatively with shrewd grey eyes. 'Do you stay in Totnes overnight?' I gave my assent. 'Where were you planning to sleep?'

'The Priory, if they can accommodate me in their guest hall. Otherwise' – I shrugged – 'anywhere warm and dry will do. Under a hedge, in a barn, even in a ditch provided it's not full of water. I have a good frieze cloak in my pack which will protect me against inclement weather.'

Oliver Cozin glanced briefly at his brother, and a silent

question and answer passed between them. Then he asked, 'What would you say to a house, all to yourself?' I stared at him in perplexity, and he went on, 'Oh, don't imagine that I'm offering you luxury. The house has stood empty these past two months, dust and cobwebs gathering everywhere. I am a lawyer and it belongs to a client of mine, for whom I am acting in the purchase of a property hereabouts. He was with me this morning, and expressed anxiety about his previous domicile, the house just mentioned, which remains unoccupied in spite of all his attempts to find a tenant for it. In normal times, such a fact would not trouble him, but with these outlaws roaming the district, he fears that they may penetrate the town and steal his goods.'

'Then why does he not remain there himself?'

The lawyer's tone sharpened. 'Chapman, you either wish to accept my offer or you do not. Nothing else concerns you.'

I hesitated. The prospect of spending a night in the comfort of a well furnished house, and one, moreover, I should have all to myself, was tempting. Yet there was something here which made me uneasy, and my instincts bade me refuse.

'But I shall be gone from Totnes in the morning,' I cavilled. 'What good will my protection be for a single night? The outlaws could strike tomorrow. Besides, how do you know that you can trust me? I might make off with some of your client's goods.'

Oliver Cozin was affronted. 'Do you think me such a fool that I can't tell an honest man when I see one? As for your other question, one night is better than none. As the blessed St Martin said, half a cloak is preferable to no cloak at all.'

I glanced at Thomas Cozin, standing at his brother's side, the two grey figures so alike that it was as though I had drunk too much ale and was seeing double. At present, their faces were expressionless, although there was, perhaps, just the tiniest flicker of worry in Thomas's eyes. He did not have a lawyer's ability to hide his emotions completely.

Was I imagining things? After all, what had they offered me but a comfortable lodging for the night? It would be foolish to refuse, even though I did not believe for a second that the outlaws would risk coming into the town. Such an occurrence had reality only in the fevered imagination of the townspeople.

'Very well,' I said. 'I accept. And thank you.'

Chapter Four

It was Oliver who led me to a house north of the Shambles, on the opposite side of the High Street, where it curves towards the West Gate. He unlocked the door and preceded me inside, picking his way carefully across the dust-laden floor and wrinkling his nose fastidiously at the musty smell. 'I suppose I'd better show you the lie of the place,' he said, a trifle grudgingly, as we stood in the stone-flagged passageway. He pushed open a door to his right. 'This is the downstairs parlour, where my old friend and client, Sir Jasper Crouchback, conducted most of his business, and behind it is the counting-house. The stairs in the corner here lead to the upper parlour and main bedchambers, none of which need concern you; for if the outlaws come, they will be sure to enter on the lower level. Follow me, and I will conduct you to the kitchens and the outhouses.'

We walked along the passageway to a stout, oaken door at the far end, now bolted and barred. With my superior height, I was able to render assistance in withdrawing the bolts from their wards; and by tugging with all my strength on the iron handle of the latch, I finally managed to loosen the wooden leaf, which, swollen by the recent spell of wet weather, had stuck in its frame. We stepped out into a paved courtyard, enclosed on either side by high stone walls. Ahead of us was another block of buildings, whose upper storey was connected to the one at our backs by a roofed-in wooden gallery, supported on struts and running the length of the right-hand wall. The kitchen, into which I was shown by Oliver Cozin, was much like all other kitchens I have ever been in, with a table in the centre, a water barrel, shelves of pots, pans and suchlike cooking utensils, and ovens built into the thickness of the fireplace brick. A ladder gave access to the storerooms and sleeping quarters of the servants above, while a door in one corner, through which we proceeded, brought us to the workshops, hen-coops, pigsties and stables. The latter had stalls for two horses which, along with the rest of the outbuildings, were again protected by high walls, and approached by an alleyway running between the house and its neighbour. An iron-studded, oaken gate kept out intruders.

After I had looked my fill, we retraced our steps.

'I suggest,' the lawyer said, 'that you sleep in the downstairs parlour and keep a candle burning all night so that its light can be glimpsed, if necessary, through the chinks in the shutters. As you have seen, the outhouses are empty, and robbers, having discovered as much, will naturally assume the house to be unoccupied as well, and venture around to the front. Signs of life might deter them from forcing an entry.'

'And if they don't?' I inquired ironically. 'What am I supposed to do then?'

The lawyer eyed me up and down. 'A great lad like you must be able to defend himself, and is probably used to doing so. You carry a good, thick cudgel and I presume you know how to use it.'

I regarded him straitly. 'These men are killers, or so I've been told. I don't imagine a cudgel to be of much use against them.'

There was a moment's silence, then Oliver Cozin grimaced. 'Chapman, you are, I should guess, a sensible man, and of greater intelligence than is suggested by your calling. You do not believe, any more than I do, that the outlaws will penetrate beyond the town's defences. Such men do not like enclosed spaces. There is nowhere to run. But my client, Master Colet, who is not a clever man' – there was a slight note of contempt in the lawyer's tone – 'and who is gripped by the general hysteria, fears for his property, and so I do what I can, even if it is just for a night.'

I frowned. 'I thought you said that this house belonged to your old friend, Sir Jasper Crouchback?'

Oliver inclined his head. 'And so it did, once. But he has been dead these five years, and now it is in the possession of his son-in-law, Master Eudo Colet.'

There was a reserve in both his tone and manner that deterred me from asking too many questions. Nevertheless, I could not stop myself from probing a little further.

'Surely,' I said, 'even if this Master Colet and his lady, Sir Jasper's daughter, are not prepared to remain in the house themselves while they conclude the purchase of another property, there can be no shortage of tenants who would be more than willing to occupy it for them. Indeed, such an arrangement would earn them money. So why are they forced to rely on the good offices of a passing traveller?'

Once again, the lawyer's eyes grew wary, while he tried unsuccessfully to appear frank and open.

'My client is a widower, and he does not wish to rent out the house. He wishes to sell. It is only the scourge of these outlaws which has made him uneasy about it standing empty.'

I shook my head. 'That does not answer my objection. As Master Colet, for reasons not known to me, is unwilling to remain here himself, then why does he not sell at once?'

'Because a purchaser has not yet been found. Now, let that suffice. You ask too many questions about matters which do not concern you. You have free lodgings for the night. Be content.' I bowed my head in submission and the lawyer seemed relieved. 'I will leave you now. Here is the key. It fits all locks, should you wish to go out before curfew. You will want food, I daresay. But I saw a supply of candles on a shelf in the kitchen, so you will not need to buy those, at least.'

I thanked him gravely and accompanied him, like any good host, to the street door, but as he was about to step across the threshold, he hesitated and turned back.

'Master Colet is . . . a valuable client,' he said, with some constraint. 'One that I should wish to please. I wonder therefore . . .' He made a determined effort to smile, trying to make his request sound as natural as possible. 'Would you be willing to remain as a lodger in this house until next Saturday? I am leaving then, for Exeter, and what you do after that is up to you. But I shall have shown myself willing, whilst here, to comply with Master Colet's wishes, and so escape his reproaches.'

'And earned yourself an even fatter fee,' I thought, 'than the one you are charging him already.' Aloud I said, 'I must give the idea some consideration before making my answer. I had not intended to stay in Totnes for more than one night.'

'If . . . if money is short, I might arrange for . . . for a small sum to be paid to you.'

I shook my head. 'My purse is, at present, as full as it will hold, Master Cozin. But it is spring, and I need to be on the road. The confinement of four walls is all very well in the winter, when the wind blows from the north, and there is snow and ice underfoot, but once the thaw sets in and the trees begin to leaf, then I like to be on the open road. But I promise that I will think about your proposal and let you have my reply in the morning.'

And with that, the lawyer had to be content. After a moment's silence, he said, 'You're an honest man. I do right to trust you. Very well, I will await your verdict tomorrow. You know where to find me, at my brother's house. And I shall accept your decision whatever it might be. I shan't try to persuade you otherwise.'

I watched him walk away, until he disappeared round a bend in the roadway, then went back inside, closing the front door behind me. The bells of the Priory were only just ringing for Vespers, and it would be light for an hour or two yet. Time enough later to go out and buy myself food and ale before curfew. Moreover, whatever Oliver Cozin might say, I wished to see all of my new domain. But before I did either, I had need to sit quietly and think. I returned, therefore, to the downstairs parlour, where I dusted the large, carved armchair with the sleeve of my tunic and seated myself, face tilted upwards, so that my eyes were not distracted by my surroundings. And thus, staring at the smoke-blackened ceiling, where cobwebs festooned the corners like folds of grey gauze, I considered my present situation.

Even if my suspicions had not already been aroused, this last exchange with the lawyer would have alerted me to something being wrong. No landlord, or his agent, offers to pay a tenant for living in his house; such a proposal is to turn the world of business dealing upon its head. That apart, however, there were other things which intrigued me. Why did the widowed Eudo Colet not wish to remain here, even though he was worried by a possible attack from the outlaws? And why was the assiduous Master Cozin unable to find a native of the town willing to oblige? Was there no neighbour ready to despatch a son, or one of his men, to play the role of caretaker? And why did there appear to be no single person eager to purchase such a handsome dwelling, even if it were solely for the purpose of renting it out to others?

There was only one conclusion to be drawn in answer to all these questions. Something had happened here; some event which had given everyone, including its owner, a distaste or fear of the house. I could think of no other explanation which fitted the facts, so I decided that while there was still enough daylight to see by, the sooner I looked it over, the better. I stood up and fetched my cudgel from beside my pack, having left both of them just inside the street door.

The downstairs parlour, which the late Sir Jasper Crouchback had also used for trading purposes – whatever those might have been – I already knew, with its panelled walls, its pair of finely carved armchairs, large table, handsome fireplace, decorated overmantel and flagged stone floor. There was also a cupboard whose shelves had most probably once contained silver and pewter plate, but whose doors now swung wide to reveal nothing but dust. The twisting corner stair, which led to the upper storey, had a delicately carved banister to help with the ascent. Altogether, this was a room whose furnishings were designed to impress.

By contrast, the counting-house behind did no more than serve its purpose. A greater air of neglect hung about it, as though it had been long unused. A table, a bench, two stools and a stout cupboard, secured by a rusting lock and chain, was all that it contained, while the beaten-earth floor showed no drift of mouldering rushes, nor any other sign of recent occupancy. The walls were a greenish-grey colour, but it was impossible to guess, at the first cursory glance, whether this was caused by dirt, or by potash and sulphur mixed with the wash of lime. There was nothing here of interest, and I returned to the passageway.

I stepped into the courtyard, which was rinsed with a pale golden light in the rays of the westering sun. The covered gallery to my right threw long, slanting shadows across the paving stones, where soft cushions of moss and tall stems of nettle and hairy bittercress were forcing themselves between the uneven flags. The well and the pump stood close to the kitchen door, which I unlocked with my key. There being nothing there that I had not already seen in the company of Master Cozin, I mounted the ladder to the storeroom and servants' quarters above. The same musty odour of damp and disuse met me here as it did everywhere else in the house, and the bareness of the boards, denuded of all hint of human habitation, only served to emphasize the fact that it was surely some months since anyone had slept here. The walls had again been lime-washed, but this time there was no doubt that red oxide had been added to the quick lime to give it a pinkish colour.

A door in the far wall led into the storeroom, which had a faint, lingering scent of apples to sweeten the less pleasant smells. But this, too, was empty except for a sack of grain in one corner. Sharp teeth had torn a hole in the cloth, and corn was spilling on to the floor. A bright-eyed mouse turned to look at me as I entered; then, with a whisk of its tail and a scutter of tiny claws, disappeared into a hole between the boards. In the corner directly opposite me was another door, and this, when unlocked, opened on to the gallery connecting the two blocks of buildings which comprised the whole.

I descended to the kitchen, locked the door from the inside, and returned once more to the storeroom, stepping out on to the covered way and again meticulously locking the door behind me. The planking shook and creaked a little beneath my weight as I walked the length of the courtyard wall, and I was glad of the handrail for support. Nevertheless, the structure seemed safe enough and in no danger of collapsing. Yet another door at the other end, when unlocked, gave access to the bedchambers and upstairs parlour of the main dwelling.

The room in which I found myself was obviously the chief of the bedchambers, judging by the four-poster bed, hung all around with blue silk draperies. A rich green damask coverlet was draped over what proved, on examination, to be a goose-feather mattress, and the walls were painted with an intricate pattern in red and white which could only have been done at considerable cost and by a skilled craftsman. There were two beautifully carved clothes chests, one supporting a six-branched pewter candelabra, bearing the stumps of pure wax candles, while the floor was still scattered with rushes and dried herbs, now brittle and brown with age. A curtain, drawn across one corner of the room, concealed two chamber-pots and a bathtub.

This room opened on to a short, narrow passage, dark and airless, which offered me the choice of two doors. I opened the one leading to the front of the house, and found myself in the upstairs parlour from one corner of which the stairs twisted down to the lower floor. Three walls were hung with tapestries, now rubbed and faded with age, but once bright with brilliant, jewel-like colours. Their fabric, however, was still intact and I guessed, from knowledge gathered on my journeyings, that they came originally from France. One depicted Tobias being greeted by the angel, Azarias; another showed Judith holding up the bleeding, severed head of Holofernes; the third told the story of Gideon overcoming the Midianites. The roof beams were painted scarlet, blue and green, their ends fashioned into the figures of saints. The wide stone hearth and chimney stood directly above that of the lower parlour, and the overmantel was even more elaborately carved and coloured than the one downstairs. Indeed, table, chairs, stools and cupboards all displayed superior craftsmanship to the furnishings below. Two rugs on the floor, and glass in the upper half of the windows, were yet further intimations of wealth and luxury.

Having looked my fill, I stepped back into the passage where, with a mere stretch of my arm, I was able to open the second door and enter the other bedchamber. This was furnished in similar fashion to its fellow, but the bed curtains and covering were of unbleached linen, and the mattress I found upon investigation to be stuffed with flock. A ewer and basin stood on top of a clothes chest, and the candle-holder contained only a rushlight. A truckle-bed, supporting a palliasse, a rough linen sheet and a couple of coarse woollen blankets, stood alongside the four-poster, evidence that a second or third person had shared the room, most obviously a servant. The window panes were of oiled parchment nailed to the wooden frame, and one of the shutters, folded back against the wall, was in danger of coming loose from its hinges. Not a room on which care or time had been lavished.

As I turned to go, a floorboard creaked beneath my feet and the noise made me jump. I realized for the first time how deserted the house felt, how eerily silent. Fear pricked along my spine and I began to sweat, aware of the presence of evil. It was here, in this room, all around me. The hair rose on the nape of my neck and my skin took on the appearance of

51

goose-flesh. I was icily cold and searingly hot at one and the same moment. My legs were giving way beneath me, I felt unable to breathe and I was perilously close to losing my senses . . .

The terror passed. Propped against the door, my hands clammy with sweat, I was nevertheless breathing naturally and my surroundings appeared perfectly normal. There was nothing and no one here, except myself, and I felt deeply ashamed of my sudden burst of panic. I needed food: it was some hours now since I had eaten my pies down by St Peter's Quay, and my stomach was crying out for more sustenance. Pulling myself together, I went back to the parlour and descended the stairs to the lower floor. I had seen everything there was to see of my temporary lodgings, and apart from the highly improbable threat of attack from the outlaws, there was nothing to be afraid of. I told myself firmly that what I had experienced in the second bedchamber was nothing more than bodily weakness engendered by hunger.

Yet I was still left with the unresolved problem of why no one could be found to remain here. There was a general aversion to the house, and, so far, I had not discovered what caused it. Perhaps if I took myself to the local inn, I might obtain some information. So I closed all the shutters and locked all the doors, before letting myself out into the street and directing my feet towards the nearest hostelry.

This I found in the lee of the castle wall – a narrow-fronted, inhospitable-looking dwelling, but whose bunch of green leaves, hoisted on a pole over the entrance, indicated that its occupant sold ale and food. I made my way inside, and when my eyes had grown accustomed to the dimness, I could see a long table down the middle of the room, benches ranged around the walls and a high-backed settle drawn up close to a central hearth, on which a few logs were burning. There were only one or two other customers beside myself, it being, by now, close to the hour of curfew; and doubtless the townsfolk were already making themselves comfortable by their firesides, barricading doors and windows against imaginary attack from the outlaws. I drew a stool up to the table, and shouted for the landlord.

As is often the case in country districts, the inn was run by a woman. She came into the ale-room from somewhere at the back; by the smell of her, most probably the brewhouse. At first sight, she appeared to be a large, motherly-looking woman, an impression immediately dispelled on closer acquaintance. Small dark eyes, set in folds of pallid flesh, shrewdly summed me up as someone likely to spend money freely, being in need of copious refreshment. She was therefore all affability; but a pair of brawny arms and a fist, the size and appearance, when bunched, of a ham, were warnings that she would stand no nonsense.

'Ale,' I said, 'and bread and cheese. And plenty of it.'

She nodded, eyeing me appreciatively.

'A hulking fellow like you could do with some cold, boiled bacon, as well, I daresay. And some buckram, nice and juicy, the first of the season?'

'Why not?' I grinned. 'In my lonely bed, there will be no one to object to the smell of my breath.'

The landlady raised an eyebrow and snorted. 'Lonely bed, is it? Then it's of your own choosing. There are girls in plenty around these parts who'd jump at the chance of keeping you warm, if you so much as crooked a finger. I'd do so myself, if I were twenty years younger.' She added a foul-mouthed sally and went away, chortling.

By the time she returned, I was the only customer left. The ale-house was too small to be a hostelry, and there seemed to be no inmates except herself and a long-faced tapster, who came to draw my ale, then vanished, silently.

'My son,' she shrugged, nodding in the general direction of his disappearance. 'A miserable dog, if ever there was one. But I need him. I can't manage the barrels on my own. Now, eat up.' She placed a laden platter before me and drew another stool close to the table. 'And while you're eating, you can tell me who you are and where you come from. It's always a pleasure to meet a stranger.'

So, between mouthfuls of bread and ham, cheese and garlic, all washed down with a good strong ale, I gave her a brief history of my life so far; a narration at which I had become adept over the years, because I always seemed to arouse people's curiosity. I also related, for the third or fourth time that day, news of King Edward's proposed invasion of France; at which she spat in the sawdust covering the floor, and remarked that men were born fools who, unhappily, never grew any wiser.

'Always fighting one another, like children. Killing each other for no good reason. Women need more say in the governing of things, Master Chapman, and then we might see common sense prevailing.' When she saw that I was not to be drawn, she gave a gap-toothed smile and changed the subject. 'Where are you sleeping tonight? At the Priory?'

I cleared my mouth. 'Better than that. I've been given a house to myself.' And I explained the circumstances.

I glanced up from scraping the last morsel of food from my plate to find her regarding me oddly.

'So! Master Eudo Colet won't be coming back, eh? Not even to protect his property.' Once again, she spat contemptuously, this time finding her target on one of the smouldering logs on the hearth. The spittle hissed and sizzled. 'Not to be wondered at, I suppose. Murder's an evil thing to be touched by at the best of times. But the death of children is particularly heinous. And when there's also the suspicion of witchcraft . . . !' She broke off, lifting her ample shoulders.

I stared at her, horrified.

'No one told me . . . I have heard of two children being murdered by the outlaws, but these, I presume, are not the ones you speak of?'

'Aye, the same pair. Brother and sister. Rosamund Crouchback's children by her first husband. Never saw him. Came from northern parts, and after she married him, they lived in London. But when he died, she came back home to her father, bringing her little ones with her. A wild, wilful girl she was, always; and when Sir Jasper himself died, leaving her everything, she said she'd married to oblige him the first time, and now she was going to marry to please herself. And so she did! Going off to London again – Bartholomewtide, it would have been, three years since – and staying away for a month or more, and leaving those pretty ones in the care of the servants. And when she came home, she was wed again, to Master Eudo Colet! An adventurer with an eye for an easy fortune if ever I saw one. And I wasn't the only one who thought so. Everyone disliked him and thought him up to no good. But the one who hated and mistrusted him most of all was Rosamund's cousin, the children's nurse, Grizelda Harbourne!'

Chapter Five

'Grizelda Harbourne?' I jerked my head up sharply at the name. 'Who has a holding near the river?'

'The very same. The holding was her father's, and when he died, not long after Sir Jasper, it passed to Grizelda.' The landlady puckered her brows. 'How do you come to know her? I thought you were a stranger hereabouts.'

'She and her friends were up early this morning, hocking, and I fell into their clutches.' I added, reddening slightly, 'Mistress Harbourne took pity on me and made them settle for less than they demanded. A kiss apiece. Then she took me home with her and gave me breakfast.'

This story seemed to afford my hostess great amusement.

'Been hocked, have you, my lad? Well, well! It's a wonder you were allowed to get away so lightly. Had I been there, you wouldn't have been as lucky.' She gave me a lascivious glance and licked her lips. My blush deepened, and she chortled loudly. 'Count yourself fortunate that Grizelda took pity on you. But she's a good woman with a soft heart. She's always protected those weaker than herself. Children and small, furry animals.' She shot me a second glance, this time tinged with malice. 'And big, dumb, ox-like creatures.' The coarse features sobered. 'Which is why she can't forgive herself for abandoning those two young innocents that terrible morning.'

'What terrible morning?' I asked. 'And why should Grizelda shoulder the blame? Where was the children's mother?'

'Dead, in childbirth, last November, around Martinmas. The child died, too. His child. Eudo Colet's. So he was left with the little ones and Grizelda and the two servants: the cook, Agatha Tenter, and Bridget Praule, the maid. Grizelda stayed with him as long as she could, for the children's sake, but she had always disliked him, and after her cousin's death, it turned to something deeper. They quarrelled and fought incessantly, so Bridget Praule told me. And finally, that winter morning, three months since, when Mary and Andrew ... disappeared' – the landlady's voice sank to a whisper and she crossed herself hurriedly, signing to me to do the same – 'she could take no more, not even to protect her little darlings. She packed her box and summoned Jack Carter to take her home to Bow Creek.

'She left the children playing upstairs, but within two hours of her departure, they had vanished, in spite of the fact that both Bridget Praule and Agatha Tenter swore it was impossible for them to have quit the house unseen. Their bodies were discovered, horribly mutilated, six weeks later, caught in some branches on the banks of the Harbourne; downstream, a mile or so from where it flows into the Dart.' The innkeeper swallowed some of my ale, her hand shaking so much that a few drops spilled from the cup on to the table, her face sallow and glistening with sweat. 'They had been murdered by the outlaws.' She gripped my wrist. 'But how had they wandered so far without anyone noticing them? How had they got out of the house when every door was within view of one or other of the servants? It could only have been by witchcraft, practised by that devil, Eudo Colet!'

'But it seems he's not been arrested on any such charge,' I pointed out. 'And the authorities would most surely have acted, had there been any proof of malpractice against him. Where was he when the children vanished? How old were they? There's so much I still don't understand.'

She answered my last question first. 'The boy, Andrew, was the elder. Six summers he'd seen, and looking forward to his seventh when he was so wickedly cut down. His sister, Mary, was a twelvemonth younger, and as pretty a little soul as you could wish to see this side of heaven. Eyes as blue as periwinkles and hair the colour of ripened corn. She took after her mother in looks, but was without the waywardness. A little angel, and her brother not much short of one; the children of Rosamund Crouchback's first husband, Sir Henry Skelton.'

I made no comment. In my experience, children, however good or placid, were rarely angelic. Recalling myself at that age, I knew I must have been a sore trial to my long-suffering mother; falling out of trees, tearing my clothes, stealing apples and playing rowdy games of football in the street.

'So, what of Eudo Colet?' I prompted, when my hostess seemed inclined to sink beneath the weight of maudlin reminiscence. 'Where was he when the children vanished?'

It was beginning to grow dusk. A flame, licking at the edge of a log, sent the shadows soaring. The landlady roused herself and shrugged.

'Out of the house,' she grudgingly admitted, 'visiting Master Cozin on some affair of business. Business!' she added scornfully. 'What did he know of business, beyond how to spend the money it brought him? For you must understand that after Sir Jasper's death, his partner, Thomas Cozin, had seen to everything for Mistress Rosamund. And very well he'd done it, too, by all accounts: she grew wealthier by the day. So no one was more dismayed than he, when she returned from London married to a man he knew nothing about. And never managed to know anything about, either, in spite of trying hard for information, like the rest of us. A mystery Eudo Colet was when she brought him home, and a mystery he's remained.'

'But there's no mystery where he was when his stepchildren disappeared,' I interrupted gently. 'You say he was with Master Cozin, who, to my certain knowledge, is a respected burgher of this town. If he vouched for his visitor, I don't suppose anyone would doubt him.'

The innkeeper, who had risen to draw me another cup of ale and fill one for herself, returned to the table. Her stool creaked protestingly as it again received her weight. She gave me a speaking look, drank deeply and wiped her mouth on her apron.

'That,' she hissed, 'is why I say it was witchcraft. Eudo Colet enlisted the help of the devil!' Once more, she made the sign of the cross.

I could see that I would be wasting my breath if I attempted to overcome her prejudice, so I merely asked, 'It's sure, is it, that the children were alive when he quit the house?'

'So Bridget Praule and Agatha Tenter testify.' She sniffed. 'Mind you, since Master Colet closed up the house, he's been lodging with Agatha and her mother, Dame Winifred, on the other side of the river. Make what you will of that.'

I made nothing of it at the moment. 'And how long was it after Master Colet returned home that the little ones could not be found?'

'According to Bridget, he sent her to fetch them almost at once. He had something to tell them, he said. She went upstairs, but ... they weren't there. At first, of course, she thought they were simply hiding, in order to tease her. But though she searched everywhere, there was no trace of them. And no one ever saw those two little innocents alive again.' Just at that moment, the bell began to toll for curfew.

I rose to my feet with the deepest reluctance.

'I must go,' I said. 'I've promised Master Oliver Cozin that I'll care for the house tonight, and I should be failing in my duty if I were to absent myself any longer. A pity. I should have liked to hear more.'

The landlady accompanied me to the ale-house door. 'Don't fret. I could tell you little else than what I've told you already. Witchcraft it was, and Eudo Colet at the bottom of it. But you say you've met Grizelda. Ask her if you wish to know anything further. She was more nearly concerned than anyone, and can give you details. So can Master Cozin and his brother, the lawyer, who's been staying with him these three weeks past. Oliver Cozin lives in Exeter, but was always Sir Jasper's friend and attorney, and has continued to manage all legal matters for Rosamund since her father's death. Including the drawing up of her will!' My hostess tapped the side of her nose significantly. 'There isn't much happens in Totnes but what I get to hear of it, one way or another.'

I stepped into the street. The sun had vanished from the western sky, staining the clouds red with its dying rays. The gates of the town were by now fast shut and the men of the Watch were collecting their lanterns from the castle guard-room before setting out on their first patrol. I let myself into the empty house, which was my home for the night, and longer if I wanted. The musty smell rose up to greet me, and, as I closed and locked the door behind me, the silence gathered, soft and menacing.

I no longer had any doubt why my footsteps had been

directed towards Totnes, nor what was required of me; but, for once, I raised no objections, nor did I try to argue with God. The killing of young children would, I hope, always have been the worst of crimes to me; but now that I was myself a father, now that I had held my own child in my arms, felt her milky-scented warmth close to my breast, it was a thousand times more terrible. Whoever was responsible for turning Andrew and Mary Skelton loose in the woods to be killed by the outlaws, was as guilty of their deaths as that set of murdering ruffians who had passed me at dawn this morning.

I walked along the passage, unlocked the door at the far end and crossed the dark and empty courtyard to the kitchen. There, after some searching, I found a bundle of tallow candles on a shelf, just as Master Cozin had told me I should. I also discovered a candle-holder, then groped around in the darkness for a tinder-box. When this proved elusive, I returned to the downstairs parlour and used the one which I always carried with me, in my pack. The fragile golden glow of the candle-flame spread slowly across the room, bringing shadows edging out of their corners like velvet-footed, nocturnal beasts of prey.

The candle in one hand and my cudgel in the other, I mounted the stairs to the second storey, my heart beating rapidly. From up here, if the inn's landlady were to be believed, on a winter's morning three months ago, two children had quit the house without anyone being any the wiser. As yet, my information was incomplete, and there might well be a half-dozen ways in which they could have escaped unnoticed; until I had the whole story from Grizelda, on the morrow, I was not prepared to accept the idea of witchcraft being responsible for their disappearance. Indeed,

I doubted of my accepting it even then, for I had already discovered that much of the wickedness in this world has its roots in the hearts and actions of men, unaided by external forces.

Nevertheless, I could not help but recall the sensation of evil I had experienced when, earlier on, I had stood in the second bedchamber, which I now realized must have been used by Grizelda and her charges. She was their nurse and had slept in the truckle-bed. It was amidst the wealth and comfort of the Crouchback household that she had acquired her taste for what she had called 'better things', as many another servant had done before her... And yet, was she a servant? Surely the innkeeper had referred to her as Rosamund's cousin, and Grizelda herself had told me that she left her father's holding when she was nine years old. A poor relation! That, without doubt, was the answer; the daughter of an impoverished kinsman of Sir Jasper, taken in to be companion to his own, and only, child. I should be very surprised to find that I was mistaken.

At the top of the stairs, I opened the parlour door and stood once more in the narrow space between the two bedchambers, the latch of each room within arm's reach. I could feel the sweat slipping icily down my back as, leaning my cudgel against one wall, I lifted the latch of the smaller chamber and stepped inside. Nothing had changed. Had I really expected it to? But, stupidly, I began to breathe more easily. My heart stopped thumping quite so strenuously, and the fingers clutching the candle-holder ceased to shake. Nor was there any recurrence of the sickness and panic of the afternoon.

I raised the candle higher, seeing again the four-poster and the truckle-bed, the clothes chest supporting basin and ewer, the rushlight in its holder, the shutter dragging loose from its hinge. Placing my candle carefully on the floor, I put the ewer and basin beside it, then lifted the lid of the chest. It opened upon a chasm of darkness, the faint scents of dried lavender and cedarwood teasing my nostrils. Picking up my candle again and holding it so as to illumine the interior of the coffer, I saw a sad little huddle of children's toys.

Reaching inside with my free hand, I withdrew, one by one, a wooden horse, with brown mane and crimson saddle, the paintwork much scratched by frequent handling; a cup and ball, the blue silk cord which should have attached them, frayed right through, leaving them in two separate pieces; a doll, whose wooden cheeks were still flushed with a high gloss of colour; some chessmen, roughly carved, and their chequered board; a small linen bag, drawn shut by a leather thong, which, when opened, revealed five smooth pebbles, used to play the game of fivestones. The floor of the chest was covered with some dark material, and this proved, on further investigation, to be a woman's gowns – two of them and obviously past their best, rubbed thin in places and patched in others. I hazarded a guess that they had once belonged to Grizelda, and that she had discarded them, when she left, as no longer fit to wear.

I replaced the various items in the chest and closed the lid, then straightened up to my full height, almost brushing my head against the ceiling. I cast a final look around the room, but there was nothing more which would add to the inn-keeper's story; no ghosts to trouble the warm, fetid air with their uneasy presence. Whatever had reached out to touch me, earlier in the day, had gone, leaving an unruffled calm behind it.

I returned to the parlour. A three-quarter moon was rising,

filtering through the glass top-half of the windows to lie in drifts of clouded silver across the dusty floor. I closed the shutters before going back to the chief bedchamber where I did the same, also ensuring that the door to the covered gallery was locked. Downstairs, I went on my rounds again, padding from parlour to counting-house, across the courtyard to the kitchens and thence to the second courtyard, making certain that all was secured. Like Oliver Cozin, I did not believe the outlaws would venture into the town, but there were thieves everywhere, and an empty house is always a temptation. Master Colet, I thought, might consider himself a very fortunate man that his property had not been robbed ere this.

As I re-entered the main part of the house, I knew a moment's temptation myself – to sleep upstairs on a feather mattress instead of downstairs, with only my cloak for blanket. But I was the night's custodian of the place, and could not afford to sleep too soundly. Too much comfort would lull my senses. I must embrace discomfort in order to discharge my promise to the lawyer. A degree of wakefulness would keep me alert for any alien noise. There was a privy in the outer courtyard which I had already used, so I placed a freshly lighted candle, in its holder, as close to the shutters as was safe, wrapped myself in my good frieze cloak and sat down in one of the armchairs, my feet resting on a stool, which I had dragged in from the counting-house for that purpose. I closed my eyes and, within minutes, was fast asleep.

That first deep slumber did not last, however, and as predicted I woke many times throughout the night, on one occasion rousing myself to prowl the length of the passageway and open the door into the courtyard, listening intently for any sound which might disturb the silence of the night. But all was quiet, not even a barking dog to intrude upon the general stillness. Another time, I rose and went upstairs, peering through a wide chink in the parlour shutters to stare down into the empty street. Nothing and no one stirred. If the outlaws were up and about their evil business, it was not within the walls and defences of Totnes.

I woke at least twice more, before falling into a doze which lasted until strong sunlight, piercing the shutters, told me that it was day. I started forward in my chair with a deafening snort, and the taste of last night's garlic foul in my mouth. The candle was almost burned down, only an inch or so of tallow still remaining. I blew out the flame, disentangled myself from my cloak, took my razor and soap, together with my tinder-box, from my pack, picked up the key and went out to the courtyard. Here, I stripped and washed as well as I could whilst working the pump with one or other of my hands, shook myself dry, like a dog, dressed again and drew up water from the well, carrying the bucket into the kitchen. There was still some tinder in the brazier which I lit, setting a pan of water over it to heat. While I waited, I considered what it would be best for me to do.

Sometime during the day, I must visit Oliver Cozin and tell him if I were willing or not to accept his offer to remain in the house until the end of the week. But before I did that, I wished to renew my acquaintance with Grizelda Harbourne, which meant a walk of some miles to her holding near Bow Creek. And for such a walk I should need sustenance: my stomach was already rumbling with hunger, making me feel quite faint. I must therefore visit the ale-house near the castle and buy myself breakfast. My mouth began to water at the prospect.

I shaved as quickly as possible and rubbed my teeth with

willow bark, as I have seen Welshmen do and for which purpose I always carry a sliver in my pocket, gathering fresh pieces
as I go. At last I had finished and, returning to the front part of
the house, I stowed away my pack, made sure all was safe,
locked the street door behind me and slipped the key into my
pocket. Then I directed my feet towards the castle inn.

Grizelda was outside the cottage when I entered the clearing,
planting leeks in a patch of ground within the paling of her
garden, but there was no sign of either pig or cow. Both sty
and field were empty and I felt a stab of alarm. Had the
outlaws indeed returned to rob her further? Or had she had
the wit to leave the beasts with her friends?

I must either have made some sound or she sensed my
presence, for she straightened suddenly, staring in my direction and shielding her eyes with her hand against the morning
sun. When she saw who it was, her wide, generous mouth
split into a welcoming grin.

'Chapman! What brings you back this way again?'

'I need to talk to you. But first tell me, where are the
animals?'

'Safe with my friends on their holding near Ashprington. I
went there last night, as you advised me to do, taking Betsy
and Snouter with me to be locked in their barn – a good,
stout building which would make any robber think twice
before trying to break in. And there they will stay, for a day
or two at least, until I get weary of trudging to and fro
carrying milk pails.'

'And nothing was disturbed when you returned this
morning?'

'Everything was exactly as I left it. And I came back very
early, before sunrise, in order to avoid the hockers.' She

smiled impudently. 'I thought you might have been out with your fellow men, getting your revenge for yesterday.'

I shook my head and reverted to the original subject.

'I'd leave the beasts where they are for as long as your friends are willing to house them. The town's full of rumours this morning that the outlaws were abroad again last night, across the river, towards Berry Pomeroy. They could return here yet. The Mayor's sent word again to Exeter, I understand, to the Sheriff, and there should be a *posse* riding south by tomorrow. But these men, as well as being dangerous, are cunning. I doubt they'll be caught without a stroke of luck, but they may well tire and move on to different ground that offers them fresh pickings. They've been in these parts a long time now. Be patient a while, and they may just vanish.'

Grizelda smiled and invited me into the cottage. 'Have you eaten?' she asked, as I followed her indoors.

'Yes, and heartily,' I answered. 'Boiled bacon, a mess of eggs, oatcakes and honey, provided for me by my friend, the innkeeper of the ale-house near the castle.'

'Jacinta! I know her. Well-meaning enough, but inclined to push her nose into everybody's business.' Grizelda looked surprised. 'You stayed the night in Totnes, then? Somehow, I thought you would be out of there and on the open road before yesterevening.' She frowned suddenly. 'You aren't carrying your pack! What's happened?'

I sat down on one of the benches, my back resting against the wall, while she poured me a beaker of her excellent ale, brewed to a rich, dark colour, and given its sharp and tangy taste by the germander I had noticed growing in her garden.

'I spent the night in Eudo Colet's house,' I said, reaching out to take the beaker from her.

She jumped, spilling some of the ale, and the brown eyes widened in horror.

'What were you doing there?' she demanded.

I told her; of my meeting with Mistress Cozin and her daughters; of my visit to the house; of the offer made to me by Oliver Cozin to play caretaker for the night; of his subsequent suggestion that I might like to remain there longer; and of my conversation with the landlady of the ale-house near the castle. 'Named by you as Jacinta,' I added, 'though she never told me how she was called.'

'And so you have come to hear the full story,' Grizelda said, sitting down beside me, on the bench. She was quick on the uptake: there was no need to explain the reasons for my actions.

'If you are willing to tell it,' I answered.

She thought for a moment, her face serious, brooding almost, and I wondered what was going through her mind. Then she shrugged.

'Yes, I'm willing, if you're interested enough to listen. But I warn you that I can shed no light on the central mystery; what happened to Andrew and Mary after I left the house that dreadful morning.' Her lips set in a thin, hard line and her face grew dark with sorrow. 'But of the events leading up to their disappearance, I can tell you as much as you wish to know, for my life had been intertwined with Rosamund's since we were children.'

Chapter Six

'My father,' she said, 'was a distant kinsman of Sir Jasper Crouchback's wife, Lucy, and there was a sufficient bond of blood between them to merit the title of "cousin". Sir Jasper acknowledged it, and did what he could to aid my parents when times were bad, and used his influence with the manor lord to get us this holding. He was also influential in having it written into the lease that it should remain in our possession for two generations, regardless of whether the heir were male or female.

'Lucy Crouchback died when Rosamund was born. She was their first child, and Lucy was not much above nineteen summers. It was a bitter blow to Sir Jasper, who had come to marriage late, being some fifteen, perhaps sixteen, years older than his wife. Everyone naturally expected him to marry again and get himself a son, but he didn't. He remained a widower for the rest of his life and lavished all his love and money on Rosamund. The result, as you might suppose, was a wilful, spoilt child, used to getting her own way in everything, and one who could wind her father around her little finger.'

'You speak without malice,' I interrupted. 'In spite of her faults, you were fond of her?'

Grizelda smiled. 'I was, and she of me, I like to think. Oh, there were times when we quarrelled, and on occasions bitterly. I should be a liar if I denied it. But it's no more than you'd expect when two girls grow up together in the same house, sharing the same toys and the same bed. But I get ahead of myself. When I was nine years old, my mother died. Rosamund was then about five, with only the old family nurse for female companionship. Sir Jasper offered to relieve my father of my care by taking me to live with him in the town, as a playmate for Rosamund. I think my father was thankful to let me go, even though I, too, was an only child. He knew nothing about the upbringing of girls.' She laughed. 'Truth to tell, I think women were always something of a mystery to him, poor man.'

'And were you willing?'

'Not at first. I remember crying and begging my father not to send me. But he told me it was for my own good, and in the end, I knew he had been right. Living with Sir Jasper and Rosamund gave me the friendship of my own sex and the kind of life of which, hitherto, I had only had glimpses.'

'Sir Jasper was a very rich man,' I said, not questioning, but stating. 'How did he make his money?'

Grizelda put her head on side, regarding me thoughtfully. 'Do you know anything about the cloth trade?' she asked.

I finished my ale and put the empty beaker down on the bench beside me.

'My mother-in-law is a spinner, and dwells in the midst of Bristol's weaving community. Her father was a weaver for most of his life. So, yes, you could say I know a little about the cloth trade.'

My companion nodded. 'Then do you know what straights are?'

'I've heard them spoken of, and always with contempt.

They are the poor, coarse lengths of cloth woven from the wool of inferior sheep, whose fleece is not considered good enough for English broadcloth.'

Grizelda laughed. 'You've obviously learned your lesson well enough to recite it by heart. But straights are not universally despised, you know, and they sell fast enough abroad, especially to the Bretons. Many a Totnes fortune has been made in Little Britain, Sir Jasper Crouchback's being but one of them. His and Thomas Cozin's boats plied from the harbour here across the Narrow Sea and back again for many years, and still do, though now the enterprise is managed solely by Master Cozin. And he, like the honourable man he is, saw to it that Sir Jasper's investment in the business continued to benefit his heirs. When Rosamund died in childbirth, last Martinmas, bearing Eudo Colet's stillborn son, she was even wealthier than her father had been.'

'And her husband is now in sole possession of this fortune? Well, it's the law. But go back a little. Tell me about your cousin's first marriage.'

'To Sir Henry Skelton. Very well. He was a gentleman of the bedchamber to King Edward. He had lands in Yorkshire, but as he was a widower with a grown-up son it was upon that son the estate devolved when Sir Henry was killed. He and Rosamund were only wed a little over two years. They met when Sir Jasper took the pair of us to London some . . . oh . . . nine years ago, would it be? Rosamund had just turned eighteen years of age, and I was four years older.' Her eyes twinkled. 'I can see you struggling with your numbers, chapman, so I will take pity and tell you that I was born the same year that the late King Henry married the Frenchwoman, Margaret of Anjou. Which, by my reckoning gives me thirty summers.'

I tried to look astonished at this information, but she was

too shrewd to be taken in by my feigned amazement.

'Admit it,' she laughed. 'You had already judged me to be as much. No, no! Don't bother to deny it. I have no wish to be thought any younger.'

'And why should you,' I asked gallantly, 'when you are such a very handsome woman?'

That made her laugh even more, but she flushed with pleasure, nevertheless. And I only spoke the truth. She was very good-looking.

'Where was I?' she murmured.

'You and Rosamund were taken to London by Sir Jasper.'

'Ah, yes. He had a house in Paternoster Row, in the lee of Saint Paul's, and we lived there for several months of each year. Sir Jasper had made up his mind, you see, that Rosamund should marry well, and there was no one in Totnes whom he could even begin to consider as a possible husband for her. She was to wed a man with a place at court and of some influence with the King.'

'Sir Jasper was for the House of York, then?'

'Most certainly. King Edward had all his allegiance.'

'And this Sir Henry Skelton, presumably, was just such a man as he had in mind for your cousin. But what were her feelings in the matter?'

Grizelda shrugged. 'I never heard her oppose his wishes. You might think that was only natural in a dutiful daughter, but Rosamund, as I have said, could be spoilt and self-willed on occasions. But in this case, she was perfectly biddable. Why do you ask?'

'Something your friend, Jacinta, told me; that your cousin said she had married to oblige her father the first time, but would marry a second time to please herself.'

Grizelda frowned, annoyed. 'That woman gossips too

much. Not but what she may be right, although I never heard Rosamund express any such sentiment myself. She certainly offered no opposition to Sir Jasper's plans for her when the marriage was arranged, although . . .' She hesitated, looking faintly embarrassed.

'Although?' I prompted.

Grizelda picked up my empty beaker and got up to refill it, busying herself so that, for the moment, she had her back towards me.

'I think the marriage, brief as it was, may have been a disappointment to my cousin. Rosamund was . . . of a passionate nature, and once those . . . those sort of feelings had been aroused in her, she needed a passionate man to assuage them.' Grizelda mopped up the drips of ale on the table, wiped around the bottom of the cup and returned to her seat, still avoiding my eyes. 'Sir Henry Skelton, as I have indicated, was some years older than she. A widower and, as far as I could observe, not a very uxorious man. Which might well be the reason why, when Rosamund came to marry again, and with no one then to check her or approve of her choice, she allowed her . . . her appetites to overrule her better judgement.'

'I understand,' I said gently, taking the beaker from her and cupping it between my hands.

'Yes.' She drew a deep breath. 'So, to continue. Fortunately perhaps, for Rosamund, the marriage did not last long. My little Andrew was born the year following the wedding, at the beginning of May, and Mary thirteen months later, but by then Sir Henry was already dead.'

'How did he die?'

'He was killed, defending his lands in the north, two months or so before Mary was born. I can't recall all the details now, but it was the beginning of greater trouble in the autumn, when the Earl of Warwick captured the King and held him prisoner in Pontefract Castle. There had been rumours during the Christmas feast that all was not well between King Edward and the Earl, but no one could quite believe it. They were close kinsmen and had been like blood brothers for so long.'

I nodded. 'I remember.' At the time, I had recently entered upon my novitiate, and the news of such stirring events, penetrating even the abbey's hallowed walls, had relieved my boredom, and distracted me from my growing conviction that, whatever my mother's wishes, I could never tolerate the religious life. 'It was the beginning of the road which eventually led Warwick into the Lancastrian camp and his death, less that two years later, on Barnet Field.'

'Your grasp of events is better than mine. But I do know that in the spring, before the King's captivity, there were insurrections in Yorkshire, because Sir Henry was summoned by his elder son to return and protect his property. It was during a skirmish with the rebels that he was killed.'

'You had remained in London with your cousin throughout her marriage?'

Grizelda replied with dignity, 'I looked after little Andrew. I was his nurse.'

I made no comment, but it was apparent to me that the relationship between the two women had inevitably altered on Rosamund's marriage. They could no longer continue on an equal footing, and the impoverished and dowerless Grizelda had been relegated to a subordinate role.

My thoughts must have shown in my face, for she said quietly, 'It meant much to me that I was still needed. I could so easily have been sent packing back to my father, but

Rosamund wanted me to stay. And in private, nothing had changed between us. We continued to be friends and confidantes.'

'And after Mary was born, you returned to Devon, to live with Sir Jasper.'

Grizelda smiled. 'You speak with confidence: Jacinta seems to have told you a great deal. But yes, you're right. We came home, and I, for one, was glad. I disliked London, a dirty, noisy place. And more traffic crowding the roads in one day than you would see in six months in Totnes. For over a twelvemonth, we were settled and happy, and I had the maid, Bridget Praule, to help with the care of the children. You met her grandam yesterday morning, at the hocking.'

'I recollect,' I said feelingly. 'What happened, then, to disturb you at the end of a year?'

'Sir Jasper died suddenly on Corpus Christi Eve. He was in the counting-house, talking to his clerk, when he just fell to the floor with a terrible groan and was taken up dead. Two months later, my own father died of a rheum, too much neglected, which turned to a fever and carried him off within a few days. I would have returned to the holding then, as my duty dictated, but Rosamund begged me to remain and continue to look after the children. They knew and loved me, she said, as I knew and loved them. And indeed, with all my partiality, I have to admit that she was not a good mother. She was by nature too indolent and selfish.

'So, I stayed. As you already know, I let Innes Woodsman run the holding for me in return for free lodging, and in this way, life continued for another two years. There were a number of suitors for Rosamund's hand during that time, as you would expect with such a wealthy young widow, especially one who, thanks to Master Thomas Cozin, was growing even richer. But none of them was successful. Not one was the man she wanted. And then in late summer, three years since, she decided to go to London to stay awhile with some former neighbours in Paternoster Row: a Ginèvre Napier and her husband, Gregory. Gregory Napier is a goldsmith with a shop in West Cheap, between Foster Lane and Gudrun Lane.'

'But you and the children did not go with her?'

'No. Rosamund had grown bored. She was restless for excitement, diversity. She said she was growing old before her time. It so happened, that August, that an elderly and respectable couple from the other side of the river, old friends of Sir Jasper, were travelling to London to visit their married daughter who lived in the Bread Street Ward, so Rosamund went with them. She was supposed to come back with them, also, three weeks later, but when Master Harrison and his goodwife called for her on the homeward journey, Rosamund told them that Ginèvre had urged her remain longer with her and her husband, and that she would make her own arrangements for returning to Totnes. That was the message they delivered, not without some distress, for I think they felt responsible for her. Nor did they care overmuch for Ginèvre Napier; I could tell, both by their manner and the way they talked about her. But there was nothing they could do. Rosamund was responsible to nobody but herself for her actions.'

Grizelda sighed, paused and then continued, 'She did not come home until October; the end, for it was only a day or so before All Hallows' Eve when she arrived in a splendid new wagonette, upholstered inside with velvet cushions, and with velvet curtains across the windows to keep out the cold. She was not alone. There was a man with her. As she descended from the wagon, the children ran to greet her.

"My dearlings," she said, stooping to kiss them, "this is your new father, Mamma's new husband, Master Eudo Colet." '

There was a profound silence in the cottage, and I became aware once more of the birds singing in the trees outside. I could also hear the snorting and snuffling of a herd of pigs, as their owner drove them into the forest to root for beech-mast and truffles. A man's voice called a greeting, to which Grizelda responded. Then the silence drifted back, deeper than before.

I had a vivid, mind's eye picture of the scene my companion had just conjured up for me; the wagonette drawing up to the door, the horses blowing steam in the cold, wintry air, the two children running excitedly to greet their mother, who had been absent for so many months and had now, at last, returned to them. I saw Rosamund – or, at least, the likeness I had created in my imagination – descend from the carriage and stoop for their embrace. And, behind her, making a leisurely descent, was the shadowy figure of an unknown man.

'What happened then?' I inquired at last.

'Nothing.' Grizelda spoke sharply. 'What could happen? She had married him, and he had the marriage lines to prove it. He was our new master, the children's stepfather. We had to accept it.'

'But you didn't like him,' I said quietly, when she appeared reluctant to say anything further.

'I hated him from the first.' Her voice was low, but vehement.

'You must have had a reason,' I urged, after another silence.

Grizelda shifted on the bench, easing her back against the wall. She seemed to relax suddenly, as though relieved to be able to talk openly at last to a sympathetic stranger.

'But that was just the trouble. I had no good reason for the way I felt about Eudo Colet, except an instinctive mistrust of the man. There was something about him from the very start that made me sure he was of peasant stock. Oh, my bucko looked very fine in the rich clothes that undoubtedly Rosamund had bought for him. But he wasn't comfortable in them. He was unused to such finery and paraded it like a peacock, whereas a gentleman who always wore that kind of apparel would have thought nothing of it. And it was the same when he bestrode a horse. Oh, he could ride, but he had a heavy hand on the bridle and the bit tore at the animal's mouth. He had been used to sturdier animals, working beasts, not the mettlesome horseflesh in Rosamund's stables.'

'And you considered him an adventurer, after your cousin's money?'

'Yes. How was it possible for me to think otherwise? And neither Rosamund nor he would ever talk about his life before they met. What he was, where he came from remained a secret which only they shared. As I said earlier, not even Master Cozin could uncover anything concerning him, although he despatched two of his servants to London to make inquiries. Rosamund was beside herself with fury when she found out, and it léd to a breach of several months between them. But she needed Thomas to run her affairs, and when she discovered that he had been unsuccessful, she forgave him.'

'What about Master Cozin's brother, the attorney? Did he ever make any attempt to get at the truth?'

'He may have done. I think it most probable, but I never heard of it. Rosamund had ceased to confide in me. I'm afraid I had made my dislike of Eudo too plain. My belief is that she would have suggested I leave and return here to live, had I not been so useful to her with the children. She had no need to trouble her head about them while I was there to look after them. She was free to spend her time as she wished, with her husband.'

'And how did they seem together?'

'To begin with, all was well. She doted on him.' Again, Grizelda coloured faintly. 'Eudo Colet gave her . . . what she wanted in a man. He provided . . . what we were talking of just now. In that respect, he was everything that Henry Skelton was not. But as time went on, there were disagreements between them. For it was obvious to me that she was far fonder of him than he of her, which only served to confirm my suspicions that he had married her for her money. In those circumstances, it was natural that, on occasions, his eyes should stray towards other women. But,' Grizelda added grudgingly, 'I don't believe he deceived her in any bolder fashion.'

'And the children?' I asked. 'Was he kind to them?'

She shrugged. 'Neither kind nor unkind. If he were forced to take notice of them, he was polite enough, but for the most part, like Rosamund, he ignored them. As long as I attended to all Mary's and Andrew's needs, there was no reason why their mother or Eudo should have much to do with them.'

I interposed here with a question I had been wanting to ask for sometime, because of a memory nagging at the back of my mind.

'What does he look like, this Eudo Colet?'

Grizelda considered, taking her time before answering. At length, she said, 'Dark of hair and general complexion. Eyes the colour of hazel nuts, a slightly crooked nose and full lips above a bushy, dark brown beard. A twelvemonth younger than Rosamund. Five years younger than me.'

'Then I've seen him!' I exclaimed triumphantly. 'Yesterday afternoon, early. I was returning to the town after eating my dinner down by St Peter's Quay, when I encountered this horseman near the Leper Hospital. He was mounted on a chestnut with pale mane and tail, but appeared uneasy in the handling of the animal. A bearded man, richly dressed.'

Grizelda nodded. 'Eudo, undoubtedly. Where was he going?'

'We didn't speak, but he was riding downhill, in the direction of the bridge.'

'Then he was returning to his lodgings. Since he quit the house, after the children's murder, he has been staying with Agatha Tenter and her mother.'

'So Jacinta informed me. She seemed to find the fact significant.'

Grizelda's head reared up. 'Significant? In what way?'

'That she didn't make clear to me, but I should hazard a guess that she suspects some sort of affection between Master Colet and Agatha Tenter. You said yourself that he had a wandering eye. Might it not have ranged as far as the cook? After all, they were together, night and day, under the same roof.'

Grizelda bit her lip. 'I never saw sign of such an attachment, but that's not to say there mightn't have been one. Agatha's a year or so older than I, but not yet in her dotage.' She gave me a sly, sidelong glance, conscious of fishing for a compliment, and hurried on, 'A good-looking enough woman, too, if you like red hair and a buxom figure.'

I said nothing, only shook my head and grinned. Almost, but not quite, by accident, I shifted a little closer to Grizelda on the bench. After a momentary start, she made no effort to put more distance between us.

'I've made you lose the thread of your story with my interruptions,' I apologized. 'Your cousin's death in childbirth must have changed many things.'

'It did. Rosamund discovered she was pregnant in February of last year. The baby was due around Martinmas. Strangely, with both Andrew and Mary she had difficulty in carrying them, but easy births. With her third child, it was exactly the reverse. She was well and happy throughout the entire nine months, with Eudo dancing attendance on her every minute of the day. To give him his due, I have never seen a man more delighted at the prospect of becoming a father; although I could not rid myself of the notion that he saw the coming child as a means of silencing much of the rumour and gossip which, even after two years, still persisted about him. But then, at the last, it all went wrong, and he lost not only his son, but his wife, as well. However,' Grizelda continued cynically, 'Rosamund's death has left him a very rich man.'

'No more,' I pointed out, 'than he has been from the moment he married her and became her lord.'

Grizelda wrinkled her nose. 'I don't think he had truly accepted, until that moment, that everything she had was his; yet another proof to me that he was not of gentle birth. He was too easily overawed by the power of money and by people such as lawyers. But after Rosamund's death, all that changed. He began to realize just how wealthy he was.' Her pleasant features hardened. 'Unfortunately for him, the partnership between Sir Jasper and Thomas Cozin had, in law, been dissolved when the former died, but Thomas, out of the goodness of his heart, had continued to share the profits of the enterprise with his old friend's daughter. But hardly was the funeral over, and Rosamund laid to rest, than Thomas announced his intention of doing so no longer. And that,'

Grizelda added, lowering her voice almost to a whisper, 'was when I began to be afraid for the safety of my charges.'

Chapter Seven

By now, the sun was high in the heavens, and the shadows which lay across the beaten-earth floor were shortening as it rose towards its zenith. It was growing warm; too warm for early April, experience having taught me that heat too soon in the year often presaged a wet and chilly summer. I was hungry, for it was past the hour of dinner, but I was too eager to hear the rest of Grizelda's story to interrupt her with a request for food. By good fortune, however, she thought of it herself, standing up and shaking out her skirt. She had on the same one of blue brocella that she had worn the previous day.

'It's time we ate,' she said firmly. 'I can offer you bread and cheese, apples and oatcakes, washed down with some more of my ale, to which you seem to have taken a liking.'

I accepted gladly everything except the ale. She made a potent brew and I had drunk enough. My head was already beginning to swim. So she filled me a beaker of water from the barrel which stood outside the cottage door, and then suggested that we, too, go outside and warm ourselves in the sunshine. So we sat on a stone bench which ran the length of the south-facing wall, eating Grizelda's excellent home-baked bread flavoured with corncockle seeds, cheese, made from the milk of her cow, oatcakes sweetened with honey, and some small shrivelled apples from last autumn's gathering, given to her by a neighbour. The rainwater from the barrel was cool and refreshing; in dry spells, she told me, when the supply ran out, she was forced to haul her water up by bucket from the river.

'Hard work,' she grimaced, 'but, luckily, I'm strong. Even luckier, I've only had to do it twice since my return to the cottage in January.'

'I'll fill the barrel to the brim before I leave,' I promised. 'It's the least I can do as repayment for your patience.'

'It's a kindness to myself,' she answered. 'It's a relief to be able to talk about what happened to someone who knows neither the participants nor the story, and so, as yet, has no theory to offer which distracts my own thoughts in the telling. It helps me to recall events as they unfolded with greater clarity.'

When we had at last finished our meal and were sitting contentedly, lapped about by the bright stillness of the morning, the succulent spring grass starred with primroses, the leaves of the forest trees rustling in a little breeze with a sound like rain, I asked her to continue; to explain why she had been so worried for the children's safety after their mother died.

Grizelda glanced down at her hands, long and strong with workmanlike fingers, folded together in her lap, and thought for a moment. Then, she raised her head, looked straight in front of her and said, 'I think it was Sir Henry Skelton's will which made me uneasy. I was in London with Rosamund and her father when it was drawn up in the spring of 1469, just before Sir Henry rode north to fight the rebels.

'It was Sir Jasper who insisted that proper provision be

made, in the event of his son-in-law's death, for Rosamund and the children; that Sir Henry's intentions should be legally set down and witnessed. Sir Jasper declared he had seen too much litigation, which benefited no one except the attorneys, because of lack of written evidence of the legator's wishes. The manor in Yorkshire would naturally be inherited by Sir Henry's elder son, but he was a very wealthy man, with money to spare for Andrew and Mary, who, at that time of course, was still unborn. Sir Jasper sent for Oliver Cozin to come up from Exeter to represent Rosamund during all the legal wrangling; and, believe me, it went on for days.

'In the end, however, it was agreed that the revenues from various business ventures in which Sir Henry had some holding would provide for the offspring of his second marriage. But Master Cozin, not content with that, was anxious to keep so considerable a sum of money in his client's family. Supposing, said he, the children should die before Lady Skelton; one or the other or both. What then? Why should the money revert to their half-brother, who was already plenteously provided for? The money settled on Andrew and the expected child must go to Rosamund or – lawyers' minds being so tortuous that they foresee every eventuality – should she predecease them and they die while still minors, to her next of kin. And, after much legal haggling, he carried the day. Such a provision was inserted in Sir Henry's will.'

I drew in my breath. 'Surely a clause which could have hidden dangers? At least, so it seems to me.'

Grizelda smiled bitterly. 'And to me. But that, Master Chapman, is because we are simple people who live among other simple people, and are acquainted with their failings. We understand the greed and cupidity of our fellow human beings. But if you are an attorney, living within the ivory tower of the law, obsessed only with torts and malfeances and other suchlike practices, how can you possibly understand what goes on in the world around you? According to his lights, Master Oliver Cozin did well for his client, and Sir Jasper was mightily pleased, boasting to us all, one evening at supper, that no one in the kingdom, not even the King himself, had a more skilful lawyer.

'And, I suppose, to give both Sir Jasper and Master Cozin their due, neither could be blamed for not anticipating Rosamund's marriage to a man such as Eudo Colet. For I don't need to point out to you, Master Chapman, that once she was dead, only the children's lives stood between him and a very substantial addition to his fortune.'

'I told you yesterday,' I interrupted, 'that my name is Roger. Now that we know one another better, could you not bring yourself to use it?'

She smiled. 'Very well, if, in return, you will promise to call me Grizelda.'

'You have my solemn word. Now, having settled that, are you trying to tell me that you suspect Eudo Colet of murder?'

She shrugged, spreading her hands. 'He was the only person who gained by their deaths. And as I explained earlier, he had grown much greedier since Rosamund died. Money for its own sake had begun to excite him.'

'But . . .' I hesitated, loath to condemn any man of so horrible a crime without having more evidence of his guilt than had so far been offered me. I continued, 'There seems no evidence to suggest that he killed the children. Unless you believe Jacinta's accusation of witchcraft.' I took another long draught of water to clear my head of lingering ale fumes.

'Tell me about the day they disappeared, or as much of it as you can remember.'

Grizelda tilted her head back against the cottage wall and closed her eyes, shielding them from the glare of the sun.

'Eudo Colet and I had never got on. He could not fail, from the first, to sense my dislike of him, as did Rosamund, who grew colder towards me. We lost our closeness and became almost like strangers to one another. But I have told you this, already. After my cousin's death, the household was in disarray, as you might well imagine, but when the first shock had passed, Master Colet made it plain that he wished us all to remain as members of the household. As far as I was concerned, he would have rid himself of me if he could, but Andrew and Mary were too attached to me, and he had no affection for either child. I was still useful to him; while I swore to myself that nothing would make me abandon my dearlings.

'But things went from bad to worse between us. Master Colet and I had terrible arguments about the children. More than once, I had to protect them from his wrath, because' – she sighed – 'there is no denying that they were often very impertinent to him. They liked him no more than I did and had always been as disobedient as they dared, flouting his orders. When Rosamund was alive, he had not cared overmuch, leaving them to her to discipline. Now, however, there was only myself between him and their ... I'm afraid I can give it no name except naughtiness. But I knew how unhappy they both were, how desperately they missed their mother, and I defended them as best I could, often drawing away Master Colet's wrath towards myself until his temper had had time to cool a little.

89

'Christmas was an uneasy season, but a sort of truce pre-vailed between us all, so that the festivities, such as they were so soon after Rosamund's death, should not be marred. But once Twelfth Night had come and gone, and the bitter January winds and rains kept us mewed up indoors, it was as though all the illwill which had festered, unspoken, over the Nativity, burst and spewed forth like the breaking of a leprous sore.

'It was a Thursday, about the middle of the month, and I had been to worship early at the Priory. I recall that as I returned home it began to snow a little, and I was hungry, wanting my breakfast. As I entered the house, I heard voices, raised in anger, coming from the upstairs parlour; Eudo Colet shouting and the children wailing. Bridget and Agatha were huddled together at the foot of the stairs, listening and won-dering whether or not they ought to interfere.

'I pushed them to one side and rushed upstairs like a Fury! Oh, I admit it! It was foolish; I should have had myself more in hand before tackling Master Colet. I can't remember now precisely what we said to one another, but enough for me to feel that I could stay in the house no longer. I yelled down to Bridget to run and fetch Jack Carter. I had urgent need of his services. Then I packed my box, although by that time, with the children clinging to my skirts and begging me not to go, I was regretting my rash decision. But it was too late. Eudo Colet would not permit me to remain in the house, even had I really wished to do so.

'By the time Bridget returned with Jack and his wagon, however, all was quiet. Mary and Andrew had cried them-selves out and, in the callous way that children have, shrug-ging off their own troubles as well as those of their elders, had started to play quite happily together. Jack Carter carried my box downstairs and placed it on his cart, I climbed up beside him, having said my farewells to Agatha and Bridget, and he brought me . . . here.' She smiled wryly. 'I was going to say home, but after so many years, it was no longer that to me; just a roof and four walls to provide me with shelter.'

'And that was the last time you saw the two children?' I asked as gently as possible. I could sense her distress and had no wish to add to it beyond what was necessary.

She nodded mutely, and it was some moments before she could trust her voice. But, finally, she went on, 'It was the following day before news reached me that Mary and Andrew had vanished within hours of my departure. Agatha Tenter sent me word by Jack Carter, who was making another journey in this direction, and I begged a lift back to Totnes with him, when he returned, in order to find out for myself the truth of what had happened.'

'And what did you discover?' I picked up and bit into the last apple, without even being aware of what I was doing.

'The house was in uproar, as you would expect, Agatha pale and haggard, Bridget crying hysterically. There was turmoil, also, in the town, with half the population out searching for the children and the other half either crowded into the downstairs parlour or gathered around the doorstep, giving advice and asking questions. Or so it seemed. Robert Broughton, the Mayor, was there, along with Master Thomas Cozin, and presently a Sergeant came down from the castle to add to the inquiries.'

'And what was the result of all this inquisition? Your friend Jacinta told me that Master Colet was away from the house when the children vanished, visiting Thomas Cozin, who, presumably, was able to vouch for him?'

Grizelda nodded with extreme reluctance.

'That is so. He apparently went out immediately after

breakfast, and both Bridget and Agatha swore that the children were still upstairs at the time. They also swore that neither Andrew nor Mary could have gone out without being seen by one or the other of them. Bridget was dusting and polishing in the downstairs parlour, and Agatha was in the kitchen, preparing the vegetables and meat for dinner. She had left the door standing wide, in spite of the coldness of the morning, to clear the steam caused by the various pots of boiling water. She had the inner courtyard within her sight for nearly the whole of the time until Bridget came running to say that Mary and Andrew were nowhere to be found. The master had returned and sent for the children, but they had completely disappeared. The two of them then searched the storerooms and bedrooms above the kitchen, and also the outer courtyard, the stables and anywhere else they could think of, but to no avail.

'At first, of course, they all assumed there must be a simple explanation; that the children had found a hiding place which no one had as yet thought of, and were intent on giving their stepfather a fright, in order to teach him a lesson for his anger of earlier in the morning. But as the day wore on without their reappearance, everyone grew worried and raised the hue and cry. Parties of neighbours scoured the streets and buildings within the town, and, until darkness fell, the surrounding countryside. By the time I arrived with Jack Carter, the children had been missing all night, and everyone was beginning to fear that some evil had befallen them. The outlaws had been scourging the neighbourhood for several weeks past, and had already carried off a child during one of their forays. It's not unusual, as you must know. They use their captives as slaves, taking them with them when they move on to other parts of the country. Nothing is too vile for those men.'

'But in this case, they murdered their victims. Or so it would appear.'

Grizelda glanced at me sharply. As she turned her head, the sun caught the right side of her face, and I saw again the thin white scar, running from eyebrow to cheek.

'You speak as though you had doubts about the children's fate,' she accused me.

'Haven't *you*?' I countered. 'Haven't other people?'

She bit her lip and looked away again, staring across the clearing to where the beech bark shone in the sunlight, as though laced with silver.

'I cannot deny,' she answered, speaking so low that I had to bend my head to hear her properly, 'that it was more than fortunate for Eudo Colet, the children being killed as they were, so soon after their mother died, for, with their death, he inherited the money bequeathed them by Sir Henry. And I was not the only one whose suspicions were aroused. There were many who probed long and deep in the expectation of finding him guilty. But, to their great disappointment, I fancy, they were unable to shake the witness of Agatha and Bridget. Not one of Sir Jasper's old friends had ever liked him, nor was he generally popular in the town. Indeed, I don't think I should be doing him an injustice if I said that I never heard a good word concerning him. But' – Grizelda spread her hands in a hopeless gesture – 'nothing could be proved against him. Agatha and Bridget both staunchly maintained that he could have had nothing to do with the children's disappearance. They were upstairs when he left the house to visit Master Cozin, and had vanished by the time he returned. The Sheriff, who came from Exeter to conduct an inquiry, was forced to exonerate him for want of proof to the contrary.'

'But did no one suspect collusion with either the cook or the maid?'

Grizelda considered this. 'They may have done,' she said at last, 'but again, there was no evidence to support such a theory. No whisper had ever linked his name with that of either woman. And to be truthful, Roger, I cannot believe that he would find either Agatha or Bridget to his liking. The girls who caught his eye were young and pretty. Bridget may be young, but she is certainly not pretty, while Agatha is three years older than I am. Besides, once the children's bodies were discovered on the banks of the Harbourne, six weeks later, there was little doubt in anyone's mind that they had been murdered by the outlaws. Certainly, that was the verdict of the Coroner.'

I stroked my chin thoughtfully. 'So,' I said, 'in spite of the cook's and the maid's protestations that the children could not possibly have left the house without their knowledge, somehow or other they must have done so.'

'Yes. But alive, and without the assistance of Eudo Colet. Loath as most people were to accept that he had nothing to do with their disappearance, in the end, it was generally agreed that, following the quarrel with their stepfather, Andrew and Mary decided to run away, managed to escape unseen and took to the forest, where they got lost and were captured by the outlaws.'

'But why should the outlaws kill them?' I wondered.

'Perhaps, after a few weeks, they saw a chance to make a bid for freedom, and took it.' Grizelda's eyes filled with tears. 'They would not be easy to control, those two. They had courage and spirit, especially Andrew.'

I frowned. 'If the truth be told, you are satisfied in your own mind, are you not, that Eudo Colet had nothing to do with your young cousins' deaths?'

The silence stretched between us. After a long time, she nodded.

'I suppose so. I must be satisfied, mustn't I? There is no other conclusion I can come to.'

I did not answer immediately, but after a while, I said cautiously, 'There may be an explanation which no one has yet thought of.' I hesitated before adding, 'I have had some success in the past in solving mysteries which others considered too difficult to unravel, and I might be able to uncover something in this case, if you so wish it.'

My companion glanced at me in surprise, then smiled uncertainly, not sure if my claim were to be taken seriously.

'I could not put you to the trouble,' she eventually protested. 'You will want to be on the road again tomorrow.'

I shook my head. 'I've made good money in Totnes, enough to support myself for several weeks before I need to restock my pack. And, as I told you earlier, Oliver Cozin has offered me the shelter of Master Colet's house until he departs for Exeter on Saturday, and I suspect he would be happy for me to remain as long as I wanted. It seems your cousin's husband can find neither tenant nor buyer for the property at present. Why is that? Although I think I know the answer.'

Grizelda nodded. 'Oh, yes. There are still rumours of witchcraft in the town; people like Jacinta of the castle ale-house believe Eudo Colet guilty of a compact with the Devil. Small blame to them, I suppose, when everything worked out so well for him, the children's deaths following so pat upon their mother's. It was the reason why he dismissed the servants and shut up the house to take lodgings with Dame Winifred and Agatha, on the other side of the river. It would never surprise me to know that he had removed from the district altogether.'

'Not according to the lawyer. If Oliver Cozin is to be believed, he is even now negotiating on Master Colet's behalf for a new property hereabouts, although exactly where, he did not mention.'

There was a sudden raucous cawing above our heads as a rook with some titbit dangling from its beak flew home to its nest among the trees. The sunlight slithered across the jet-black plumage and tipped the ragged wings with gold. Grizelda watched the bird until it disappeared, when she lowered her eyes again and turned to me.

'So,' she said at length, 'Eudo Colet intends to remain to plague us, does he? I thought that surely he would go away and leave us all in peace to mourn the dead.' She lifted her chin and I saw the jawline harden. 'Do you really believe that there is anything you can possibly discover that has eluded the vigilance of the rest of us?'

'That I don't yet know,' I answered. 'I can but try, so long as I have your blessing. You are the person most nearly concerned with the dead, both by blood and friendship, and therefore the one to be most distressed by memories if I proceed.'

Once more, she tilted her head back against the wall, eyes closed, thinking. I did not try to persuade her one way or the other; the decision must be hers, and hers alone. But I waited with bated breath for the reply, my curiosity by now fully aroused, and with the bloodhound scent of the chase hot in my nostrils. And yet, because I felt sure that God had led me to this place, once again to do His bidding, I did not truly doubt what her answer would be.

I was not disappointed. Without opening her eyes, she nodded.

'Very well. If you can find out anything further, you have my blessing. But I must warn you that I think you will not succeed.'

I leaned forward, my hands on my knees. 'Perhaps. But did it never occur to you, or to anyone else, that Master Colet might have made a compact with the outlaws to steal the children and do away with them later? These things do happen. In Bristol, unwanted kinfolk are still sold into slavery with the Irish, in spite of the fact that the trade has been banned by both State and Church for more than two hundred years.'

Grizelda looked horrified, but argued that such a possibility would have been considered by the Sheriff, if by no one else.

'Yet, if so, it must have been dismissed in the end. For how could the outlaws have spirited the children out of the house without themselves being seen? Or how could a rendezvous have been arranged between the children and their captors without Mary and Andrew's connivance? And I should tell you that the gatekeepers on all the town gates were questioned most minutely, but not one of them remembered seeing two small children on their own. Indeed, not a single person was found who had even the smallest recollection of sighting either Mary or Andrew, within or outside the walls that morning.'

'But they got out somehow!' I placed my hand over hers, where it gripped the edge of the bench, and she made no attempt to free it. 'Are you seeking to discourage me?' I asked. 'Are you regretting your decision to let me probe further into this affair?'

She looked me full in the eyes then, smiling and shaking her head.

'No. I just want you to understand the difficulties you are facing. I wouldn't wish you to think that others had been lax in their duty and not given every consideration to even the most unlikely probability.'

I grinned. 'In short, you are trying to check my conceit before I make a fool of myself and have to admit that I am no cleverer than my elders and betters.'

'No, no!' she laughed. 'I only meant . . . Oh, I don't know what I meant! You confuse me.'

'Do I?' I raised my free hand and stroked her cheek, the skin soft and smooth despite its weather-beaten appearance. Then, as much to my own surprise as I think to hers, I leaned forward and kissed her on the lips.

Chapter Eight

'That,' I said, a trifle breathlessly, 'is in return for the kiss you gave me yesterday morning.'

'Did I kiss you yesterday?' The brown eyes mocked me, but I thought I also glimpsed a tenderness in them. 'So I did. I remember now. When we parted.' She cocked her head to one side, as though to ask, 'What response do you wish me to make?'

I had no answer to her unspoken question. She was unlike any other woman I had ever known or thought myself in love with. So far, these had all been women younger than myself; and while Grizelda was, indeed, thirty to my twenty-two, in maturity she gave the impression of a sibyl, wise beyond her years.

Moreover, I guiltily recalled that on the several occasions when both Jacinta and Grizelda had talked to me of Rosamund Colet dying in childbirth the previous Martinmas, I had not once remembered that my young wife, Lillis, had also died of the selfsame cause around that time. There had been no well-spring of grief nor bitter recollection to bring tears to my eyes or a lump to my throat. I had quite simply forgotten that I, too, was a man bereaved, left with a child to care for. I felt suddenly and deeply ashamed.

'What is it?' Grizelda asked gently. 'Something is bothering you. There's unhappiness in your face.'

Perhaps there was no other woman, under such circumstances, to whom I would have given an honest answer, but with Grizelda I felt that I could tell her the truth. She heard me out in silence, drawing a little away from me, but still retaining her clasp on my hand. When I had finished my confession, she smiled.

'You have too tender a conscience, my friend. No one is able to control his or her thoughts, not even the most disciplined and saintly amongst us. It is how you translate those thoughts into actions that matters, and will matter to God on the Day of Judgement. Or to the Devil, if we happen to find ourselves before Old Scratch.' I crossed myself hastily, and again she smiled. 'You are a good man, Roger. Don't expect too much of yourself. There are times when we all have to accept what we are.'

'Do you?' I queried.

'Oh yes!' She spoke cheerfully, if a little ruefully. 'I realized many years ago that to be jealous or envious of those who had more than I did was not necessarily sinful. Oh, I was told that such feelings were wrong, but only by those who wished to keep what they had to themselves and deny me any share in it. Once I understood this, I was able to acknowledge my failings and to condemn myself less harshly. Even so, you told me yesterday that I was too severe on myself. Well, now I tell you the same. You did not love your wife, but you did your best for her. You married her when she found herself with child, and I daresay you made her as happy as you could during the brief months you spent together. Be content with that. It's as much as God has a right to ask of you.'

I eyed her a little askance, wondering if I should cavil

at what any churchman would condemn as blasphemy, but knowing that if I did so, I should be a hypocrite. Had I not entertained similar thoughts myself from time to time? And no priest worth his salt would condone the arguments I had with God, nor the direct way I approached Him, instead of through the Virgin or the Saints. Grizelda and I had many ideas in common. Maybe that was what drew me to her.

I debated silently whether or not a renewed advance on my part would be welcomed by my companion. I wished she did not make me feel quite so young and inexperienced. But while I hesitated, the moment was lost. Something landed with a thud at my feet, barely missing striking me on the forehead. With astonishment, I saw that the missile was a short, thick length of branch, stripped of its leaves and trimmed into a handy weapon. A piece of bark was peeling away from the core, and could have caused a nasty, ragged gash had it hit me. Looking up swiftly for my assailant, I saw Innes Woodsman standing on the opposite side of the clearing. Gathering up the piece of wood, I rose menacingly to my feet, and Innes, after staring defiantly for a moment or two, withdrew strategically into the trees.

'I seed you kissin' her!' he shouted. 'You leave 'er be! She's a bad woman!'

I advanced a few paces, letting my arms hang loosely by my sides. He retreated a little further, with equal deliberation, unsure of my intentions. Then I sprang with such suddenness that he lost valuable seconds before he realized what was happening, and so fast that I was on him before he had taken more than a couple of steps. I bore him to the ground, pinioning his wrists together with my hands so that he was unable to make a grab for his knife.

'This is the second time in as many days you've tried to

harm me,' I accused him through gritted teeth. 'I think I'm about due for a reckoning, don't you?'

He looked up at me with a hatred I was shrewd enough to know was really meant for Grizelda. 'She's a bad woman!' he repeated. 'You let 'er be.'

For answer, I tightened my grip on his bony wrists and tried to ignore the rancid smell of him – sweat and dried urine and mouldering leaves – which, at this little distance, was all-pervasive.

'Why do you vilify Mistress Harbourne so?' I demanded.

'Let him go, Roger,' Grizelda said from behind me. She had advanced so quietly that I had not heard her approach. 'I told you yesterday, he means no harm.'

'I beg to differ,' I answered shortly, and turned my attention back to my captive. 'Well? What have you to say for yourself? I'm waiting.'

'She turned me out of my home,' was the sullen response, which rose to a mewling whine. 'You're hurting my wrists. I ain't strong. You'll snap 'em in two if you're not careful.'

I was unmoved by this complaint and, kneeling astride him, dug my knees into his fleshless hips.

'This cottage belongs to Mistress Harbourne, who graciously permitted you to use it until she needed it herself. And what is her reward? Not gratitude for benefits received! Oh, no! Rather, attacks on her person and abuse.' I bent closer to him, valiantly ignoring the blast of stinking breath. 'Now, let me make this clear! If I hear that you have tried to harm her just once more – just once, mark you! – I shall hunt you down and thrash you within an inch of your miserable life.' I rose, abruptly releasing him, and watched in silent contempt while he scrambled to his feet and made off amongst the trees without so much as a backward glance. I turned to Grizelda. 'You must promise to tell me if you have any more trouble from him.'

She led the way back to the cottage.

'You're very kind,' she said, 'but you have no need to concern yourself with me. I'm perfectly capable of looking after myself.'

'That man has a knife,' I persisted, 'and bears you a grudge. I would much prefer that you allowed me to send word to the Sheriff. Innes Woodsman could well prove dangerous, not simply to you, but to others.'

Grizelda resolutely shook her head.

'No. That I forbid on pain of my greatest displeasure. In Innes Woodsman's eyes, I have done him an injury, and I refuse to add the insult of having him taken into custody.' And when I would have protested, she again betrayed impatience. 'No! I'll not argue with you. My mind is made up on that point.'

'But yesterday, you told him one more chance. He's had that chance and thrown it away.'

'Roger! If you value our friendship, say no more on the subject.'

I realized with a tinge of sadness that the former mood between us had vanished, and was not to be recaptured. It was by now midday, the sun standing directly overhead and the shadows reduced almost to nothing. I should be on my way: what was there to keep me? Besides, I must visit the Cozins' dwelling and inform Master Oliver that I accepted his offer to remain in Eudo Colet's house at least until Saturday, and longer if he wished it. And there might be some information to be gleaned from him, if I went about the matter carefully.

'I have to go,' I said. 'Sleep with your neighbours for as

long as they'll allow it, but if you must stay in the cottage at night, bolt the door and shutters.' I did not add that the woodsman worried me far more than the outlaws, sensing that such a sentiment would prove unacceptable to Grizelda in her present mood. 'Do I still have your permission to inquire into the disappearance of the children?'

'Yes. But I repeat, I'm afraid you'll have no success. For, reluctant as I am to admit it, I don't believe there is anything more to discover. The truth is the sum of what we already know. Wasn't it William of Occam who adjured us to make the least possible number of assumptions when trying to explain things?'

I kept my promise to top up Grizelda's water barrel before departing, making two trips with the bucket down to the river's edge and returning without too much spillage. But it was hard work, even for the great strong lad that I was in those days, and I offered up a prayer of thankfulness for the recent rains, which had filled the cask three quarters full.

As soon as I had completed my task, I set off towards Totnes, for the journey took over an hour on foot. But I hardly noticed the weary miles as I trudged along the forest paths, my mind being too busy with everything that Grizelda had told me. All very well, I thought, for her to quote William of Occam; and while I had the greatest respect for old Dr 'Singularis et Invincibilis', and his axiom *entia non sunt multiplicanda*, there were none the less many occasions upon which I had found that the simplest assumption was not necessarily the right one. And William had been in his grave for well over a century. With the arrogance of youth, I decided that modern life and the people it produced were of a far greater sophistication and complexity than he could possibly have anticipated. Of course, I'm wiser now: I realize that every generation thinks the same.

By the time I passed once again through the West Gate, it had grown hot enough for me to remove my leather jerkin and the cap from my head. The gatekeeper, a ruddy-faced man with huge forearms bared to the elbow, greeted me in the friendly manner of one who is having an easy day.

'All quiet, then, friend?' I asked, and he nodded.

'Aye. Mind you, it's not often like this. Most times it's nothing but clatter.'

'I don't doubt it for a moment.' I smiled, at my most conciliatory. 'Not a job I could do. I haven't the patience.'

He was flattered and disposed to gossip, in order to enliven the tedium. I saw my chance and took it.

'Are you the regular keeper on this gate?'

'Mostly.' He sucked his teeth, probing with his tongue to dislodge some sliver of meat or bread that had lodged itself among them. 'I have a deputy for when I'm sick or on festival days, but he's a young lad, green and none too bright, so I'm on duty as much as possible.'

'And you were here, no doubt, that day last January when the stepchildren of Master Eudo Colet went astray?'

The gatekeeper raised two bushy eyebrows and regarded me quizzically.

'So! You've ferreted out that story mighty quick. Yet I'll swear I only saw you for the first time yesterday morning, when you passed through the gate near dinnertime. You were chatting to Tom the drover. I remember thinking to myself that I'd not seen you around these parts before. You're a pedlar if I'm not mistaken. What have you done with your pack?'

'It's at my lodging,' I answered. 'As for the story about the children, I had it from Jacinta at the castle tavern, when I supped there last evening.'

The gatekeeper laughed. 'Oh, her! She has a nose in everybody's business, that one. Bound to, I guess, in her calling. And that son of hers can't be much of a companion. A miserable cur, with very little to say for himself.'

'I barely saw him, but yes, you're right, he did seem a taciturn fellow. To return, however, to Andrew and Mary Skelton. The story captured my imagination, as I suppose any unresolved mystery is bound to do.'

My companion interrupted me. 'No mystery, friend, and not unresolved, neither. The varmints went adventuring in the woods and fell into the hands of the outlaws. That's all there is to it.' Here, obviously, was a man of whom William of Occam would have approved.

'But according to the cook, Agatha Tenter, and the maid, Bridget Praule, they couldn't possibly have left the house without being seen. Or so I've been informed.'

The gatekeeper gave a roar of laughter and clapped me on the back with one of his enormous hands.

'They would say that, wouldn't they, to safeguard themselves? Who'd take the word of a couple of silly, emptyheaded women? And it's as plain as the nose on your face, that whatever those two say, the children escaped somehow, or their bodies would never have been found, six weeks later, on the banks of the Harbourne.'

'They didn't pass through this gate, though, or surely you would have seen them?'

'As it happens, I didn't see them, no. But as I told all the civic busybodies who came inquiring, there were the usual number of carts going in and out that day, piled high with their various cargoes. And not knowing then that anything was amiss, I let them all pass through, once the toll was paid, without searching the contents. So, who's to say that those two children weren't curled up somewhere between bales of cloth being transported to the quay, or hidden away under some sacking?'

I considered this answer to the problem with a sinking heart. The man was right; it was a possibility which could not be lightly dismissed, and one which Grizelda had not seen fit to mention. Nor had it occurred to me, though I felt now that it should have done. Both of us had been blinded into looking for a more sinister explanation; she by her hatred of Eudo Colet and I by my desire to dazzle her with my cleverness.

'All the same,' I persisted, 'you did not, with your own two eyes, see either Andrew or Mary Skelton?'

'I've told you, no!' The gatekeeper showed a touch of impatience. 'Nor were they marked by either of my fellow gatekeepers, for we were all questioned together by the Sheriff, in the guardroom of the castle.'

'Would those men have any cause to lie?' I queried.

He gave me a pitying look, as though I were a fool, irritating but harmless.

'Why should they? They'd nothing to gain by denial.'

'Not unless they were in league with the outlaws,' I agreed, musing aloud rather than making any real accusation.

But the effect on my companion was to swell his chest to almost twice its normal size and banish all his former comradeship. The massive arm, which had been laid in friendly fashion across my shoulders, now tightened its grip until I could almost hear the cracking of my bones. The big red face advanced to within half an inch of mine.

'Now, listen to me, chapman! I've known these men all my life. Boys and men, we've grown up together. They're good, honest, God-fearing citizens of this borough, and I'll not listen quietly while anyone, let alone a stranger, implies otherwise. If you value your hide,' he added menacingly, 'you'll not repeat that suggestion.'

'You mistake me,' I said hurriedly. 'It was not meant as it sounded. I was merely clearing my mind of even the remotest possibilities before searching elsewhere for a solution.'

The arm about my shoulders relaxed a little, but was not immediately removed. Nor did the ruddy face so close to mine lose one jot of its grimness.

'There's no solution to find, my friend. It's there, plain for all to see. Those two children got out of the house and clear of the town one way or another, and with all the cunning that younglings bent on mischief employ in such matters. I don't hold with Master Eudo Colet no more than the next man, but you can't hold him guilty of a crime he hasn't committed because you don't like him. If that were the case, there are a great many acquaintances of mine, and of yours, too, I daresay, who'd end up on the gallows, dangling at the end of a rope.'

'You're very right,' I heartily agreed, at which he finally released me and grew more amiable. I ventured a further inquiry. 'You referred to the children just now as varmints. Yet they have been described to me as two little innocents, almost contenders for sainthood.'

The gatekeeper snorted violently. 'Sainthood, is it? I've never known any youngling who'd qualify for that description, and I doubt you have, either. No, young Andrew and his sister were no better – nor no worse, mark you! – than other children of their age from what I saw of them. But saints they weren't. Whoever told you that, took you for a fool, my lad.'

I shook my head. 'The landlady at the castle ale-house described the girl as a little angel, and her brother not far short of one. And I'd take my oath she meant every word. I was doubtful, remembering myself at that age. But recollecting that Mistress Cozin had called them a pair of holy innocents, I thought maybe Jacinta was right after all. And Mistress Harbourne was devoted to her charges.'

The gatekeeper regarded me curiously, his animosity fading and his tufted eyebrows climbing once more up his forehead.

'Dang me, chapman, you've been busy since you got here! Been in touch with half the town, I reckon. This affair of the young Skeltons seems to have taken a powerful hold on your imagination. But Jacinta Jessard's a maudlin old woman who thinks any child with a whit more manners than that graceless son of hers a veritable wonder, while Mistress Cozin is a sweet and pleasant lady who'd think no ill of anyone, let alone a child, for all she's three young minxes of her own to give her the lie. As for Grizelda Harbourne, of course she'd think her little dearlings perfect. She was mother, aye and father to them, too, from the moment they were born, for their true mother had no time for them. A selfish piece, Rosamund Crouchback was, with never a thought in her silly head except her own pleasure. So, no, you'd hear nothing but praise from Grizelda, that's only natural. But take it from me, they could be just as naughty and mischievous as other children when the fancy took them, which is why I say they made their way out of the town somehow or another on that morning. There'd been great trouble between them and Master Colet, I understand. Enough, at any rate, to drive Mistress Harbourne to leave the house, and for that, they'd want to punish him. How better than to disappear for an hour or two and cause him an agony of worry?'

I had to concede that there was much sense in his argument, but had no opportunity to counter it with the fact that Eudo Colet had benefited from the children's timely disappearance and subsequent murder. At that moment, a party of men who had been hocking in the surrounding districts, entered the gatehouse and claimed the immediate attention of the gatekeeper. He knew all of them well, and was concerned to know what success they had had that morning. There was much chuckling, winking, nudging and grinning, while the leader of the group held up a leather pouch, jingling with coins, given as recompense by those women who were unwilling, or too maidenly, to pay the forfeits demanded of them.

'A good haul for the Priory coffers,' he said, 'although not all, by any means, found it necessary to be parted from their money.'

Again, there was a deal of chaff and self-congratulatory laughter, and I could see that it was time to move on. I could no longer hope for the gatekeeper's undivided attention, now that his friends had arrived with their list of triumphs and failures – their catalogue of who had and who had not been game to pay the price demanded of them. I walked on along the High Street, pausing momentarily to cast a glance at Eudo Colet's front door as I passed, then followed the curve of the road round by the pillory until I came to Thomas Cozin's house, in the lee of St Mary's Priory. I raised my hand and knocked.

As on my visit of the previous day, the door was answered by the little maid, Jenny, but the youngest daughter of the house was not far behind, anxious to discover the identity, and interest to herself, of any visitor. She emerged from the downstairs parlour and smiled cheekily when she saw me.

'It's that handsome pedlar you fancied, Joan! And you,

Elizabeth!' she shouted up the stairs.

I blushed and the maid remonstrated, 'You'd best watch that tongue of yours, Mistress Ursula! Your sisters'll have your hide for garters, if you go on provoking them like you do.'

'I – I've come to see Master Oliver Cozin,' I stammered. 'He – He might be expecting me. Is he within?'

'I'll see, if you'll step inside a moment.'

Jenny vanished into the parlour and I heard her run upstairs. Ursula Cozin and I were left confronting one another, with me shuffling my feet, while she compressed her lips to stop herself giggling aloud at my embarrassment. The gatekeeper had been right, about this one, at least. This youngest daughter of Thomas Cozin was most certainly a minx.

'I wasn't telling a lie, you know,' she remarked pertly. 'Joan and Elizabeth both admired your looks. My mother did, too, I could tell, though of course she didn't say anything. Papa would have been so hurt, for he's not the handsomest of men, as you must have noticed, but we all love him dearly.' The candid grey eyes gave me renewed appraisal. 'I think you're quite nice, as well.'

'Ursula, go upstairs. Your mother wants you.' Oliver Cozin's dry voice preceded him, as he stepped into the passage. He waited silently until his niece, dropping him a primly obedient curtsey, had disappeared from view, before letting his somewhat forbidding features relax into a smile. He gave an indulgent shake of his head, but made no comment, merely asking, 'Why did you wish to see me, Master Chapman?'

'I have come to say, Your Honour, that I am willing to remain in Master Colet's house for a day or two yet, if that arrangement is still to your liking. Certainly until Saturday, when you leave for Exeter, and maybe a day or so longer.'

'Ah!' He looked relieved. 'Yes, I should be pleased if you would do so. I am going, this afternoon, to visit Master Colet and he will be happy to know that his property is being cared for. The outlaws were out and about again last night, it seems, in the vicinity of Berry Pomeroy, so you have my blessing to lodge in the house for as long as you wish. The longer the better as far as I and my client are concerned.'

I gathered up my courage. 'On one condition,' I said.

The lawyer was startled. 'Condition? What condition?' he demanded stiffly, but his eyes were wary.

'That you permit me to ask you some questions,' I answered.

Chapter Nine

'Questions? What questions?'

Oliver Cozin's manner was terse. He was not a man used to being interrogated, particularly by the likes of such as me. Normally, he did the asking and others gave the answers. I was determined, however, not to be intimidated. I had promised Grizelda to try and uncover the truth, and that was what I intended to do.

'I know why Master Colet can find no one willing to rent or buy that house,' I said. 'There is still a lingering fear that Andrew and Mary Skelton were somehow spirited away by witchcraft before they were murdered by the outlaws.'

There was silence, then the lawyer sniffed. 'You seem to have been very busy, chapman,' he said, echoing the gatekeeper's words. 'I didn't take you for a gossip. I'm disappointed.'

I felt the anger rise in my chest and steadied myself to speak without choler.

'You must admit,' I reproved him, but calmly, 'that the circumstances of my tenancy were unusual. Did you expect me to be lacking in curiosity? I'm as nosy as my neighbour; as nosy as you, too, would have been, I suspect, in similar circumstances.'

He looked affronted, but before he could reply to this direct attack, there came the patter of feet, and Mistress Joan, the eldest of Thomas Cozin's three daughters, rounded the bend of the stairs and descended to the parlour. She sketched a curtsey and sent me an upward glance from green-flecked hazel eyes, beneath long, sweeping lashes.

'I'm sorry to disturb you, Uncle, but Mother wishes a message delivered to Mag, in the kitchen.'

'Very well.' Oliver courteously held open the door until his niece had passed through, then shut it firmly and turned again to me.

'I suppose,' he conceded, 'it was always possible that you might discover the reason behind my request. But, having done so, I should have hoped that there the matter would have ended. What further interest in the story can there be? My client, Master Colet, was fully exonerated of any complicity in the children's disappearance, either natural or ... supernatural. So why do you raise the subject?'

'I have promised Mistress Harbourne to find out, if I can, the truth of her charges' murder. If, that is, there is anything more to be discovered.'

The lawyer was now seriously displeased. The narrow face froze into immobility, and the chilly grey eyes grew even colder as he stared down his finely chiselled nose. But yet again, before he had time to speak, there was another diversion as Mistress Elizabeth, the second daughter, came tripping lightly down the stairs on small, scarlet-leather-shod feet, her green woollen gown hoisted in one hand to display a neatly-turned ankle.

'Well, Miss?' her uncle barked. 'And what do you want?'

'I ... I have a message for Mag, in the kitchen.'

'Your mother has already sent one message by Joan, not two minutes since.'

'Ah . . . !' Mistress Elizabeth thought swiftly. 'Mother forgot something she particularly wished to say concerning the eel pie for supper. I am charged with the additional message.'

'Oh, very well!' For the second time, Oliver Cozin held wide the door until his niece had departed, which she did with a provocative swing of the hips. Fortunately, I was the only one to notice it. Much put out, the lawyer resumed his seat beside the table, while I stood awkwardly, twisting my hat between my hands.

'And how, may I ask, did you come to make the acquaintance of Grizelda Harbourne?'

I had barely had time to explain when the child, Ursula, followed her sisters downstairs, a strand of chestnut-brown hair escaping from beneath the white lawn hood. The bodice of her blue wool gown was partially undone, the result of careless lacing in the first place.

'Joan and Bess, did they pass this way, Uncle?' And sensing that, if she tarried, she would bear the whole brunt of Oliver's annoyance at being so constantly interrupted, she gave me a wink, mouthed, 'I told you they liked you', and whipped out of the room, closing the door behind her.

'Really!' The lawyer's irritation boiled over. 'I do not know what is going on in this household today! You seem to have a very unsettling effect on my brother's family, chapman. Now, what were you saying? Yes, yes, I remember. You were telling me how you came to meet Grizelda Harbourne. So, you have promised to discover the truth for her, have you? But everyone knows the truth, and I cannot see what Mistress Harbourne hopes to gain by once more muddying the waters. There was a full inquiry by the Sheriff at the time. The testimony of Bridget Praule and Agatha Tenter, and indeed of my own brother, was sufficient to clear Master Colet of any blame.'

115

'Yet there seems no doubt,' I persisted doggedly, 'that he, and he alone, benefited from the children's deaths because of Sir Henry Skelton's will, which you helped draw up at the instigation of Sir Jasper.'

The thin face suffused with blood. 'Are you accusing me of some impropriety? This passes all bounds! I suppose you are indebted to Grizelda Harbourne for this knowledge, also. I cannot possibly discuss my client's private affairs, and would not, even if I could. Please leave this house immediately.'

'No, wait, brother.' There was a fourth interruption, as Thomas Cozin himself descended to the parlour and drew a second chair close to the table. He motioned me to sit on the bench running along the facing wall. 'I could not help overhearing the latter part of your conversation, and Grizelda Harbourne is right, Oliver, to be mistrustful of Eudo Colet. I realize that he is your client and that you are chary of saying anything against him, but you like him no more than the rest of us. The man's an adventurer, that much was obvious from the moment Rosamund brought him home. His antecedents are shrouded in mystery, and we have never managed to find out who or what he really is, nor where he comes from. The girl made a foolish marriage, and we all thought it, even if we did not say so. What did you want to know, chapman?'

I spread my hands. 'I am a babe when it comes to legal matters. I wished to confirm that Mistress Harbourne was correct when she told me that Eudo Colet was the rightful inheritor of the money left to Mary and Andrew Skelton by their father.'

Thomas glanced at his brother, but Oliver folded his lips together and made no reply. Thomas shrugged and turned back to me.

'He was Rosamund's husband,' he answered simply. 'Every-

116

thing she had was his. She would have inherited the money, a considerable sum, mark you, had she outlived her children, so, by default, it was bound to be Eudo's. No provision was made in the will – I know, for Jasper showed me his copy of the document – for the money to revert to the Skelton family. Indeed, quite the reverse. In the event of the children's deaths, it went to Rosamund or her heir! It was all wrapped up in lawyer's parlance, but its intention was abundantly plain.' Thomas cleared his throat and glanced sideways at his brother. 'I recall thinking at the time that, in certain circumstances, it could prove to be a most dangerous clause, but Jasper seemed mighty pleased with it.'

Oliver was goaded into speech. 'As things stood when the will was drawn up,' he said huffily, 'there was nothing to fear, and our concern was to ensure that the money stayed in the Crouchback family in perpetuity. It was a skilful piece of negotiation on my part; even Sir Henry and his lawyers admitted it. And may I remind you, Tom, that no one anticipated Sir Henry's death. The rebellions of Robin of Redesdale and Robin of Holderness seemed very unimportant affairs in the beginning. No one could possibly have foreseen what would happen.'

Thomas Cozin gave an ironic little smile. 'What you don't say, but I will, is that Jasper, dear friend though he was, was undoubtedly a greedy man. He enjoyed getting the better of other people, and in this case, he saw an opportunity to acquire part of his son-in-law's fortune to add to that of his own family. It was never to be allowed to return to Skelton hands. And, as is so often the case with grasping people, he was too shortsighted to see beyond his immediate objective; to guess at any chain of events which might endanger the lives of his grandchildren.'

Oliver rose abruptly from the table.

'I warn you, Tom, to guard your tongue. No crime has been proved against Eudo Colet, and in my estimation, never will be, because there is nothing to prove. Andrew Skelton and his sister wandered out of the house, lost their way and were murdered by the outlaws. Now, let us leave it at that. And so will you, chapman, if you have any sense, or you may find yourself under arrest for spreading malicious rumours about my client. You may stay in his house for as long as you wish, but confine yourself to caretaking and tell Mistress Harbourne that you have thought better of your promise to meddle. She's a sensible woman and will understand, much as she abhors Master Colet – and that without good reason from what little I could see on my infrequent visits to the house, for he always treated her civilly enough when I was about. And now, God be with you. I shall be here until Saturday, should you need me, but I will not undergo any more inquisitions nor listen to unfounded rumours.' And he mounted the stairs with a slow, self-conscious gait.

Thomas rose from the table, and I with him. He leaned towards me, lowering his voice.

'You mustn't mind Oliver,' he said. 'He has a crusty way with him, but he has a good heart. We're twins, as you can see, and I know him as well as I know myself. The death of those two children preys on his mind more than he'll admit to, being as how he was the one who negotiated that clause in the will. At Jasper's behest, it's true, but it was a tricky business and wouldn't have been accomplished without Oliver's legal brilliance. He feels responsible, and that annoys him.'

'Did he *never* suspect Master Colet of being implicated in their disappearance?' I inquired.

Thomas shook his head. 'Oliver was at home, in Exeter, when the children vanished, and by the time he had been sent for, and reached here four days later, it had been well established that Eudo Colet, short of sorcery, could have had nothing to do with Andrew and Mary leaving the house that morning. The man was here, in this very room, with me when it happened. Nevertheless, the rumours which persist about Eudo Colet, among the lower orders of townspeople, keep the gossip alive, and that, as I said, imbues Oliver with a false sense of guilt, which, in turn, makes him angry.'

'Why did Master Colet come to see you?' I asked. 'If Mistress Harbourne is to be believed, you were no longer linked to him in business. You did not even like him.'

'True, on both counts. But you cannot turn a man from your door simply because of personal prejudice. And I had no reason to believe that he had been a bad husband to Rosamund. On the contrary, she doted on him. It was those two poor, innocent children she neglected, but he could not be saddled with the blame for that. She left them to Grizelda's care from the moment they were born, long before she met him. Much as it grieves me to speak ill of my old friend's daughter, Rosamund was spiteful and selfish, never mindful of anyone's comfort but her own.'

'So,' I prompted, 'why did Master Colet come to see you?'

'What? Oh! Yes. He came to ask me to reconsider that very decision of mine to sever business links with his late wife's family. He wanted to become my partner, as Jasper had been. He would be willing, he said, to put a substantial part of the Crouchback fortune into the making of straights. The market in Brittany, he understood, was greater than it had ever been.'

'You refused him?'

119

'I'm afraid I did.'

'May I ask why?'

Thomas stroked his chin, submitting, somewhat surprisingly, to this protracted catechism, but still keeping his voice low.

'Well, for one thing, I should have found it difficult to work with a man I dislike so much. For another, I did not gain the impression that his heart was in the request. Don't ask me why. It was simply a feeling.'

'He had not approached you before that day? Not at any other time since Mistress Colet's death?'

The grey eyes, inherited by his youngest daughter, were suddenly bright and shrewd.

'You are suggesting that it might have been a trumped-up excuse to come and see me?'

I shrugged. 'I find it . . . suspicious, shall I say, that it was that morning out of all the others that he was absent from home and in such reputable company.' Thomas Cozin graciously inclined his head. I continued, 'And that it was while he was here, talking to you, that the children vanished.'

My host thought about this, rubbing his nose with a bony forefinger. After due consideration, however, he pursed his lips doubtfully.

'It alters nothing, chapman. Facts are facts. The children were there when he left the house, not there when he got back. If you doubt me, question Bridget Praule and Agatha Tenter; if you can shake their witness, you'll do more than the Sheriff or any of his sergeants were able to do.'

I had every intention of speaking to both women, and would have asked him for their directions had not Oliver Cozin called peremptorily down the stairs, 'Tom, what's keeping you? Has the chapman gone yet?'

I put a finger to my lips, mouthed my thanks, tiptoed to the door and let myself out into the passage. As I quietly lowered the latch, I heard Thomas reply, 'Oh yes, he's gone, Noll. What is it you wanted?'

I opened the street door, but was not allowed to escape so easily. There was a sudden scurry of feet on the flagstones behind me, and Ursula Cozin seized my arm.

'It's men's turn to hock today, chapman. Aren't you going to ask me for a forfeit?'

I tried to look severe. 'Go back to your school books,' I said. 'You're too young for such matters.'

'I have nine summers,' was the indignant answer. She smiled pertly. 'Well, if I'm not old enough for your taste, would you like me to summon one or both of my sisters? I should choose Elizabeth, if I were you. She is younger and less of a tease. Joan's very high and mighty at present, ever since she had her first proposal of marriage. Of course, Father refused the offer. The young man had no money and his way to make in the world, being nought but the Benjamin out of six brothers.'

I suppressed a smile at this ingenuous confidence. 'If you wish to do something for me,' I said, 'tell me where I may find Bridget Praule and Agatha Tenter.'

Ursula pouted. 'Oh, very well, but you won't find either of them as pretty as me. Or as Elizabeth or Joan, if it comes to that. Yet am I, in my sisters' case, being over-generous?' She doubled up with mirth at her own wit, revealing herself as the child she truly was. Recovering her poise a little, and conscious of self-betrayal, she told me, with as much dignity as she could muster, that Bridget lodged at her grandmother's cottage, between St Peter's Quay and the Magdalen Lazar

121

House. Agatha Tenter, now living once again with her mother, Dame Winifred, was to be discovered on the other side of the bridge, within the Pomeroy parish bounds.

'And for that, I think I deserve a kiss.' Ursula leaned forward, brushing my cheek with soft, petal-like lips. 'God be with you, chapman. Oh, here are my sisters returning from the kitchen. I should escape while you can.' She gave me a friendly push towards the open door.

I needed no second bidding and was out in the street almost before I knew it.

I left the town this time by the East Gate, pausing for a brief while to put the same questions to the gatekeeper as I had posed to his fellow on the West Gate. But I got no more joy than before. Yes, he remembered the day in January when the Skelton children had disappeared – who could forget it? – but he had seen nothing of them. All the gatekeepers had been interrogated by the Sheriff and all had told the same story. And yes, he supposed it possible that Andrew Skelton and his sister might have concealed themselves among the contents of a wagon, although he himself obviously inclined towards the idea of witchcraft. However, as he made it plain that he had no liking for Eudo Colet, I took this with a grain of salt and considered it more wishful thinking, rather than outright conviction on his part. I thanked him and passed through into the Foregate.

The street ran downhill to the town mill and the bridge across the Dart at the bottom. To the left spread the Priory fields and orchards, while to the right, another stockade enclosed an area known as the Pickle Moor and a straggle of shops and houses. It had been my intention to visit first Dame Winifred's cottage, on the other side of the river, but a sudden thirst and gnawing hunger reminded me that it was several hours since I had eaten dinner with Grizelda. I could pay a visit to Jacinta at the castle tavern, but did not wish to retrace my steps. There must be ale-houses outside the walls; I had only to ask directions.

A cart, empty of any burden, lumbered through the gate behind me, a thin whippet of a man perched up behind the horse, the reins slack in his hand. A pair of brilliant blue eyes considered me dispassionately from a weatherbeaten face beneath a thatch of dark hair, salted with grey. I hailed him with a friendly 'Good-day!' and he drew to a halt alongside me.

'Can I help you, friend? You have a lost air about you.'

'I'm looking for an ale-house,' I confessed, 'where I can quench my thirst. I thought you seemed like a fellow who might know of one.'

He roared with laughter at that, revealing a flash of surprisingly sound white teeth in the wrinkled, sunburned features.

'Your instinct was right, chapman. I know every ale-house and tavern within a ten-mile distance of this town. But you need search no further than the one I'm off to, now, close by St Peter's Quay. I note you were heading for the bridge, but it's not so very much out of your way, and you can ride with me, if you've a mind to. I've just delivered a load of flour from the mill to the baker's, and I've an hour to spare before my next journey. I'd be glad of your company.'

I thanked him and heaved myself up into the empty cart, where a fine dusting of flour still whitened the boards.

'St Peter's Quay will suit me very well. I have a visit to pay near there, in any case.' My newfound friend twitched the reins and the horse plodded along a path to our right, between some cottages, and so to a gate in the stockade. 'I think you must be Jack Carter,' I hazarded.

'The same.' He grinned, glancing over his shoulder. 'Who's been speaking of me?'

'I'll tell you when we're settled with our ale,' I promised. 'It might prove a longish story.'

We made our steady way around a tidal marsh whose land had been drained by a broad, stone-built dam, which kept back the encroaching river.

'Is that the Weirland Dam?' I asked my companion.

'Aye, that's it. Built more'n two hundred years ago, if accounts can be believed. 'Tis sure it's been there all my lifetime and the lifetime of my father and his father afore him.'

A heron swooped low over the marshy reaches, where clusters of kingcups raised great, golden heads to the sky. Clumps of reeds stood sentinel between tall, spiked grasses and purple loosestrife, not yet in flower, but with leaves showing a tender young green. Some of the land had been reclaimed and built over.

Matt's tavern was a low, thatched building flanked on one side by a scattering of cottages rising uphill towards the Leper Hospital, one of which, from Ursula Cozin's direction, must belong to Granny Praule. Inside, the ale-house was full of men who all knew one another and were on terms of friendly familiarity. Their elliptical speech argued the case for most of them following either the same trade, or for their being employed in similar callings.

'Dockers and sailors, mostly,' Jack Carter confirmed, when I asked him. 'Put your money away, chapman, I'll stand the first shout. You can pay later. Matt! Two stoups of ale and be quick about it, or you'll have a couple of corpses, dead of thirst, on your hands.'

The leather-aproned landlord grinned good-naturedly, and

there was a deal of chaff from the rest of the drinkers.

'Who's your companion, Jack?' demanded one wag with a ginger beard. 'Looks big enough to drain the whole of Devon.'

I answered in kind, and it was some time after Matt had brought the ale to our bench near the door that Jack and I were able to resume any private conversation. But, gradually, the rest of the company lost interest in us, and I nudged the talk in my chosen direction by inquiring of Jack Carter if he knew which was Granny Praule's cottage.

'Last before the Lazar House at the top of the rise,' was the prompt reply. He took a gulp of ale and wiped his mouth on the back of his hand. 'What's your business with that old crone?'

I told him, and saw him furtively make a sign to ward off evil.

'You were sent for, I believe, that morning the Skelton children disappeared, to fetch away Mistress Grizelda Harbourne?'

He nodded solemnly. 'Near hysterical, she was. White as a shroud and shaking so much she had difficulty in speaking. Agatha Tenter had warned me, before I went upstairs, that there'd been a terrible falling out between them. Mistress Harbourne and Eudo Colet I'm talking of. And some falling out it must have been to make her look like that, I'm telling you! I didn't see *him*. He was keeping out of the way, I reckon. Putting no rub in the path of her leaving. They'd never got on, it was common knowledge. I didn't say nothing. Just dragged her box downstairs and called for their stable-man to help carry it out to the cart and heave it aboard. By that time she'd joined me, still looking like she'd died and gone to Hell, and told me to take her home, to her father's holding.'

'Did you hear the children at all, while you were in the house?' I asked him.

Jack swallowed more ale. 'Oh, yes,' he said, 'I heard 'em all right. Or, leastwise, the girl. She was singing.'

Chapter Ten

The clatter and hubbub of the ale-room was growing less as the dockers gradually returned to work, leaving only the sailors to while away the rest of the afternoon with drink and sleep before going aboard their now cargoless vessels to spend the night. Tomorrow, the empty holds would be loaded with fresh merchandise, and the following morning, the vessels would weigh anchor for Brittany or Spain or Ireland or wherever else they happened to be bound.

At Jack Carter's instigation, the landlord refilled our cups, before going to the assistance of his pot-boy who was having difficulty fixing a tap to a new cask of ale. I watched absent-mindedly for a moment or two, then turned my head towards my companion.

'What was she singing?'

'What was who singing?' Jack's attention had plainly strayed during the last few minutes.

'Mary Skelton. You said you heard her singing while you were bringing Mistress Harbourne's box downstairs.'

'Oh, you're back at that, are you? Yes, I heard the girl, but what she was singing, I couldn't tell you. A pretty, clear, high-pitched voice she had, but I've no ear for music, chapman, and can't tell one tune from another.'

I murmured sympathetically, being afflicted with the same lack myself, as my fellow novices at Glastonbury used to complain whenever I chanted too loudly during a service. Nevertheless, I urged, 'Can't you recall even a snatch of the words?'

The carter rubbed his chin, already faintly shadowed with black stubble.

'You're asking too much of me,' he complained. 'I tell you, I've difficulty holding a song in my head for three minutes, let alone three months! Oh well, if it's important to you,' he added good-naturedly, 'I'll see if I can remember something.' He placed his elbows on the table and cupped his chin in his hands, frowning in fierce concentration. After perhaps a minute, he uttered, 'I think ... Yes, I'm almost sure it was a lullaby.' He nodded his head vigorously. 'It was. I recollect a refrain of lollay, lollay, lullow.'

He hummed a few tuneless notes which I could not identify; nor was I any more successful when he whistled them. And there were too many lullabies to soothe sleepless babes for me to be able to guess. Furthermore, did it really matter what Mary Skelton had been singing that January morning? The strange thing was that the child had been capable of singing at all after being at the centre of such a terrible quarrel between her stepfather, herself and her brother, and then between her stepfather and her nurse. Yet Grizelda had told me that both children were playing calmly by the time she left, as though the affair no longer concerned them. Why? What was in their minds? Had they already decided on some desperate course of action before the angry exchange with Eudo Colet took place? Had they deliberately provoked him to a fight for reasons of their own?

There were too many as yet insoluble questions, but Bridget

Praule and Agatha Tenter might be able to supply some of
the answers. I should be on my way. I finished my ale and
rose to my feet.

'You're not going?' Jack Carter demanded, aggrieved.
'There's time for another shout before I need collect my next
load from the sawmill.'

'I'm sorry,' I said, 'but the afternoon is already advanced.
Which did you say was Dame Praule's cottage?'

That made him laugh, dispersing his ill-humour.

'Never tell me you're going to beard Granny Praule in her
den?' he guffawed. 'She'll eat a good-looking young fellow
like you alive. You'd never think it to see her now, but she
was the prettiest girl in these parts, and for miles around,
when she was in her prime. I can remember my father saying
that when he was a lad, she was the toast of every tavern
between here and Plymouth. She finds it hard to forget those
days, and to accept that time hasn't dealt favourably with her.
But if you're set on going, you'll find her in the last cottage
as you go up the hill towards the Lazar House.'

I thanked him, and we parted with mutual goodwill and
the promise of seeing one another again before I left Totnes.

The early brightness of the day had dimmed as evening
approached. The sun's radiance was veiled behind a thin,
grape-coloured cloud, which spread across the hillside on
which the town was built. A trio of gulls, crying desolately,
hovered and swooped as they searched for food along
the river banks. In the distance, the stockade of the Leper
Hospital, which fenced its inmates off from the rest of the
world, made it look like some embattled fortress. Which,
indeed, I suppose all such places truly are.

Granny Praule's cottage, the last of four, was crumbling
gently into ruin, with a shutter hanging loose from one of its

hinges, its thatch badly in need of repair and a gaping hole in one of the walls into which sacking had been stuffed to keep out the draught. The door stood wide to catch the warmth of the day while it lasted. I knocked and entered upon being bidden to do so, the dimness within bringing me to a standstill while my eyes grew accustomed to the contrasting light. Gradually, however, the interior became clear, and I was able to discern that Granny Praule and her granddaughter were provided with only the bare necessities of life; I could not help wondering how Bridget bore with such poverty after the comparative luxury of the Crouchback house.

I was greeted with a cackle of delight, which I would have recognized anywhere after my encounter with Granny Praule yesterday morning.

'Dang me if it ain't you again, lad! Come for another kiss, have you? I'll be only too happy to oblige.'

'I've come for a word with your granddaughter,' I answered hurriedly, 'if she's here.'

A girl rose from the bench at the far end of the room and came towards me. She had been peeling apples and had an apronful of rind, which she tipped out of the open doorway on to the track.

'It'll be a bit extra for Tom Lyntott's pigs when he drives them in from the forest this evening.'

'Aye, fatten 'em up,' agreed her grandmother, 'then maybe Tom'll give us a leg or a loin for salting, when he kills 'em next Martinmas. That'll see us nicely through the winter.' She gnashed her almost toothless gums together. 'There's nothing I like better'n a nice bit o' salted pork. Well, young fellow,' she added, 'here's my granddaughter. What do you want to see her for? I'm very disappointed you've not come to see me!' She gave another cackle. 'I'd do you a power o' good, an' you'd let me. More'n young Bridget ever could. Takes after her father, God rest his soul. A bit too pious for my liking, always on his knees. Couldn't abide him, if you must know. Nor could my Anne, poor cow, for all she married him. But they managed to produce Bridget between them, though only God and His saints know how.'

Bridget remained unperturbed by these strictures on her parents.

'Give over, Granny,' she reproved the older woman calmly. 'Chapman don't want to hear all our business.' She smiled at me. 'Come and sit up the other end o' the room. And, Granny, don't you disturb us.'

'Thought he'd come to hock me,' the old woman whined in mock indignation. 'It's men's turn today, chapman,' she reminded me, and screeched like a barn owl.

I escaped to the far end of the cottage, although there was little enough space between us and she could have overheard every word I said, had she been so minded. But she suddenly seemed to abandon all interest in me and, leaning her head against the wall behind her, fell asleep with that special facility of the old and the very young. I sat down beside Bridget Praule on a rough wooden bench drawn up to a table which rocked with each unguarded movement, one of its legs being an inch or so shorter than the other three. Bridget pushed aside her knife and the remaining apples, folded her slender arms on the board and twisted her head to face me.

'What do you want?' she asked. 'Granny calls you chapman and I'll take her word for it, but you don't have a pack with you, so you've not come to sell me anything.'

'I've come to ask you some questions,' I said, 'and hope that you'll favour me with some answers, about the disappearance and murder of Andrew and Mary Skelton.' The thin, childish face looked wary, and I went on quickly, 'I have the blessing of Mistress Harbourne.'

'You know Grizelda?' The pale blue eyes lit with pleasure and the snub little nose wrinkled as she smiled. 'Are you some distant friend or kinsman come to visit?'

So once again, I recounted the history of yesterday and today, and when I had finished, Bridget sighed.

'I'm sorry you're not a member of her kinfolk,' she said. 'Grizelda must be lonely with no one of her own. Now that her father and Sir Jasper and Mistress Rosamund are all dead, she's alone in the world.' Her voice sank to a whisper. 'Even the children were taken from her. It's cruel.' The words became almost inaudible, and some were completely lost. '. . . can God allow it?' I heard her murmur.

I put one of my big hands over one of her rough and calloused little ones. 'We have to have faith,' I answered gently, 'and put our trust in Heaven.'

She nodded. 'I know, but sometimes it's hard.' She smiled bravely. 'What is it you want to know?'

'Anything you can remember about the morning the children disappeared. Take your time. There's no hurry, and I shall be grateful for the smallest recollection.'

Bridget, becoming aware of her hand still enclosed in mine, blushed and withdrew it before giving her undivided attention to my request. I judged her to have some fifteen or sixteen summers, but she could have been older. She would, I guessed, always look young and immature for her age. There was nothing of her; she was like a little sparrow, with the same brownish colouring and tiny, brittle bones.

'How long had you been in the Crouchback household?' I asked, when she seemed not to know how to begin.

'Oh, it must be four years,' she said after a good deal of

ticking off on her fingers. 'My mother was alive then, and Mistress Colet was still Lady Skelton. But Sir Jasper was dead. I think he died the year before I went there. My mother was clever with her needle and had done sewing for my lady, and she got me the job when the former girl married and went to live with her husband, over Dartington way.'

'How many servants did Lady Skelton keep?'

'Me and Agatha Tenter, the cook, and Mistress Harbourne. I've heard my mother say that in Sir Jasper's time there were two grooms lived in the loft above the outhouses, but Lady Skelton kept only one horse after her father's death and hired what others she needed from the livery stables near the castle. She also hired one of their stablemen to come in each day to take care of her own mount and tend to its wants.'

'So you remember the days before Mistress Rosamund married Eudo Colet. Were things very different then?'

Bridget chewed her underlip thoughtfully. 'It was quieter,' she volunteered at last. 'We were a household of women, except of course for Master Andrew, who was too little to count. I suppose,' she added shrewdly, 'it was too quiet for my lady, who suddenly went off to London and came back married to Master Colet. Took us all by surprise, that did, though Grizelda was uneasy, and predicted mischief when Mistress Rosamund didn't return with Goody Harrison and her husband. Goody Harrison . . .'

I interrupted quickly. 'Mistress Harbourne has already explained the circumstances to me. She hated her cousin's new husband on sight, she tells me.'

Bridget lifted her narrow shoulders. 'She never had much good to say for him,' she admitted. 'Said he was an adventurer, after Mistress Rosamund's money.' There was a pause, then Bridget continued, 'Mistress Harbourne was always kind to me, but I think she was unjust to the master. He was a very fond husband, as far as I could see, and let my lady have her own way in most things. He didn't object when she said she still wanted to be called Lady Skelton; though most of the townspeople addressed her as Mistress Colet in a nasty, sneering way, as much as to say she'd made her bed and now she could lie in it.'

'You like Eudo Colet?' I queried.

Again Bridget hesitated. 'He didn't treat me ill,' she said finally. The pale blue eyes met mine. 'But no, I didn't truly like him, though I couldn't tell you why.'

'Try,' I encouraged her.

Bridget stared, a little nonplussed, seeking for words to express what had, up until now, been merely an inchoate feeling. She blurted out at last, 'He . . . He had no right to the master's chair. He was no better than me, than Agatha. He couldn't read nor write, like Grizelda could. His speech was rough, though he wasn't from hereabouts. Grizelda spoke true when she said he belonged in the stables or the kitchen.'

They had all resented him, this man of whom they knew nothing, but who was so evidently one of their own kind put in authority over them. And Grizelda, who was his superior in every way, had, understandably, resented him more than the others. I straightened my aching back and eased my cramped legs by stretching them out under the table, before harking back to my original request.

'Tell me about the morning of the children's disappearance.'

'Grizelda had gone to church,' Bridget said, 'and I was helping Agatha get the breakfast. Master Colet was still upstairs and so were the children. Things hadn't been easy in the house since the mistress and her baby died. Master was lost without her. He was still bewildered. Still trying to find his feet, not knowing quite where he was or what to do. Most of all, he didn't know what to do with Master Andrew and Mistress Mary. He didn't like them, and they didn't like him. Played all sorts of pranks on him if they thought they could get away with it. Made his life a misery, they did.'

'Did they play pranks on everyone?' I interrupted.

'Master Andrew, he was very high-spirited, and his sister, she followed where he led. But they didn't mean any harm. It was just their way and we all put up with it. But the master found it hard. Well, as I was saying, I was helping Agatha with the breakfast, which was being laid in the downstairs parlour. It was bread and milk for the children, cold beef and saffron porridge with honey for the master and Mistress Harbourne, ale and small beer for them all. We'd carried the food across from the kitchen and were just putting it on the table, when we heard the master shouting upstairs. Shouting at the top of his voice, he was. Then Master Andrew started shouting back, and Mistress Mary, she began wailing. But the master just yelled louder and louder until both children were crying, and the noise was something dreadful. I looked at Agatha and she looked at me, neither of us knowing what to do for the best. "Ought I to go up?" she asked, but I said no, not to interfere or we might find ourselves turned out of the house.'

'Could you hear what Master Colet was shouting about? What was he accusing the children of doing? Or not doing?'

Bridget shook her head. 'I don't think it was anything in particular. They were always slow getting dressed if Grizelda wasn't there to chivvy them along, and the master used to get annoyed if they were unpunctual for meals. I think he saw it as a kind of insult to himself, if they came late to table.'

I nodded. A man unsure of his position, aware that he was mocked behind his back, would be sensitive regarding such matters.

Bridget continued, 'Then Grizelda came in. As soon as she heard what was going on, she just flew up the stairs without even taking off her cloak and began screaming at the master. They must have moved out of the parlour and into one of the bedchambers, because their voices got fainter. But I did hear her yelling that he was a wicked, hard-hearted man to bedevil two innocent children in such a way, and he answered that she was a harpy who should be tied to the ducking-stool. I can't remember everything that was said. I couldn't hear a lot of it. But then, suddenly, it all went quiet.'

'And after that?' I prompted.

Bridget shivered and wrapped her thin arms around her body.

'After that Grizelda came to the top of the stairs and asked me to run as fast as I could for Jack Carter. She was leaving, she said, and needed him to carry her box.'

'Which you did?'

'Yes. I ran down to his house in the Foregate without even stopping to put on a cloak or pattens. It was a very cold morning, but I didn't think about it at the time. I was that upset, I didn't know properly what I was doing. Jack's wife lent me a shawl and I rode on the cart coming back.'

'And when you got home?'

'Mistress Harbourne was standing at the top of the stairs, all white and shaking. She had her box ready, beside her, and Jack and the stableman lifted it out to the cart.'

'There were no further exchanges between her and Master Colet?'

Bridget shook her head. 'The master didn't come down for

breakfast until after she'd gone. And the children didn't come down at all. The master said they were too upset, but I reckon they did it just to spite him, 'cos I heard one of them singing.'

'Ah!' My attention sharpened. 'Jack Carter said it was Mistress Mary. He heard her, too, but couldn't recall what she was singing. He thought it was a lullaby, with a refrain of "lollay, lullow", or some such matter. Can you remember?'

Bridget nodded. 'But I'm not certain it was Mary who was singing. I thought it was Master Andrew. It sounded more like a boy to me.'

'But did you know the song?'

'It was a lullaby Grizelda used to sing them to sleep with. I've heard her sing it many times, but I can't recollect the words.' Bridget paused, thinking hard. 'There was a refrain, I remember, which began "Lollay, lollay, little child, Little child, lollay, lullow . . ." ' A longer pause ended in a regretful shake of her head. 'No, the words have gone. I was never any good at learning. Grizelda used to try to teach me my letters, but I can't hold things in my head.'

'It doesn't matter,' I reassured her. 'It's not important. Go on with your story. You say Master Colet came down to breakfast when Mistress Harbourne had departed? What happened next?'

'When he'd finished, he said he was going out to see Master Cozin on business. He went upstairs to get his cloak and hat. Agatha had gone back to the kitchen by that time, but I was clearing the table. I heard him talking to the children, asking them if they were sure they didn't want anything to eat, and I heard Master Andrew shout, "We said we didn't! Leave us alone!" And I heard the latch of the bedchamber door rattle as he banged it shut. Master came down looking very upset, and I can't say I blamed him. I asked him if I should go up to the children, but he said to get on with my work and let them be. They might be in a better mood when he got back. He wouldn't be long away. He asked if I knew anyone who might be a suitable nurse for them, now that Mistress Harbourne had gone, and I said I was sure he'd have no difficulty finding someone among the women of the town or the Foregate who would be willing to take on the job.'

'And then he went out?'

'Yes. But before he left, he called "God be with you" up the stairs, and Mary answered him.'

'What did she say?'

' "And with you, too!" I remember being glad, because it showed that one of them, at least, was willing to end the quarrel and not sulk all day.' Tears welled up suddenly in Bridget's eyes and spilled down the thin cheeks. 'If only I'd known what they were planning, that I'd never see either of them alive again, I'd have defied the master and gone up to them. The silly, little varmints! Why did they run away?'

'You do think, then,' I said quietly, 'that they escaped and were not, as some people believe, spirited out of the house by witchcraft?'

She shuddered and crossed herself. 'I . . . I don't know,' she blurted out at last. 'After the master went, I was in the downstairs parlour, dusting and polishing, from the moment he left until he came back, so they couldn't have gone that way, of that I *am* certain. And Agatha was in the kitchen, preparing dinner. She must have seen them if they'd quit the house by either the passage door or the bedchamber door opening on to the gallery. The kitchen door was wide open all the while, she says, because of the steam from the cook-pots. But, also, the children must have gone through the kitchen if they wished to reach the outer courtyard, and Agatha swears that they didn't.'

I frowned to myself. Was it not possible that two determined children might have been able to scuttle across the inner courtyard and through the kitchen without being seen, in spite of Agatha Tenter's being there? A cook, of necessity, is forced to move about while practising her art; there are plates to warm, meat to turn on its spit, herbs to chop, water to boil, spillages to be mopped up, spices to grind with pestle and mortar, and a dozen other distractions almost every five minutes. Could Andrew Skelton and his sister have moved so fleetly and silently, taking advantage of a moment when Agatha's back was turned, that they had escaped her notice?

I sighed. It was possible, but barely so. A person alone in a room can sense almost immediately when a second presence has been added. And if Agatha had not actually glimpsed the children, she would have been conscious of the chill blast of air cutting the room in two when they opened the second door into the outer courtyard.

I turned again to Bridget. 'I understand that when Master Colet returned, he sent you to fetch the children. But you couldn't find them.'

The girl started to tremble, and I put my arm about her shoulders for comfort.

'No,' she whispered, and a hand crept up to her mouth. 'At first, of course, when they didn't answer, I thought they were hiding; playing a game. So I kept calling their names and searching for them. But they weren't anywhere to be found. They had completely vanished.'

Chapter Eleven

I wondered how often I had heard that same phrase in the past two days. Completely vanished. The words mocked my impotence to see through them to the truth. How had the Skelton children left the house? Why had they left the house? When I knew the answers to those two questions, it maybe that the mystery would be solved.

The second question was easier of solution than the first, the explanation having already been presented to me on more than one occasion. Andrew and Mary had intended to stay out until curfew in order to teach their stepfather a lesson, and had managed to pass beyond the town walls without being noticed. As the keeper on the West Gate had said, not an impossibility, given the amount of traffic in and out of Totnes. The first question, however, posed greater difficulties unless I could shake the testimony of either Bridget Praule or Agatha Tenter.

'Are you sure,' I asked Bridget gently, 'that there was no moment, no one single instant, when you left the downstairs parlour for any reason, or your attention was so distracted, that the younglings could have crept down the stairs, through the room into the passage and thence into the street?' But before she spoke, I already knew what her reply would be.

'None at all!' She gave a vigorous shake of her head. 'I was in the parlour for the whole time the master was absent, and did not stir outside of it. I must have seen the children had they descended. Master Colet was not gone much above an hour. He liked his dinner promptly at half past ten o'clock and would not have been late returning.'

She had grown agitated, afraid that she was being accused of lying, and again I patted her hand.

'I'm not questioning your word, Mistress Praule, only clearing the last shreds of doubt from my mind. When did Master Colet decide to close up the house and look for new accommodation?'

'After the children's bodies were discovered. Until then, you see, we all hoped and prayed that they would be found alive and well. And if they had made their own way home, they would have come straight to the house, so we had to be there in case that happened.'

'And how did your master seem to you throughout that time of waiting?'

'Oh, he was very upset. Wouldn't eat much. Left half his meals, even though Agatha tried to tempt him with all his favourite dishes. He couldn't sleep, either. I remember, several times, looking out from my room in the loft and seeing, across the courtyard, a chink of light between his bedchamber shutters, which meant his candle must still have been burning. And once, when he shouted at me for some silly mistake I'd made, he apologized and told me to take no notice: he wasn't himself, he said. He said, too, that if anything had happened to the children, people would blame him because he was the only person to gain by their deaths. I told him Agatha and I both knew he could have had nothing to do with it, and if need be, so we'd tell the Crowner.'

'What did he answer?'

'He thanked me, but said that people would still try to blame him by accusing him of evil practices. Which is just what they did do. After it was known that the children had been murdered, even though it was plain to anyone of sense that the outlaws must have killed them, poor little lambs, the neighbours began to shun him, and make the sign to ward off evil if they passed him in the street. It didn't seem to matter that the Crowner decided he was innocent, people still believed him guilty, including Mistress Harbourne. She was one of the ones who stirred up most hatred against him.'

'You sound sorry for Master Colet, in spite of not really liking him.'

'I am,' Bridget retorted warmly. 'I don't care to see anyone wrongly accused. Liking or not liking has nothing to do with it.'

I smiled and squeezed her hand before releasing it. 'You've a gentle heart, Mistress Praule, and a sense of justice. So, when Master Colet decided to shut up the house, you returned here to live with your grandmother, and he went to lodge with Mistress Tenter and her mother?'

'Yes. It's not easy to find new berths in a town this size, though I'm hopeful of a fresh place before the summer's out. And the master needed a billet while he cast about him for a new home and sold the old one. He'd no friends in Totnes to turn to, and had no wish, he said, to stay at an inn. But neither did he want to quit the district altogether, so when Agatha offered to take him home with her, he agreed most readily.'

'But surely Mistress Tenter and her mother – although I speak as one knowing nothing about them – surely they are unable to offer Master Colet any of the comforts he has been accustomed to?'

Bridget rubbed the tip of her nose with a forefinger stained brown from the constant peeling and preparation of vegetables.

'I don't think that would worry him. It's ... Well, I think it's more what he was used to before Lady Skelton married him. He might even prefer it.'

She was far shrewder than her innocent, childish face suggested. Eudo Colet had very probably found solace in adversity in being with his own kind, as many another man had done before him.

I thanked her and stood up, glad to stretch my legs properly at last, but almost banging my head against the cottage roof. Bridget giggled, and a voice from the far corner cackled, 'Dang me, if you ain't one of the tallest fellows I ever laid eyes on, chapman! What was your father? One o' they Dartmoor giants?'

'No, a small man, and dark with it if my mother was to be believed. Of Celtic stock. It was the men of her family who were tall and fair-haired.'

Granny Praule snorted. 'I'd accuse no woman of playing her man false, but I'm willing to swear there's no Celtic blood in you. Saxon, you are, m'lad, through and through.' She added peevishly, 'You're not going already? Bridget, have you given the lad a cup of my damson wine?'

Bridget started guiltily and began to apologize for her oversight. I hastened to her rescue.

'Granny, I need to keep a clear head on my shoulders at the moment, and I'm sure your damson wine is too potent to allow any such thing. In fact, I'll wager yesterday's takings against anything anyone likes to name, that you make the best and strongest damson wine this side of the Tamar.'

She gave a toothless grin which split her wrinkled face from ear to ear. 'You're not wrong. It's a recipe I had of my mother and she of hers, and she again of hers. You'll taste none better anywhere in the kingdom. So bide awhile,' she wheedled, 'and try a drop.'

I refused, however, thanked Bridget Praule for her help, asked for more exact directions to Dame Tenter's dwelling than Ursula Cozin had been able to give me, and took my leave, stepping into the roadway and breathing deeply to clear my stuffy head of the rancid smells of the cottage. The Priory bells were ringing for Vespers, and I judged, therefore, that I still had an hour of daylight in which to visit Agatha Tenter and regain the town before sundown and the closing of the gates.

But here I was confronted by a problem. Eudo Colet lodged with the Tenters, and his presence could prove a hindrance to my mission. Indeed, as mother and daughter had taken him in, it was to be presumed that they championed him against all comers, and would resent as greatly as he would himself, any questioning on my part. Both Sheriff and Coroner had exonerated him of any blame for the children's deaths, and here was I, a stranger, once again muddying the waters. I should be lucky to escape without the handle of a broom broken across my back. If I had foreseen this difficulty earlier, and I took myself severely to task for not having done so, I could have brought my pack and knocked on Dame Tenter's door with good, if not honest, reason. Yet if I toiled back up the hill and then down again, much precious time would be lost. I could, I supposed, wait until the morrow, but I had made up my mind to speak to Agatha that day and was set on doing so, against all rhyme or reason. I therefore turned my feet towards the bridge and trusted that God would send me inspiration.

He did not fail me. Halfway across the narrow, uneven

span of arches which linked the west and east banks of the
Dart, I realized that I could, with a clear conscience, introduce
myself to Eudo Colet as his tenant. What might lead on from
that, I once more trusted in God to reveal. He had surely
brought me to Totnes in order to uncover the truth of this
matter, and therefore He could not disappoint me.

On the opposite bank of the river was the township which
both Ursula Cozin and Bridget Praule had referred to as the
Brigg, its cottages stretching away on either side of a dusty
track, towards the forest and the castle built by Henry de
Pomeroy two centuries earlier. Bridget had told me that
Dame Tenter occupied a dwelling close to the river, downstream a little, beyond the ford used by all horse-drawn traffic,
which the bridge was too dangerous to bear. So I turned my
feet along a narrow path edging the bank, until I came to an
isolated cottage, its pink clay walls glowing in the late afternoon sunshine. It stood in the middle of a neatly fenced
garden, where a bed of herbs gave forth a heady, aromatic
scent. A patch of stitchwort, growing by the gate, was already
in flower, the white-starred petals beginning to furl against
the waning of the light, the lance-shaped leaves and fragile
stems supported by the woven slats of the wattle. In the clear
April evening, the whole place looked warm and welcoming,
unlike Sir Jasper Crouchback's house, which seemed perpetu-
ally in shadow, as though happiness and laughter had been
little known within its walls.

I was being fanciful. I pushed open the gate, walked up the
short path to the door and knocked. After a moment or two,
it was opened by an elderly woman, who I guessed to be
Dame Tenter.

A voice from within called, 'Who is it, Mother?'

I raised my own voice a little. 'I've come to see Master Colet, if he's here.'

The woman who came to the door, wiping her hands in her apron, fitted Grizelda's description of Agatha Tenter; something more than thirty summers, buxom, with rosy apple cheeks and a fringe of dark red hair showing beneath her white linen hood. Her eyes were the bright blue of speedwells, her chin delicately pointed, and only her nose, sitting squatly in the centre of her face, marred what could otherwise be described as a handsome countenance.

'Who are you?' she demanded. 'And what do you want with Master Colet?'

Her manner was abrasive, but I gave her as admiring a glance as I could conjure up, removed my hat and bowed.

'My name is Roger and I am by trade a chapman. Master Oliver Cozin, the lawyer, has, however, seen fit to install me as tenant in Master Colet's house, in the hope that I may afford it some protection should the outlaws penetrate the town's defences. I am engaged to remain there until Saturday, and longer if it is possible for me to do so. I felt, therefore, that I should make myself known to Master Colet, so that he can see for himself what sort of fellow I am, and ask me any questions he deems necessary.'

Agatha eyed me suspiciously for several seconds, then mellowed a little. She moved back and held the door wide for me to enter.

'Master Colet is not here at present, but we expect him back very soon.' She nodded towards a stool near the central hearth and added, 'You may be seated.' And she began turning the spit over the fire where she had a rabbit roasting.

The older woman, a small, wizened creature who appeared to be of little account in her own home, retired to a corner

147

and resumed her spinning without vouchsafing me a single word, seemingly indifferent to my presence. I held my hands to the small fire burning on the hearthstone, for the evening air had grown chill during the past half-hour. Now that I was here, I did not know quite how to begin. Agatha solved the dilemma for me.

'You have no doubt been informed of the trouble surrounding Master Colet,' she remarked abruptly. 'Your free tenancy cannot have failed to arouse your curiosity, and, moreover, I should be surprised if the general gossip had not reached your ears by this time. But I'd be grateful if you would take care to say nothing of it in Master Colet's hearing. He is extremely distressed by any mention of the subject.'

'Understandably,' I murmured, 'if he is an innocent man.'

'Of course he's an innocent man,' she snapped, the blue eyes sparkling with anger. 'He has been found blameless by both Coroner and Sheriff on my testimony. And on that of Bridget Praule,' she added as an afterthought.

I hesitated before saying, 'Mistress Harbourne might not agree with their findings.'

'You've not been talking to that woman, have you?' Agatha's face grew red, and not altogether because of the heat from the flames. 'What does she know of anything? She wasn't there when the children disappeared. She'd gone, and good riddance to her!' The tone was scathing. 'She never liked Master Colet from the moment she first set eyes on him. She saw him as a cuckoo in her nest; as coming between herself and Lady Skelton. She'd always preened herself on being my lady's cousin, and so privileged in the household. A husband for my lady threatened her position. My lady had no further time for her. All her attention was for Master Colet, and Grizelda could not forgive him. She's still intent

148

on bringing him down with her lies and insinuations.'

'You are certain, then,' I inquired idly, as though having but small interest in the subject, 'that your master could have had nothing to do with the Skelton children's disappearance?'

'Of course, I'm certain, you dolt! They were there, in the house, when he left, and not there when he returned. That I can vouch for.'

'Then how did they get out? For it's certain they did, or else they would not have come by their deaths.'

She resumed her task of turning and basting the rabbit whilst casting me a look of pity.

'They went down the front stairs, of course, when that stupid wench, Bridget Praule, wasn't looking. The girl's a day-dreamer. Whenever she helped me in the kitchen, I had to scold her for inattention: she was never thinking of what she was supposed to be doing. And afterwards she was too scared to admit that that was what must have happened. But I made my views plain, first to the Sheriff, and, later, when the bodies were discovered, to the Coroner.'

I nodded as though satisfied, making no answer and continuing to warm my hands at the fire. Was this, then, the answer to the riddle? It made sense and had obviously appealed to the logical minds of Authority. I was back with William of Occam again, and his belief that the fewest possible assumptions are to be made when explaining anything. Yet Bridget had not seemed to me to be a dreamer. Even more importantly, unless she were clever enough to pull the wool over my eyes, she had revealed herself as someone with a deep regard for the truth. I was convinced that had she thought for a moment the children could have escaped through the downstairs parlour without her seeing them, she would fearlessly have admitted as much. My suspicions began to turn towards Agatha Tenter, so anxious to maintain both her employer's innocence and her own standing in his eyes. If the children had gone through the kitchen to the outer courtyard, perhaps she had deliberately ignored, or even abetted, them.

Yet, what could have been her purpose in doing so? I was convinced that she was more than a little in love with Eudo Colet, and would therefore have done nothing to cause him anxiety or annoyance. On the other hand, if she were in league with him to get rid of the children, she could have eased their passage to the outside world, even suggesting to them how they might pass through the gates unseen. Perhaps their stepfather had picked a quarrel with them on purpose, adding fuel to the flames of their resentment until Grizelda returned, knowing that she would fly to the children's defence and using it as an excuse to dismiss her. But what then? He could have had no sure knowledge that Andrew and Mary would leave the house, nor, if they did, that they would be captured and murdered by the outlaws. I stared into the heart of the fire, seeking for an answer to the puzzle, but none was forthcoming.

The cottage door opened and a man entered, instantly recognizable as my horseman of the previous day. He was even wearing the same clothes, but now the red leather riding boots were dusty with walking, his horse presumably having to be stabled some way away. Dame Tenter had no outbuilding where such a noble beast could be housed, but the cottage did, I noticed, boast a second bedchamber, now given over entirely to Master Colet's use, if the makeshift bed in one corner of the living-room were anything to judge by.

He did not see me immediately, being intent on imparting his news to Agatha.

'I have been with Lawyer Cozin again, and he's sanguine that my latest offer for the property near Dartington has satisfied its present owner. I can look forward, he thinks, to being settled in before Rogationtide. Nothing remains now but to sell . . .' He broke off abruptly, becoming aware of my presence. 'Who, in Jesu's name, is this?'

I rose swiftly to my feet, making obeisance.

'I am Roger the chapman, Your Honour. Master Oliver Cozin may have mentioned me to you. I am your tenant, *pro tempore*.'

The full lips, set in their hedge of dark brown beard, curled into a sneer.

'Oh, yes. The lawyer mentioned some pedlar who had been granted free lodging in my house. So why aren't you there, protecting it? That, I thought, was the agreement. It's nearly sundown and the town gates will soon be shut against you. These outlaws are dangerous men, and grow bolder by the night. Any time now, they'll breach the Totnes stockade, and an empty house will be a godsend to them. What are you doing here anyway?'

'I came to make myself known to your honour, and to inquire if you had any instructions for me. I thought you might have entertained some misgivings concerning Master Cozin's decision to install me without first consulting your wishes.'

'I trust Oliver's judgement in most things,' Eudo Colet rasped, seating himself in a carved armchair, made comfortable by a velvet cushion, which had plainly been brought with him from the Crouchback house. 'I have no interest in the matter, nor anything to say to you. You are free to leave here as soon as you please.' He gave a blustering laugh.

I regarded him thoughtfully. Most surely, this was someone

elevated above his natural station in life, who felt in duty bound to wield an authority which did not sit easily upon his shoulders. He was not a man of Wessex, of that I was certain. There were none of the broad vowels or Saxon diphthongs in his speech, and it was probable that he came from the east or north of the kingdom, where, centuries ago, the Danes had imposed upon the English a fashion for pronouncing words alien to those parts of the land where their writ had never run.

I could not see the chin beneath the bush of beard, but I suspected that it had no strength. A weak man, I guessed, open to the influence of others and whose vanity was easily fed, but, for all that, lacking in confidence, as bullies generally are. I did not like Eudo Colet, yet in some strange way, he aroused my pity, as he had done Bridget Praule's. There was a kind of doom about him, as though Fate had marked him down at birth as one of her victims.

'Then if your honour has nothing further to say to me, I shall be going,' I promised, stooping to retrieve my cudgel from where I had laid it, on the floor. I turned to take my leave of Agatha Tenter.

Her eyes were fixed worshipfully upon Master Colet. I had not been mistaken. She was besotted by him; and I had to admit that he was both young enough, and sufficiently good-looking, to be found attractive by many women. Rosamund Skelton had obviously been willing to cast aside all scruples about marrying beneath her, in order to make him her husband. What Eudo Colet's feelings were for Agatha, I had no means of knowing, but few men are above taking advantage of a woman's love if it can serve their own ends, myself included. Myself, perhaps, most of all when I remember Lillis.

'God be with you, Mistress Tenter, and with your good mother.' I smiled at the old lady in her corner, but she made no response. 'Thank you for your hospitality. And now, I'll be on my way. Master Colet, God be with your honour.'

'And don't come nosing around here again,' Agatha said, suddenly vicious. She added for Eudo Colet's benefit, 'He's been talking to Grizelda. She's still bent on making trouble for you, isn't she, chapman?'

I answered steadily, 'Mistress Harbourne is anxious to find out the truth about her charges. She grieves for them, as is only natural.'

Eudo Colet flushed angrily, the colour rising from beneath his beard in an unbecoming tide.

'She maligns me, if she speaks ill of me,' he answered, with an air of injured innocence. 'She knows it, as do most others who try to smear my good name. Ask Agatha, here, or Bridget Praule. Or Master Thomas Cozin. They will all tell you that I could have had no hand in my stepchildren's disappearance. Furthermore, my argument with Mary and Andrew was stormy, but brief, and would have been quickly over had it not been for Grizelda's interference. Their sulks never lasted long, believe you me.'

'Oh, I do, your honour. Jack Carter told me that he heard one of the younglings singing while he was taking Mistress Harbourne's belongings downstairs. A lullaby, or some such. He had no reason to lie, as far as I can see.'

'You seem to have been busy quizzing half the town, Master Chapman,' Agatha Tenter interrupted nastily. 'People who stick their noses into other people's affairs, may find themselves in trouble. I should be careful, if I were you.'

'Indeed, I shall, Mistress Tenter! Once again, I bid you all goodnight.'

But as, in the final rays of the dying sun, I made my way back across the bridge, and as I climbed the Foregate into the town, I had much to think about, not least that last remark of Agatha Tenter's. Had it been intended as a threat? Who could say?

It was growing dark, and suddenly I shivered.

Chapter Twelve

I came slowly to my senses from the depths of a deep, untroubled sleep. Something had woken me, but as yet I was unsure what it was.

Before turning in, I had eaten well at the castle ale-house, free of Jacinta's conversation, as she was visiting a neighbour who had just been delivered of twins. This much I prised out of her taciturn son, who answered all my questions with a series of grunts and a few grudging phrases. There were a half-dozen other men present: a couple of guards from the castle garrison, a stout and respectable burgher of the town and three travellers who had obtained lodgings at the Priory guest-house for the night. I was grateful for the landlady's absence; and while I ate my boiled bacon and peas, washed down with a cup of Rhenish wine, I turned over in my mind the events of the day and tried to sort out my impressions. But I was too tired to do them justice, and by the end of the meal, I was nodding over my empty platter, the wine spilling from the cup in my hand. I paid what I owed and left.

I decided that I could not endure another long and wakeful night, like the one before, so I dragged the flock mattress and two woollen blankets downstairs from the smaller bed-chamber, and made myself comfortable. Too comfortable, perhaps, for, having stripped off my outer clothing and cleaned between my teeth with my strip of willow bark, I was sound asleep almost before I had rolled beneath the covers . . .

And now, for some reason I could not immediately fathom, I was wide awake, sitting bolt upright, my hand already reaching out towards my cudgel. I listened intently, but the house was silent except for the slight nocturnal groans of settling timber. Yet something had disturbed my rest, penetrating the veils of sleep which still clung about my eyelids. Or was it simply the echo of a dream?

After a few minutes, I lay down again, pulling the blankets around my ears, finally convinced that I was mistaken. A finger of moonlight silvered the floor as it probed its way between the shutters.

I was drifting on a cloud of pleasant dreams, a child again, back in my home in Wells. My mother had sent me out of doors to play, while she swept the cottage floor with a broom she had made from stems freshly gathered that morning. These stems had been carefully stripped of their flowers, which made a good yellow dye, or, when mixed with woad, a green one. She was a thrifty housewife, my mother, but she had need to be since the death of my father. As she sent dust and old rushes flying through the open doorway, she began to sing, her voice very faint, high-pitched and far away . . .

I was wide awake again, the hair beginning to rise on the nape of my neck and droplets of icy sweat breaking out all over my body. I propped myself on one elbow, straining my ears, suddenly realizing with horror that this was no dream, but reality. The sound came from above me, a child's voice, very thin and reed-like, some way off, but the words clearly audible in the stillness. I recognized them as part of a lullaby my mother used to sing on those many nights when, as a young child, sleep proved elusive.

> Lollay, lollay, little child,
> Child, lollay, lullow,
> Into this uncouth world
> Incummen so art thou.

I shivered, aware of a coldness in the room. I battled against the impulse to burrow down into the mattress and throw the blankets over my head; to block my ears with my fingers until that eerie keening had ceased. The wraiths of darkness seemed, to my fevered imagination, to be circling all around me: hobgoblins, spectres and phantoms of the night; unhappy spirits rising from yawning graves.

The voice came again, still clear and high, but this time with a slight quaver in it, like a child who is comforting itself and trying to be brave. A boy's voice or a girl's? It was hard to tell. I only knew that the sound was piteous, that it was asking for help, drawing me on like the sailors of old who heard the sirens' call, only to be dashed to pieces against the rocks . . .

> Lullay, lullay, little child,
> Child, lollay, lollay,
> With sorrow thou comest into this world,
> With sorrow shalt wend away.

I forced myself to rise from my lowly bed and, with trembling fingers, sought for the tinder-box which I had left on the parlour table. Twice I tried to rub the flint against the steel, and twice failed; but the third time, I managed to steady

157

my hands long enough to strike a spark. The tinder flared and I held it to my candle, the flame illuminating the room and bringing the shadows creeping stealthily out of their corners. I must have dragged on my hose and shirt and laced up my tunic, but I had only a hazy recollection afterwards of having done so. Then I picked up the candle-holder in one hand and my cudgel in the other, and began to mount the stairs.

The voice continued its singing, enticing me forwards. Just for a moment, as I reached the top of the flight, it wavered and broke, the final notes of the verse sounding louder and closer at hand. I spun round on my heel, raising my candle above my head, letting its pale radiance play across the walls and furniture of the upper parlour. The carved saints at the end of the roof-beams stared down with sightless eyes, the reds and blues, greens and yellows of their robes leaping out at me, jewel-bright, before subsiding back into shadow as the light slithered over them and passed on. The tapestry Judith, holding up the head of Holofernes, was transfixed in the moment of her triumph, the embroidered gouts of blood, dripping to the ground of the Assyrian's tent, looking almost real in the glow from the candle . . .

There was no one there: my ears had tricked me. And now the singing started again, in the distance. I stepped through to the tiny, airless landing. The door of the children's room was shut, but the one leading into the larger bedchamber stood ajar, and I could hear the words of the lullaby with even greater clarity.

> Lollay, lollay, little child,
> Why weepest thou so sore?

I entered the room, once more raising my candle aloft, and

looked around me. With a jolt of fear, which made me tremble from head to foot, I saw that the further door, leading to the courtyard gallery, was open, letting in a blast of cold night air. Almost certain that I had locked it the previous day, and not having been up here since, I knew an overpowering impulse to turn and run downstairs and out into the street; to seek sanctuary in the Priory from whatever restless spirit haunted this unhappy house. I was shivering violently, my tongue cleaving to the roof of my mouth, my hand shaking so much that drops of hot tallow spattered the red and white walls. And beneath the horror ran a more mundane fear that I might let the candle fall, setting light to the old, dry and brittle rushes which remained scattered across the floor.

> Needs must thou weep,
> It was ordained of yore.

The voice soared to a high, pure note, like the pealing of a silver bell, then ceased abruptly. In the moments of utter silence which followed, I waited, my heart thumping in my chest, for it to begin again. Nothing happened. The stillness became first oppressive, then menacing. Finally, summoning every ounce of courage, I crept towards the paler oblong set in the blackness of the wall and stared out into the moonlit night.

Shadows filled the inner courtyard. I could make out the shapes of well-head and pump outside the kitchen door, which, I noted with relief, appeared to be shut. The windows, too, were closed, displaying no chink of light. Immediately ahead of me stretched the covered gallery, and the door at its further end also presented a blank and shuttered face. My candle-flame paled into insignificance against the beams of the waxing moon, and I snuffed it out. I could find my way downstairs sure-footed now that my eyes had grown accustomed to the dark. I waited, unmoving, my ears alert for any resumption of that ghostly singing; any last echo, however faint, of the childish treble whose sex I still could not determine. The beating of my heart had quietened a little, making it easier to breathe, and I drew in a mouthful of the early morning air. For surely, I decided, it must have long gone midnight. It was the dead time of darkness when nothing stirs. No noise, not even the cry of the Watch, disturbed the town which slumbered all about me.

I leaned against the jamb of the door, waiting to regain control of my limbs, vainly telling myself that I had imagined the whole. It must, after all, have been an extension of my dream. It was my mother's voice, long since stilled by death, that I had heard. After a moment or two, I felt it possible to move and gently eased my body away from its support. As I did so, a flash of movement at the other end of the covered gallery riveted my attention.

The door leading into the lofts and the servants' quarters above the kitchen stood wide open, where, only seconds before, it had been fast shut. It had swung inwards on silent hinges, revealing an archway of blackness. There was no glimmer of light nor any sign of life, but the solid, iron-studded oaken leaf could not possibly have moved of its own accord. My heart began to thump once more, and I found it difficult to swallow. I cursed myself for having prematurely doused my candle; for having too eagerly embraced the notion that what had happened had been due to nothing more than my imagination. I hesitated, tempted to turn and flee, but a voice inside my head urged me not to be a coward. I crossed myself, placed my candlestick on the floor, took a firmer grip of my cudgel and advanced along the gallery, the boards creaking a little beneath my weight.

The moonlight made my passage easy, so that I was able to keep my eyes on the cavern of darkness ahead without worrying too much about my feet. Thus it was that I saw the faint movement beyond the storeroom door; the merest flicker of black upon black, but sufficient to reassure me that the events of the night were indeed real and not imagined.

'Hello!' I called. 'Who's there? Stand fast, whoever you are. You're trespassing!'

My voice sounded strange and unnatural, and the profound silence which ensued left my words echoing through my head without form or meaning. Then suddenly there came again that weird, almost unearthly singing.

> Lullay, lullay little child,
> Child, lollay, lollay,
> With sorrow thou comest into this world,
> With sorrow shalt wend away.

I could stand it no longer. I lunged forward, pounding along the gallery with long, hasty strides, not noticing how the boards were shaking beneath my feet. As I reached the middle, there was a terrible groaning, the ominous crack of splintering wood, a rending shriek as the old and rotten planking gave way, fragmenting into a gaping hole. I grasped desperately at the handrail in an attempt to save myself, but it was too late. My hands were slippery, unable to get a grip, and I fell, feet first, to the courtyard below.

It was not a long drop, perhaps only a distance of seven or eight feet, but I could have done myself more hurt than I did. As it was, I struck my head on the flagstones, a blow which made my senses reel, and twisted one leg beneath me. How long I lay there, stunned, I have no idea, but it could not have been many minutes. Cautiously and painfully, I dragged myself upright, using my cudgel, which, by God's providence, had fallen close at hand, as a prop to aid me in getting to my feet. My left ankle was very tender when I first put it to the ground, but after hobbling to and fro across the courtyard several times, the pain grew less and it was able to take my weight. I had been extremely fortunate to escape without any broken bones.

A glance in the direction of the covered gallery showed it irreparably damaged. Apart from the roof, which now sagged drunkenly in the middle, the walkway stood in two separate parts, the flagstones beneath strewn with fragments and splinters of wood, some of them sizeable pieces of timber. It would take the craft of a master carpenter, aided by his apprentice, to try to put it right, although in my estimation it was past repairing; a structure long neglected and rotted by the effects of the weather.

I realized that I had almost forgotten my original fear in the aftermath of my fall and concern for my body's well-being. Now, it returned in full force, and I gazed up at the storeroom door above me, in terror of seeing some ghostly, childish face peering over the end of the broken balustrade. There was nobody there, and the door was shut. At first, I thought it a trick of the moonlight, and stood on tiptoe, craning my neck, getting as close to the rickety structure of the gallery as I dared, but I was not mistaken. Whoever, or whatever, had opened the door had now closed it.

Again plucking up my courage, I decided to search the kitchen building. I hobbled towards the door and tried the latch, but it was barred and bolted. Moreover, the keys were not upon my person. Before retiring to rest, I had placed them for safekeeping beneath the mattress. Once more, fear pricked along my spine. Doors had been opened that night, but whether by witchcraft or by human agency I had, as yet, no means of knowing.

Before I had time to give the matter much thought, however, I was struck by another consideration, and one of more immediacy. As I did not have the keys upon me, I was unable to re-enter the front part of the house except by the bed-chamber door, to which my only access was the gallery, now broken. I was trapped in the inner courtyard unless, by some chance, the intruder had also unfastened the door into the downstairs passage. But it, too, was locked and bolted.

Desperately, I cast about for some way out of my predicament. The moonlight aided my search, its pale beams showing me imperfections in the stone of the wall, outside the counting-house window, which might provide me with a foothold. I judged that the floor of the gallery at either end was still firm enough to support my weight, and if I could manage to scale the wall and heave myself over the balustrade, I would be able to re-enter the main bedchamber.

I laid my cudgel on the ground and began the ascent, my hands still slippery with fear. But as so often throughout my life, my height was to prove a blessing. A jutting stone some eight or nine inches above the ground and close to the gallery, enabled me to gain a foothold, and, by dint of clinging to another protruberance with my right hand and stretching my left arm as far above my head as I could reach, I was able to catch hold of one of the balusters. After a moment in which to steady myself, I swung my right arm across and grabbed a second baluster, allowing myself to hang by my arms from the broken structure, which creaked and groaned a little, but showed no signs of total collapse. Encouraged, I began to haul myself up by my hands until, after much sweating and heaving, I managed to fling first one arm, and then the other over the balustrade. This way, I obtained sufficient purchase to pull myself up until I found kneeholds between the uprights. Eventually, exchanging kneeholds for toeholds, I managed to get one leg across the handrail and, moments later, was crouched outside the open bedchamber door, gasping heavily from my exertions. My hands were scratched and bleeding, my whole body aching unpleasantly from head to foot. I straightened and stepped into the shelter of the room, closing the door behind me.

Yet again, for the past quarter-hour, or for however long my climb had taken me, I had forgotten my terror, but now, as before, it came flooding back. I picked up my abandoned candlestick, blundered downstairs and felt with trembling fingers for the bunch of keys beneath my mattress. They were still there and I gave a groan of relief. Somewhere at the back of my mind had lurked an unacknowledged fear that they might have been stolen from me by my ghostly visitor. I sat down in the armchair and closed my eyes, my mind whirling with a hundred thoughts, none of which made any sense in my present distressed condition. I had heard a child's voice, to that I was ready to swear, but both Mary and Andrew Skelton were dead. So who could it have been, if not the unhappy shade of one of them?

After a while, I forced myself to my feet, relit my candle, took the keys and walked the length of the passageway to the door at the far end, which I unlocked and unbolted before stepping out into the courtyard. All was silent and everything just as I had left it; the broken planks scattered across the flagstones, the gallery in two parts, sagging towards the middle, the doors at either end fast shut, the windows blank and sightless. My cudgel lay where I had dropped it when I began my climb, close to the counting-house wall, and my fingers fastened round it with a sense of the utmost relief. It felt thick and solid in my palm, an old, familiar friend and protector on whom I could rely in times of trouble. I knew its every knot and imperfection, felt the comforting weight of its rounded end. I swung it gently to and fro for several moments, first in one hand, then in the other, making sure that I had done no harm to wrists or shoulders. Satisfied, I went back indoors, turning the key in the lock and lowering the bar.

My next task was to return upstairs and fasten the bed-chamber door securely. For good measure, I dragged one of the clothes chests across it, as close to the jambs as possible. Yet, even as I did so, I realized the futility of my action, for if the presence in the house that night were inhuman, no barriers could gainsay its access. If, on the other hand, the voice belonged to flesh and blood, there was no way in which the intruder could reach the door across the broken gallery.

I found that I was shivering again. My limbs felt heavy and extremely cold. I went downstairs and sat for a second time in the armchair, unable to bring myself to lie on the mattress. I needed to be alert, to have all my wits about me in case . . . In case of what? What could I do against the spirits of the grave? My teeth were chattering, and at last I was forced to wrap myself in the blankets, even though they hampered my movements. I left my arms free, however, and propped my cudgel against the chair, within easy reach.

I must not sleep, that was the thought uppermost in my mind as I tried to stop my eyes from closing. For, in spite of my terror, my lids constantly drooped and my senses swam. And, of course, in the end, there was no way I could prevent myself from losing consciousness ...

When I at last awoke, the early morning sunlight was creeping through the shutters, harbinger of another fine, warm day. Painfully, I got to my feet, tenderly stretching each part of my body, feeling along each limb with cautious fingers, examining my bruises. The latter were plentiful, some already turning an angry purple, others were still a sickly yellow. But there was little else wrong with me, apart from the general feeling of having been soundly beaten. I went into the yard and stripped, holding my head beneath the pump and allowing the cold, clear water to trickle through my hair and down across my neck and shoulders. Then I hauled up water from the well, ignoring the effort it cost me, and emptied bucket after bucket over my aching body. Water has great healing properties and, after a while, I began to feel better. I rubbed myself dry with the piece of rough linen I always carried in my pack for such a purpose, dressed again and was almost ready to face the prospect, when I had shaved, of breakfast at the castle ale-house.

Before that, however, I had things to do, the first being to inspect more closely the broken strut where the boards of the gallery had given way. There was no doubt, after a closer examination, that the planks were rotten and had shattered beneath my weight and heavy-footed pounding, but the rest of the walkway was in no better condition. Why, then, had it collapsed at that particular spot? I picked my way through the fallen timber and looked carefully at the strut which had supported it. The top was cut cleanly through, no jagged splinters protruding as there should have been had the structure been torn apart by accident. Someone had taken a sharp knife or cleaver to it, weakening the whole fabric of the gallery. Someone, too, had lured me on to walk across it.

But why? Such a short fall could not possible have killed me. It could, however, have injured me, and that quite seriously. Even at the time, I had considered myself lucky to escape as lightly as I did. I might well have broken an arm, a leg, a shoulder, or twisted my ankle more severely, and been laid up in the Priory's infirmary for weeks. By which time, my interest in the disappearance of Mary and Andrew Skelton would have waned – or so, at least, my attacker would happily have imagined. But who was my attacker? Who wished so strongly for the matter to be forgotten? Who found my interest a threat to his peace of mind? Above all, who would have another set of keys to let himself in and out of the house at will? There was only one answer. Eudo Colet.

I went across to the kitchen door, unlocked it, mounted the ladder to the servants' quarters and opened the shutters. Here, where the dust lay thick on the floorboards, there should have been evidence of only one set of footprints; my own from the day before yesterday. Now, however, the dust had been scuffed into lines and whorls, evidence of some attempt at obliteration. I passed into the storeroom and again let in the morning sun. The same scuff marks were everywhere apparent. This was not the work of a spirit. A human foot had made this effort to wipe out all trace of its owner's presence. And who, in the dark, would be aware of the dust on the floor, except someone who knew how long the house had stood unoccupied? Yet again, the name of Eudo Colet came to mind.

I tried the door which opened on to the gallery, but it remained fast shut until I unlocked it with my key. It swung easily and soundlessly inwards, and when I stooped and touched the hinges, my fingers were smeared with a thick, black grease. Most certainly, my nocturnal visitor had been no denizen of the after world, but made of flesh and blood, like me. Yet it had been a child's voice singing, I would swear to that; a child's voice, thin and high and pure. I began both to shiver and to sweat. There was something deeply evil here, and as yet I did not know what it was. I still was no nearer to the truth.

Chapter Thirteen

Half an hour later, I stepped outside the front door, and almost at once became aware of a general sense of expectancy and fear. At the corner of High Street, where it curves downhill towards East Gate, a group of people were engaged in earnest conversation, and it was plain that this was no idle morning gossip. Opposite, an upper casement of a house had been flung wide open and its mistress, her hair not yet dressed and braided, leaned out, calling to a man on horseback, who had reined in his mount below. A second horseman, in the livery of the Mayor, entered through the West Gate behind me and clattered over the cobbles as though his life depended on it.

One of my neighbours emerged from the dwelling next to Master Colet's and shouted across to his friends, 'What's to do? Our man, Jack, has just returned from the bakery and is full of some tale of murder, but who's been killed, or where, he doesn't know.'

The horseman slewed around in his saddle.

'It seems the outlaws were out and about last night and slaughter done. It's reported that Mayor Broughton has sent to Exeter for the Sheriff to come in person, and it's expected that when he does, he'll raise another *posse* to try to smoke

out these fiends for good and all. Accompany me as far as
the Mayor's parlour and we'll hear what His Worship himself
has to say.'

The lady added from her eyrie, 'I heard they struck twice,
in two separate spots well removed from one another, which,
if true, is something new and means that they may have
joined forces with a second robber band.' She shook her
head sadly, the unbound hair, still dark in places but liberally
streaked with grey, swinging mournfully about her face. 'What
lawless times we live in! What my dear mother would have
made of it all I dare not think. The saints be praised, she's
safe in her grave these fifteen years.'

The two men murmured sympathetically and prepared to
move on, greeting several other acquaintances who had,
meantime, appeared at doors and windows, attracted by the
sound of urgent voices. Before he could join the horseman
on the opposite side of the street, however, I seized my
neighbour's arm.

'Sir,' I said, releasing his sleeve as soon as he turned his
indignant gaze my way, 'you won't know me, but my name is
Roger. I'm a chapman by trade, and I've been lodged next
door by Master Oliver Cozin, the lawyer, to keep an eye
upon the house for Master Colet. Did you...? Did you,
by any chance, hear anything last night, during the hours
of darkness?'

The man's lean features registered alarm. 'Hear anything?
Like what, pray? Dear Heaven, are you saying that the outlaws may have breached the town's defences? Colin!' he
called to his friend, but fortunately the horseman was still
deep in talk and did not hear him.

'No, no, sir!' I interrupted hurriedly. 'This had nothing to
do with the robbers. This noise was more like the singing of

a child. But whether the voice was that of a boy or a girl, I was unable to distinguish. Did either you or any member of your household hear it?'

'The singing of a child?' My gentleman grew irascible. 'What nonsense is this? We've more serious matters to deal with this morning than your nocturnal fancies, as you're no doubt aware.' His gaze narrowed. 'Didn't I see you supping at the castle ale-house last evening? Mmm. I thought I wasn't mistaken. And downing some of Jacinta's best Rhenish if I remember rightly. No doubt, it went to your head and made you tipsy. In future, leave such drink for your betters and stick to ale. All right! I'm coming! I'm coming!' he added, as the horseman, whom he had addressed as Colin, finished his conversation and grew impatient to move on.

Walking beside his friend's horse, he vanished round the bend in the roadway, intent on his quest for further information. I tipped my hat and bowed to the lady opposite, but she, suddenly becoming conscious of her state of undress, whisked herself inside and slammed shut the casement. The other people, too, disappeared indoors, anxious to let husbands, wives or masters know of the night's happenings and of the possible arrival of the Sheriff later in the day.

With my own inquiries to make, I put off eating for a while and directed my feet away from the castle ale-house towards the West Gate. The same man I had talked to yesterday was on duty again today, and was at that moment arguing fiercely with a cowherd who wished to drive his animals from the Rotherfold to pasture, on the other side of town.

'You must take them by South Street and the Foregate. Clear passage must be left within the walls in case my Lord Sheriff and his men arrive.'

''E'll not be 'ere until nightfall,' the cowherd protested

angrily. 'Maybe not until tomorrow. 'E ain't long been sent for, so I 'eard. It's a long way round by South Street. Why should me and my beasts travel all that way?'

'Get along with you, you lazy varmint!' the gatekeeper exclaimed wrathfully. 'You ain't entering here, and that's a fact. If you give me any trouble, I'll see you set in the pillory, so I will. Stand aside, now! You're interfering with those about their lawful business.'

Grumbling, the cowman turned about and departed with his herd, to the great inconvenience of those trying to enter into the town, and for the next several minutes, the gate-keeper's attention was fully occupied. I was, however, able to speak to him at last, and was greeted civilly enough as an old acquaintance, although not with quite the geniality of the previous day, when traffic had been slack.

'What can I do for you, then, friend? Here's a terrible night's work by all accounts.'

I agreed, but briefly. There were already more travellers approaching up the hill from the Leper Hospital, as well as from along the Plymouth road.

'Yesterevening,' I said urgently, 'near to curfew, did Master Colet enter by this gate?'

'Master Colet?' The man rubbed his nose thoughtfully with one ham-like fist. 'Close to curfew?' Slowly, he shook his head. 'No. I saw nothing of him. Why do you ask?'

'No reason,' I answered hastily. 'I . . . I thought I recognized him in the street last night, as I left the castle tavern. But I was most likely mistaken.'

'Most likely you were.' The gatekeeper shrugged his massive shoulders and turned away to greet the next arrivals.

'You're sure?' I persisted. 'You'd have known Master Colet if you saw him?'

He gave me a look of withering scorn. 'And him living within a few yards of the gate for more than two years? Do you think my head's stuffed with wool? Of course I'd know him! Get along with you, chapman! I've work to do. Now then, lad, where are those sheep bound for? Pasture or the Shambles?'

So, Eudo Colet, if he had followed me from Agatha Tenter's cottage, had not entered by the West Gate. I would make further inquiries at the East Gate later, when I had broken my fast.

Jacinta herself welcomed me as I stooped beneath the lintel and seated myself at a table near the doorway. She hurried across as soon as she had finished serving two travellers with their meal of oatmeal, boiled bacon and salt herring.

'Here's a to-do,' she said, wiping her hands on her apron. 'You've heard, no doubt. Indeed, the whole town must have heard the news by now. Two attacks by the outlaws last night, as far afield as Dartington and Bow Creek. And murder done in the latter place, they're saying.'

My blood ran cold.

'Bow Creek? That's where Grizelda Harbourne has her holding. Is she safe? Who's been murdered? Have any names been mentioned?'

Jacinta plumped down on a stool opposite, one hand creeping up to her mouth.

'Grizelda! I'd forgotten her, God forgive me! But I know nothing but what people are saying; that great damage was done that way. A house burned down. And a body discovered in the ashes, early this morning, by two woodsmen on their way to work in the forest. Now, lad, what can I bring you?'

But my appetite had deserted me. I was gripped by a terrible fear that something had happened to Grizelda. I jumped to my feet, ignoring the landlady's protests that I could not leave until I had eaten.

'I must go at once,' I said. 'I must find out if Grizelda is safe.'

A gleam appeared in Jacinta's eyes, the outlaws momentarily forgotten as she scented gossip.

'So, that's the way the wind's blowing, is it? A little long in the tooth for you, I should have thought, but a handsome enough woman. And age brings experience, they say.' She let out a raucous cackle of laughter.

I ignored her and made for the ale-house door. All I could think about was getting to Bow Creek as quickly as possible. By now, the morning's traffic had increased so much, both in and out of the town, that I had no difficulty obtaining a ride on an empty haywain, which had been relieved of its load and was returning in the direction of the Harbourne River. The driver, who had lodged overnight in the Priory guest-hall, knew no more of events than I did, and was hurrying home to reassure himself that his wife and children had not been harmed.

'I can't help worrying, although my holding's a good half mile to the west of where they say the robbers struck, towards Luscombe way.'

Nevertheless, his natural anxiety caused him to make all speed, and we covered the ground between Totnes and Ashprington while the sun was still low, and the eastern sky streaked with the faint, luminous pink of early morning. One or two fleecy clouds now and then obscured the face of the sun, but they were trembling and insubstantial. It was going to be another warm and rainless day.

I said goodbye to the hayman on the outskirts of the village, making my way through the trees by the narrow track which

Grizelda and I had traversed together two days earlier. My nose picked up the faint and acrid smell of burning, and I quickened my pace, half-hoping that I might see some evidence of the outlaws' villainy when I reached the huddled cluster of houses, which would mean that Grizelda's holding was safe. But although there was a great deal of feverish activity, with some of the younger women crying hysterically into their aprons, or clinging, pale and wide-eyed to their menfolk, there was no sign of damage; no smoking ruin which would indicate that it was here and not elsewhere that the outlaws had struck.

A sergeant, wearing the Zouche livery and despatched from the castle garrison to make inquiries, was gentling his uneasy horse as the villagers swarmed around him, the men all talking at once, anxious to give their different versions of what might, or might not have been heard or observed during the night. I approached a stout, elderly matron, seemingly calm enough to answer questions, standing on the edge of the little crowd.

'What's to do? Rumours in the town say that a house was burned to the ground by the outlaws, and someone murdered.'

The woman nodded, without turning her head to glance at me, but keeping her eyes fixed on what was happening in front of her.

'Rumour says true for once, then. Grizelda Harbourne's cottage was utterly destroyed, and a body's been discovered in the ashes.'

For a moment, my voice failed me. Finally, however, I managed to croak, 'Grizelda's?'

My informant did look round at this, a little frown puckering her forehead.

'Thanks be to Our Lady, no! Are you a friend of hers, lad?'

As I waited for the agitated beating of my heart to subside, I considered the question. Could I honestly claim to be Grizelda's friend? I had only met her the day before yesterday. Yet, in that short space of time, I had not only grown to know and like her, but I also wished to know her better. What her feelings were for me, though, I had no idea. Perhaps I had no right to lay any demands upon her.

'Let's just say I'm a chance acquaintance of hers, but one who is worried for her safety. You know for a certainty that it was not her body found in the ashes?'

The woman smiled broadly. 'Lad, look over yonder. Wearing the blue gown. Grizelda. There, she's seen you. She's coming towards us.'

By the time the woman had finished speaking, Grizelda had skirted the crowd and was beside me, her handsome face, a moment ago so dark and brooding, transfigured by a welcoming smile.

'Roger! What brings you here? Oh, I'm so glad to see you!' She held out both her hands.

I took them in mine. 'I came to see if you were safe,' I told her, 'only to learn that it is your holding which was attacked last night, and your cottage which is burned to the ground. And a body among the ruins! I was afraid...' Unable to finish, I took a tighter grip on her fingers.

'You thought me dead. And you cared.' The smile faded and she drew a deep, shuddering breath, a tear trickling slowly down one cheek. 'Forgive me,' she went on, 'but it's so long since anyone had kindness enough for me to worry about my fate.'

I drew her into my arms, to the great interest of the elderly dame standing beside us, and kissed her gently between the eyes.

'Tell me exactly what's happened,' I urged her.

Grizelda rested her head against my shoulder.

'There's little to tell. Last night, I slept yet again at my friends' holding, as you advised. But in the late afternoon, just as I was leaving the cottage, Innes Woodsman waylaid me and begged me, if I were not sleeping there myself, to let him use it for the night. He must have kept watch on it the previous evening and taken note of my absence.'

'Begged you or threatened you?' I interrupted.

'Oh, his manner was sufficiently humble for me to agree to his request. And he had a deep-seated cough which was tearing at his throat. Dear sweet Saviour! Why did I not follow my inclination and refuse him! He would still be alive!'

'He was burned to death, then, not murdered?'

Grizelda indignantly tore herself free of my arms. 'He was murdered by those devils just as surely as if they had stabbed him with a knife. Indeed, a knife would have been quicker and cleaner, I have no doubt.'

I frowned. 'But why would the outlaws burn down your cottage? What could it possibly avail them?'

'Revenge,' she answered simply. 'They returned for my pig and my cow. But, as I told you yesterday, I have lodged Snouter and Betsy in my friends' byre and sty, along with their own beasts. When the outlaws found them gone, they grew angry and set fire to the house. I was the one they intended as their victim.'

Yet could Innes Woodsman not have escaped in time? I wondered. But the thatch would blaze fiercely, as, too, would the building's wattle framework. A man sleeping soundly might well find himself trapped before he had time to come fully to his senses. And even had he managed to avoid the furnace, he would have run full tilt into the murdering hands of his oppressors. It might so easily have been Grizelda had she not heeded my warning that the outlaws would probably return, and followed my advice to stay with friends.

As though reading my thoughts, she smiled suddenly and once more clasped my hands.

'I have you to thank for preserving my life. You urged me to caution. I cannot express my gratitude enough.'

'You have no need to be grateful,' I told her, stroking her right cheek and feeling the faint, thin line of the scar which ran from her eyebrow halfway down her face. 'You did what your own common sense dictated. But what will you do now? Will you remain with your friends?'

The crowd was dispersing, the villagers returning to their homes, the day's work still all to do. The sergeant prepared to depart and report back to the captain of the castle garrison. Later, he would no doubt be summoned to wait upon the Sheriff, whenever his lordship arrived in Totnes. He glanced round until he saw Grizelda, then, riding towards her, leaned from the saddle to speak.

'Mistress Harbourne, my condolences. Also, my heartfelt thanks for accompanying me to your holding and bearing witness as to the corpse. Not a pleasant charge to lay upon one of your sex. I must congratulate you on your courage. My lord Sheriff may wish to hear your testimony for himself. Where may he find you, if he needs you?'

Grizelda hesitated for a moment, before replying, 'In Totnes. At the house belonging to Master Eudo Colet.'

The sergeant nodded briskly and rode away, leaving me staring stupidly at Grizelda.

'I'm sorry,' she said, laying a conciliatory hand upon my arm. 'I was just about to tell you. I have nowhere else to go now. My friends cannot keep me indefinitely. Their holding is small and they have growing children. They are willing to look after Betsy and Snouter for me, but for myself, I have now no means of earning my keep. I cannot and will not be a burden to them.'

'And . . . Master Colet has agreed to this arrangement?'

She grimaced wryly. 'Not yet. He knows nothing of it. But I am sure that even he will not say me nay in the circumstances. The Crouchback house was, after all, my home for the best part of my life, and where else should I go in my hour of need? And it will only be until I can find myself a place as housekeeper to some respectable household. That should not be difficult. I am known in Totnes.'

'So you will require me to quit the house?' I asked, speaking as steadily as I could.

Grizelda raised her eyes to mine, holding them with a look which was half amusement, half defiance.

'That will be up to Master Colet when he gives his yea or nay to my request.' She grew sober, her lips compressed. 'I hate having to throw myself on his mercy, but I know of nothing else to do. I have lost everything, even my clothes. I have only what I am wearing. Without a roof over my head, I am like to become a parish pauper.'

I said thoughtfully, 'Before you commit yourself to sleeping once again in your old home, there are things I must tell you. But first, are your friends at hand? Would they, from the kindness of their hearts, supply me with food and drink? I have had no breakfast. I have money in my purse. I can pay them.'

'Were they here, they would be offended by any such suggestion,' Grizelda assured me. 'But they have already returned to their holding. They are poor people and cannot afford to waste the daylight hours unnecessarily. They know

179

my intentions. We have said our adieus. But I have some acquaintance with the goodwife you were speaking to earlier. I might prevail upon her to provide us both with bread and ale.'

The stout woman proved obliging, and Grizelda and I sat on a wooden bench outside the goodwife's cottage eating oatcakes spread with honey and drinking mead. Our ears were filled with the gentle humming of the bees from the hives at the bottom of her garden.

When I had finished recounting to Grizelda the events of the previous night, she sat silent for several minutes, frowning into space. The sun was hot on our faces, and all about us the woods which surrounded the village clearing spread warm and fragrant, sloping down to the banks of Bow Creek.

At last, she said slowly, 'You think now that it was Eudo Colet, trying to frighten you away?'

'To maim me, injure me, so that I could no longer pursue my inquiries. Yes, I'm sure of it. The stay of the gallery had been cut clean through. It had not broken.'

'And you think this attempt was made because of your visit to Dame Tenter's cottage?'

'Again, yes. There was time enough for him to follow me and enter the town before curfew. He must still have keys to the house in his possession. He could easily have entered the back yard and concealed himself in one of the outhouses, or in the kitchen building itself. What would there be to stop him?'

Grizelda chewed her lower lip. 'But what of the child you heard singing? That could not have been Master Colet. His voice is not deep, I admit, but it has nothing of a green boy's high pitch.'

'Nor of a young girl's.' I nodded. 'No, it's that that worries me and makes me still a little fearful for anyone remaining alone in that house at night.'

'You think he employed witchcraft?' Grizelda asked, her breath catching in her throat.

I shrugged my shoulders. 'That's a question I can't answer. We all know that the powers of darkness exist, and can be harnessed. But to accuse a man without proof is not something I should wish to do. It's a hanging matter.'

'You believe, however, that I should be on my guard if Master Colet agrees to my lodging there?'

'I think you must take care. I should prefer it if he'd let me stay there with you, but I think he'll seize on your request as a means to rid himself of an unwanted guest, without having to resort to any more of his tricks.'

Grizelda's head reared up sharply. 'Do you suspect Eudo of trickery? For trickery's not witchcraft, although I sometimes think that there is kinship between them.'

I pressed a hand to my forehead. I had a nagging pain between my eyes and a slight feeling of sickness in my stomach; the undoubted results of a disturbed night and a delayed breakfast. I took another long draught of the goodwife's excellent mead and felt a little better.

'The truth is,' I admitted, 'I don't know what to think any longer. I am confused, and cannot see the part played by Master Colet in the disappearance of his stepchildren. Indeed, except for last night's occurrence, I might begin to think that there was none. Now, why does that vex you?'

'Because I think you too easily fooled,' Grizelda responded tartly. 'There *is* some connection between him and the outlaws if only we could find it. But enough of that for now. I must get to Totnes without any further delay and present myself at Dame Tenter's.' She smiled suddenly. 'Will you give me the pleasure of your company on the journey? I'm sorry for what I said just now. I don't really think you easily fooled. Far from it. But I think you won't regret getting back on the road and putting these unhappy events behind you. You'll be your own man again, Roger, and I believe that to be the most important thing to you in the whole wide world. And dare you look me in the eye and tell me that I'm not right?'

Chapter Fourteen

I accompanied Grizelda as far as the Foregate, where we separated just beyond the stockade, she to cross the bridge to visit Eudo Colet at Dame Tenter's cottage, I to make my way uphill to the East Gate. During our walk together, she had shed a few tears over the loss of her own cottage, a weakness she immediately condemned, and which she attributed to the shock of seeing Innes Woodsman's charred body.

'For you must understand,' she apologized, 'that I despise women who cry. And Our Lady knows that I have had enough unhappiness in my life to give me practice at controlling my grief. But I cannot help feeling responsible for Innes's death.'

'Nonsense!' I declared stoutly. 'And as the Novice Master used to tell me, in the days before I gave up the religious life, it's as great a sin to take too much guilt upon your shoulders as it is to take none at all. Every man and woman must accept responsibility for his or her own actions.'

This seemed to comfort her, and she was calmer by the time we parted company. After seeing her safely over the bridge, I climbed the hill and sought out the keeper of the East Gate. He, too, was busy, diverting as much of the afternoon's traffic as he could away from the town in anticipation of the Sheriff's visit.

'For you never know,' he said, mopping his forehead on his sleeve, 'his lordship might make all speed from Exeter, and the sun's well overhead. It must be turned midday already.'

'I doubt we'll see anything of him much before evening,' I offered by way of consolation, quoting the cowherd. 'His Worship's messenger has to reach Exeter first, and you know how ponderously the law reacts to any situation. Tell me. Did you, by chance, let Master Colet into the town last evening, shortly before sunset?'

The gatekeeper gave a final wipe to his face and sniffed.

'Aye, that I did, and let him out again first thing this morning as soon as the Angelus sounded. Last in, first out. But I thought you might have know that. Aren't you the man lodged in his house by Lawyer Cozin? It came to me that Master Colet must have passed the night there.'

It was on the tip of my tongue to answer, 'And so he did,' but instead I merely asked, 'Was he mounted?'

'No, afoot, now you mention it.' The gatekeeper sounded surprised. 'Now that's strange, for he's proud of that beast of his and rarely walks anywhere. Odd, but I thought nothing of it at the time.'

I murmured my thanks and made my way through the postern gate, before I could be questioned more closely. So! I had my answer. Nevertheless, I thought it prudent to make inquiries of the Priory porter, for Eudo could have sought a bed in St Mary's guest-hall. The porter, however, disclaimed all knowledge of Master Colet.

'But you were here, on duty yesterevening? And you know him?'

The porter, a lay brother, wrinkled his nose and nodded.

'Yes on both counts. And indeed, I've always found Master Colet a pleasant enough gentleman, whatever others in this town might tell you different. I've spent an evening or two in his company, at Matt's tavern or the castle ale-house. Mostly he kept to himself, but I've known him when he's been drink-taken, and then he could make a man laugh at his antics. He was never drunk, you understand,' the porter hastened to add, 'but on occasions, the ale loosened his tongue a little.'

'What sort of antics?' I asked, frowning.

The porter shrugged. 'He could sing a bit. Ballads, ditties. Quite a few of 'em, the funniest ones, not fit for a lady's ears, I can tell you. And once, when a strolling flute-player came visiting Matt's, Master Colet took the instrument from him and played it well enough. He could caper a few steps, too, when the mood was on him. But, as I say, for the most part he was quiet and sober as befitted the husband of Rosamund Crouchback. Now, there was a woman with a fine notion of her own importance. She was always the same from girlhood, though, ruined by her father's indulgence. I wouldn't have been a servant or a poor kinsman in that house, not if they'd offered me a free barrel of the best malmsey wine every day for the rest of my life.'

I spared a smile for what seemed to be the porter's idea of paradise, but was too wrapped up in my thoughts to pay him any further attention. I bade him good-day, continuing my climb towards the pillory on the brow of High Street. I had much to mull over. In the past hour, I had learned that Eudo Colet had spent the night within the town walls, that he had not stayed at the Priory, and that he had sufficiently sweet a voice to entertain fellow ale-house guests without giving them cause to complain of his singing. I supposed it just possible that he had sought out lodgings other than at St Mary's, but somehow I could not bring myself to believe it. He had entered the East Gate on foot and walked up High Street under cover of the encroaching darkness. Then, he had kept watch on the house until my visit to the castle tavern had offered him the chance to slip along the alleyway and unlock the gate into the outer courtyard. But even had I remained within doors all evening, he must have been able, at sometime or another, to let himself in without being noticed. He had keys to all the locks, and the peculiarity of the Totnes houses made it possible to be in one part of the building without having any idea of what was happening in the other, separated as they were by that inner courtyard.

What Master Colet did next was conjecture on my part, but of sufficient likelihood to make it seem that I had watched him do it. He had taken a knife from the kitchen and hacked through the stay of the gallery, a structure he knew to be already weakened by neglect and decay; he had then returned to the loft to wait until the small, chill hours of early morning, when he had crossed the gallery, treading lightly and with the utmost care, to lure me from my bed with his singing . . .

But it had been a child's voice, not a man's, which had sung those poignant words; a voice which had sometimes been close at hand, and at others, far away. Was it possible that Eudo Colet had not been alone? And if not, who had been with him? I cursed silently to myself. It seemed that as soon as one door opened upon daylight, another closed, leaving me once again floundering in the dark.

I was so engrossed by my thoughts that I traversed the busy market-place and shambles, weaving my way between the throngs of townspeople, without really being aware of anyone. I did not even feel the hand laid upon my arm until the fingers nipped me.

'Master Chapman,' said a voice at my elbow, 'why do you

not have your pack with you? I was hoping to buy some ribbon.'

I turned what I'm sure must have been a sleepwalker's face towards my indignant questioner, to find myself accosted by the child, Ursula Cozin, attended by the faithful Jenny. The grey eyes which regarded me were the same colour as her father's, but there the similarity ended. Whereas Thomas Cozin's gaze was calm and a little diffident, his youngest daughter's was pert and provocative; and the plump features, snub nose and pouting, pretty mouth were all her mother's.

'I . . . I'm sorry,' I stammered, 'but my wares are not for sale today.' I sought desperately for some further topic of conversation, which seemed to be expected of me. 'Is . . . Is Mistress Cozin still pleased with the length of silk she purchased?'

'Oh yes.' The eyes sparkled with affectionate laughter. 'Mother's very vain, you know, and she adores new finery. She even brought it out to show Master Colet, yesterevening.'

'M – Master Colet?' I gibbered like an idiot, and Ursula stared at me in some astonishment. 'Master Colet called on your family last evening?'

The head was tilted consideringly to one side. 'Indeed. He came to see my uncle on business.'

'Did . . . Did he stay long?'

A gurgle of laughter escaped my young lady. 'I'm glad to know that there's someone else as nosey as I am. My parents call it my besetting sin, but I say it's just natural curiosity. How am I to know what's going on in this town if I don't ask questions concerning my neighbours? If you really want to know, Master Colet stayed for the night. My father pressed him to do so as curfew had sounded, and he considers it unsafe at present for anyone to walk abroad after sunset. He sent to a neighbour for the loan of a truckle bed, as my uncle is using ours during his visit, and it was put up for Master Colet in the downstairs parlour because he had to leave very early this morning, and so could let himself out without disturbing anyone.'

Within the hour, I found myself confronting yet another of the Cozin household; this time, Master Oliver. And with him came Grizelda.

I had returned to the house after my encounter with the child, Ursula, dazed and confused by this brutal shattering of all my notions. Eudo Colet had spent the night with the Cozins, his movements accounted for by respectable people. But who, then, had been my nocturnal visitor? I had thought and thought about it, my mind going round in circles, my aching head clutched in my hands, until I suddenly discovered that I no longer cared. By the time Lawyer Cozin presented himself at the door to inform me that my tenure of the house was no longer necessary, I could have shouted aloud with joy and willingly embraced him.

'Mistress Harbourne, whose holding was razed to the ground last night by the outlaws, has obtained permission from Master Colet to lodge in her old home until she is able to settle her affairs to her greater satisfaction. I believe,' the lawyer added austerely, 'that you already know Mistress Harbourne and have no need of my introduction.'

Grizelda smiled and stepped past him into the passageway.

'Eudo has agreed, albeit with very bad grace, to my tenancy. It suits his purpose as well as mine, otherwise I think he would have been less inclined to oblige me. But my being here will allow you to be on your way, which you must surely wish for soon, whilst I can remain until a more permanent occupant is found for the house.'

The lawyer nodded briskly in agreement. 'Mistress Harbourne is right. I thank you for your good offices, chapman, but you may now take your leave with a clear conscience. You are absolved from your promise to remain as custodian until Saturday.'

He inclined his head and turned away. I wondered whether or not to mention the broken gallery, but decided against it. It would involve an explanation of my clumsiness which I was not prepared to give at present, and, possibly, recriminations. He might even demand that I pay for its mending. So I watched him go in silence. But as soon as he had vanished from sight, I turned to Grizelda.

'I don't like leaving you here alone,' I said, regarding her anxiously, and proceeded to tell her of all my discoveries since parting from her that morning. When I had finished, I added earnestly, 'You could well be in some danger. I wish you would let me stay here with you.'

'No you don't,' she answered quietly. 'I can see it in your eyes. You need to be gone. You are straining at the leash, like an animal at the end of its tether. Besides, I have my good name to think of. To be staying with you alone, under one roof, would give rise to more gossip than I care to think of.' She placed her hands on my shoulders, reaching up to kiss my cheek. 'I have looked after myself from childhood, and no one and nothing has worsted me yet. Never fear, I shall be a match for whoever, or whatever, haunts this house. Nor,' she went on, trying to suppress the laughter in her voice, 'shall I be visiting Jacinta's tavern.'

I pushed her hands from my shoulders.

'Is that what you really think?' I asked furiously. 'That I was drunk? That I dreamed the voice and the singing? Then let me advise you to examine the broken stay of the walkway, and you will see what I saw; that it has been cut through and is not the result of my drunken blunderings.'

'Roger—!' she began, reaching out to me once more, but I pushed her roughly aside and picked up my pack and cudgel.

'I bid you good-day, Mistress Harbourne. You're right. I shall be glad to be away from here.' I lifted the latch and stepped into the street.

'Roger! Please wait! Don't go like this, I beg you!'

There was distress in her voice, but I was too hurt and angry to heed it. I thought she had believed my story, but now I could see that she had merely been humouring me, privately considering me a drunken sot, lying to account for my clumsiness. She stumbled after me across the cobbles, clutching beseechingly at my sleeve, but I shook her off and lengthened my stride.

'Let me be!' I shouted over my shoulder.

Her steps faltered and stopped. As I rounded the bend in the street, I glanced back briefly. She was standing motionless, desolate, her arms fallen limply to her sides. Just for a moment, I felt an impulse to return, but I had my pride and I had been insulted. I carried on down the hill and passed through the East Gate without so much as a nod to the keeper.

The April afternoon was hot and the roads dusty from lack of rain. Behind me, the little town, high on its hill, sparkled like a jewel in the sunshine, and in a meadow which bordered the Dart, two lambs played, enjoying the unseasonal warmth. In a walled garden, the gate stood open to reveal fruit trees, vegetables and sweet-smelling herbs. The sky was an unbroken blue, and a flock of starlings flew across the face of the sun, like a cloud of blown petals. Presently, I left the cultivated strips by the riverside and plunged into the woods, dark, yet glowing. Here and there, the dense leaf mould crackled with a scattering of last year's oak leaves, as yet unclaimed by the earth. All about me lay a forbidding hush, and tree trunks, overgrown with brambles, slowed my progress, bringing me at last to a halt.

With a shock, I realized that I had no idea where I was going. For the last few miles, I had simply walked without any sense of purpose or direction. My one thought was to get as far away as possible from Totnes. Now, finally coming to my senses, I knew by the position of the sun that I must have been travelling north-westwards and would eventually arrive – if I returned to, and followed, the course of the river – at the great Cistercian abbey of Buckfast. If I reached there before nightfall, I could sleep in the guest-hall or, if it were full with more important travellers, in one of the abbey barns.

After walking some way further, I emerged into a broad ride where, to my right, I caught a distant gleam of water among the trees. I followed it to the river's edge, and found myself once again among the small settlements and holdings stretched along the banks of the Dart. A narrow ribbon of track threaded them all together, and I walked until I discovered a likely looking cottage with a well-stocked vegetable patch, a fat pig rootling and snorting in its sty, and an equally fat and contented cow in the field behind it. Moreover, a comfortably rotund and well-fleshed goodwife was tending her herb garden. Here, without doubt, there would be food in plenty, and enough to spare for a passing stranger.

I was not disappointed, and was soon seated with my back against the wall of the cottage, a plate of bread, cheese and small, green leeks on my lap, a cup of ale on the bench beside me, while my hostess went eagerly through what remained of the contents of my pack. From the open kitchen doorway

came the smell of slow-burning peat, warming the big earthenware pans of milk until the rich, thick clots of cream rose
to the surface.

'Have you been troubled by the outlaws this far north?' I
asked after several minutes of companionable silence.
'They're hunting all around Totnes.'

The goodwife's face clouded with anxiety.

'So we've heard,' she answered, 'but as yet we've seen
nothing of them, God be praised! It's lawless times we live
in, that's for certain. And what are the Sheriff and his men
doing, I'd like to know! Enough pence go into their coffers
to keep the highways and byways clear of such evil, if they
would only get up from their fat backsides and risk their
precious hides now and then. How much for this leather
strap? I need a new one for sharpening my knives.'

'You may have it as payment for my meal,' I told her; and
when she demurred that such simple victuals were no more
than she would provide for any wayfarer like myself, I
insisted, adding, 'The lord Sheriff's been sent for from Exeter
by Mayor Broughton, and he's expected to raise a *posse* to
ride after these devils, and root them out. They struck twice
last night, towards Dartington and along the banks of Bow
Creek. There was a holding burned to the ground in the latter
spot, and a man killed, charred to a cinder, as he slept.'

The goodwife clucked in dismay. 'My man's away to
pasture, with the sheep. I hope he's safe.'

'You've nothing to fear in daylight,' I assured her. 'That's
when the wolf-heads go to their lair and sleep.' And I finished
my ale.

She brought me another stoup and some pastry coffins,
containing apple and honey, together with a clot of fresh
cream, before returning to tend her herbs.

'Sit there as long as you wish, lad. You won't bother me.' And she bent once more over the plants, her fingers expertly plucking out the weeds from among them.

I took her at her word. The food and ale had made me sleepy, and the afternoon sun was still warm on my face. I stretched my legs their full length, settled my back more comfortably against the wall and closed my eyes. The varied scents of spring teased my nostrils, and for several long minutes I let my thoughts drift, relaxed and filled with contentment.

This mood did not last, however. Conscience pricked me about Grizelda. I had reacted with unnecessary harshness to her teasing. Most likely she had not meant what she said; and at a time when I should have offered sympathy and understanding, after the loss of her home and the death of Innes Woodsman, I had chosen to be angry with her. Why? Because, whether she believed my story or not, I felt guilty at leaving her to her fate when I suspected she might be in some danger? Because I had needed an excuse to be on my way, having suddenly grown tired and confused with a tangle of facts and events which I found impossible to unravel?

It had seemed to me earlier in the day that God Himself was telling me that I was mistaken; that He had not directed my feet towards Totnes; that there was no mystery concerning the disappearance of Andrew and Mary Skelton. They had managed to escape unseen from both house and town and had been killed by the outlaws. But I realized now that I had deliberately deluded myself. In the sweet silence of the warm afternoon, with a quiet mind and a body at rest, God's voice once again made itself heard, urging me to retrace my foot-steps. I sighed, but for the moment stayed where I was, trying to get my reluctant thoughts in order.

193

Two small children had vanished from their home without being seen by either of the servants in charge of them. Both Bridget Praule and Agatha Tenter swore that this was impossible. But knowing the cunning of the young, and recalling my own youthful shifts and ploys to escape the watchful eyes of my mother, I was perfectly ready to accept that it had happened. More difficult for me to accept, however, was the fact that Eudo Colet, the one person with anything to gain from his stepchildren's deaths, had been in no way involved in their disappearance and subsequent murder. Yet he had been out of the house, visiting one of his most respected neighbours, at the time they had vanished. They had been there when he left, gone when he returned. Both maid and cook testified to that fact, and would not be shaken.

So, what did I and others know about Eudo Colet? Very little before his arrival in Totnes as husband of the town's richest heiress. His origins were shrouded in mystery, but his air and manner proclaimed him of lowly birth; a man who had used his good looks to ensnare a vain and wealthy woman. A common enough story, and one told over and over again throughout the ages. Nevertheless, it demonstrated Eudo Colet to be a man of few scruples, as all adventurers are, of necessity. Grizelda had pressed me to consider the possibility that he had links with the outlaws, and who was to say that she was wrong? Who knew what dubious connections he had formed in his youth? He might himself have once been a felon. Perhaps some chance meeting with a member of the robber band had renewed an old friendship; and with his wife recently dead in childbirth, and his newly acquired wealth burning holes in his pockets, Master Eudo had seen a way to help himself to an even greater fortune. But this posed me a problem: by what reasoning had he been able to persuade the children to escape secretly into the countryside, where his murderous cronies awaited them?

I jerked upright on the bench, now thoroughly wide awake, and stared around at the sun-dappled garden. The goodwife was still busy about her weeding and had not noticed my sudden start. I sank back once more against the wall, but this time did not close my eyes.

I remained uneasy concerning this notion of Grizelda's; it seemed too much dependent on chance and luck. But neither could I dismiss it, my experiences of the past night convincing me that Eudo Colet had tried to get me out of his house, either by injury or by playing on my superstitious fears. And his only reason for doing so must be my visit to Dame Tenter's cottage and my poorly concealed interest in the fate of Mary and Andrew Skelton. Moreover, I had mentioned the lullaby heard by Jack Carter on the morning of the children's disappearance, which must have suggested a means by which he could be rid of me. The discovery that Master Colet had indeed spent the night within the town walls, confirmed this suspicion, only to have doubt cast upon it by Ursula Cozin's information. But Mistress Ursula had said that the guest slept on a truckle bed in the downstairs parlour, so that he could be away at first light without disturbing the rest of the household. And now that I had leisure to consider her words, I realized that if Eudo Colet could let himself noiselessly out of the house in the morning, he could equally well have done so during the night. My turmoil of mind following Ursula's revelation, had merely been the result of tiredness due to lack of sleep. Another excuse for leaving, the belief that I had reached a dead end, was knocked from under me. I had no longer any choice but to return.

I got to my feet, thanked the goodwife for her welcome, added a spool of fine silk thread to my gift of the leather strap, hoisted my pack on to my shoulders and, grasping my cudgel, set off back the way I had come, towards Totnes.

Chapter Fifteen

The first shadows of evening were stroking pasture and garden as I made my way along the track, steadily putting the miles behind me. On the far horizon, black-fingered clouds stretched towards the sun, an intimation that the spell of fine weather might soon be over. There was a chill in the air, and the distant hills were lost behind gathering mist. Here and there, plumes of smoke rose from a cottage roof as the good-wife began her preparations for supper.

I was careful, on this return journey, not to stray into the forest, but to keep to the course of the river and in sight of habitation. It was not yet time for the outlaws to be up and stirring, but there were others who hunted alone, or in twos and threes, lying in wait for the unwary traveller. I had always been capable of protecting myself against these enemies, and my cudgel was my trusty friend, but it would be untrue to say that I had never suffered injury, and I had no wish at present to risk my hide.

The track broadened as I reached the great tidal marsh, just north of Totnes. Golden-headed kingcups were beginning to close with the fading light, and clumps of reeds and grasses were slowly drained of colour as banks of clouds diminished the sun. Lights from the Foregate pricked the gathering darkness and, high on the hill, torches had been lit on the castle walls.

I was nearing East Gate, skirting the fences of St Mary's Priory, when I heard the rattle of wheels behind me. I had been vaguely aware for some minutes past of a cart approaching, and now, turning my head, I saw a gaily painted wagonette, its wooden sides picked out in yellows, reds and greens, and between its beribboned shafts, a patient-eyed mule plodding decorously over the rough and stony ground. A willow framework supported a canvas covering, and within the body of the cart was a tumble of bedding and brightly coloured costumes. Three young men walked alongside the wagon, one at the head of the mule, his hand on the bridle, the other two lagging a little, and all of them plainly footsore. Shoes and hose were white with dust, their tunics well worn and, in places, threadbare. A flute and tabor were tied to the slats at one side of the cart, but even without them, I should have had no difficulty in recognizing this little party of vagabonds as travelling entertainers. Early spring was the time when such bands took to the roads, mumming and miming, juggling and dancing, after spending the winter, if they were lucky, in the household of some great lord, or, if less fortunate, earning a few pence in the streets of a town. And if all else failed, they had a home of sorts in their covered wagon.

The youngest of the three, the one leading the mule, was a thickset lad with a shock of red hair, blue eyes, turned-up nose and a round, jolly face, peppered with freckles. I recognized him on the instant, and without stopping to think that I had to be mistaken, put out a hand and gripped his arm.

'Nicholas!' I exclaimed. 'Nicholas Fletcher!'

He turned a startled gaze in my direction before giving a good-natured grin.

'My name is surely Fletcher, sir, for my great-grandsire was a maker of arrows. But my baptismal name is Martin.' He knotted his sandy brows. 'Although I do have an older brother called Nicholas.' The grin widened. 'A brother twice over in fact, for he's not only my parents' child, but also a Brother of the Benedictine order at Glastonbury Abbey.'

'Of course!' I said, clapping a hand to my forehead and cursing my own stupidity. 'Forgive me, but you're as like as two peas in a pod.'

'You know him?' Martin Fletcher asked delightedly, while his two friends crowded round, eager to discover what was happening. 'You're acquainted with Nick?'

'We were novices together,' I explained, 'but the cowl and tonsure were not for me, and I never took my vows, unlike your brother.'

I have mentioned Nicholas Fletcher somewhere before in these chronicles, the fellow novice who taught me how to pick locks, a dubious talent learned during his childhood travels with the troupe of jugglers and mummers to which he and his family belonged. Had he ever talked of a brother? Maybe, and I had forgotten.

'Well,' beamed that younger sibling now, clapping me on the shoulder, 'fancy that! We're on our way to Totnes to try our fortune with the castle garrison. Men get tired, mewed up in barracks, with only themselves for company. Even drinking and whoring can pall, and then they're glad of other amusement. Are you making for the town yourself? Do you know it?'

'I've been lodging there some days already,' I answered, 'and am returning for the night. I've ... I've had a berth of a sort, but now I've lost it. I was hoping to sleep in the Priory guest-hall.'

'Then we'll join you, if we may,' said Martin Fletcher. 'If it's fine, we sleep in the wagon, but it's beginning to look like rain.' He indicated his two companions. 'These are my friends. Peter Coucheneed, he's a juggler and a good one, and the other is Luke Hollis, who plays the flute and dances. As for me, I rattle the tabor and mime a little.'

The first named, Peter Coucheneed, was very tall and stringy, with a high, domed forehead, and going prematurely bald. The second man, Luke Hollis, was squat and fat with a pot belly and an unruly mop of thick, dark hair. The contrast between them was ludicrous, and no doubt earned them a laugh before ever a ball was juggled or a note played by way of entertainment.

'And I'm called Roger,' I said. 'A chapman by trade and now by name, although Brother Nicholas would have known me as Stonecarver or Carverson, for that was how my father earned his living. So, shall we go the last short distance together? If you're ready for some victuals, there's an ale-house near the castle I can recommend.'

The four of us entered by the East Gate, although the keeper was reluctant to let the wagon through.

'Mind you keep it off the main highway,' he ordered, after much negotiation. 'There's still a chance that the lord Sheriff might arrive before curfew.'

In reply to my companions' questions, I explained about the outlaws and the state of fear pervading the countryside.

'However, I doubt his lordship will be here before tomorrow morning,' I said, as we climbed the hill towards Jacinta's tavern, 'but you'd do well to find a place for the cart where it won't impede the Law's progress when he and his sergeants finally appear.'

But this was easier said than done; the wagonette, although

200

not big, was of sufficient width to block most of the alleyways, and the Priory porter expressed strong doubts about allowing it to stand in the courtyard.

'My Lord Sheriff will be received here, in the forecourt, and neither His Worship the Mayor nor Father Prior will wish to see it cluttered with a mummers' cart, in however obscure a corner. My advice is to return to the Foregate.'

'What about the castle?' I suggested to Martin. 'After all, that's where you're bound.'

But the officer of the garrison was also discouraging.

'Alas, no entertainment this evening, my friends,' he said, looking sadly at the painted cart. 'Any other time but now, and we'd have welcomed you with open arms. But the lord Sheriff, whenever he arrives, will expect to find us fresh and alert, and we'd not be that after a night's carousal; for what's an entertainment without drink to go with it? Nor can I offer hope for tomorrow, for we'll be off chasing these damned wolf-heads as soon as his lordship gives the word.'

'We'd best get back to the Foregate,' Peter Coucheneed sighed, 'and be on our way first thing in the morning. There's no custom for us here. We've picked a bad time.'

Martin and Luke Hollis nodded in agreement, but I was not so despondent.

'Folks will be in need of cheering up when the *posse* has left, and some of the townsmen with it. Stay for a day or two, and I think you'll have no regrets. There's good money to be made in a place like this, as I discovered. Many of the burghers have well-lined pockets. As for the wagon, no call to make up your minds to lie outside the walls just yet. I have a friend in High Street who might let you use the outer courtyard of her house, where there's also stabling for the mule. The poor creature looks as though it's about to drop between the shafts.' And I briefly explained the circumstances, naming no names but that of Grizelda, and leaving unmentioned all that had gone before the burning of her cottage.

My suggestion was received with thankfulness, tempered by doubt that anyone would allow a band of strolling players within her pale, or be persuaded to take their honesty on trust when she knew nothing of them. But I said that my recommendation would guarantee their welcome, adding that with fear of the outlaws hanging over the town like a pall, Mistress Harbourne might well be glad of their company. I was less confident than I sounded, for Grizelda and I had parted on bad terms, but I was sanguine enough to hope that my humble apology would be accepted.

After some discussion, it was felt to be wisest if Martin and I went alone to make the necessary request, leaving Peter and Luke to sup ale in Jacinta's tavern, where we would rejoin them later.

'For you're her friend and Martin has a respectable face,' Luke said, adding frankly, 'Peter and I are like to scare her out of her wits if she sees us staring at her out of the dark. God fashioned us both to make men laugh, but together, and at night, I don't deny we can be frightening.'

Both Martin and I refuted the claim vigorously, but in the end agreed that there might be some sense in the argument. So, we went together to knock on Grizelda's door, where a torch in an iron holder at one side of the doorway had been lit, casting a smokey, amber glow across our faces. At least she would be able to recognize me without any difficulty.

It was some moments before she answered our summons, but at last the heavy oaken door swung inwards and Grizelda, a lantern held aloft in one hand, stood before us.

'Who's there?' she asked. 'What do you want?' Then the light from her lantern found me out and she stared in astonishment. 'Roger? What are you doing here? I thought you well on your way by now.'

'I came back,' I answered contritely, 'to beg your pardon. Once my temper had time to cool, I realized that you were only jesting.'

She made no reply and in the silence the lanternlight passed from my face to that of Martin Fletcher. 'Who's this?' she demanded.

I hastened to introduce him and explain our errand. 'He and his friends need shelter for the night for their mule and wagon. I thought you might be willing to stable both in the outer courtyard.'

'We'd be no trouble to you,' Martin assured her fervently. 'And we'd be gone as soon as the town gates open in the morning. But with these wolf-heads on the prowl, we don't fancy sleeping in the open ground of the Foregate.'

'There's a stockade to the south of the Pickle Moor,' she retorted.

I had not expected Grizelda to be so ungracious, particularly as she herself had just been a victim of the outlaws.

'A poor defence, broken in several places. And nothing to the north,' I reproached her.

She rewarded me with scarcely a glance, for the most part keeping both her eyes and the lanternlight fixed on Martin.

'I'm sorry,' she said, 'but I'm here alone. A woman has her reputation to think of. To be allowing three strange young men within her walls is to put it at risk, especially in this town, where there are eyes and ears at every casement.'

I was astonished at the coldness of her manner, and realized that I must have hurt her far more deeply than I had imagined. I was about to argue the cause of Martin and his friends, when I became aware of a movement in the passageway behind her. It was little more than a shifting of the darkness, the faintest blur of whiteness denoting a face, but enough for me to feel sure that someone was there.

'Who's that?' I asked sharply, starting forward.

Grizelda whirled about, raising the lantern higher, sending long shadows dancing up the walls. But the passageway was empty. She turned on me fiercely.

'Why are you trying to frighten me?' she snapped.

'There was someone there,' I told her urgently. 'I saw him.' Why was I so certain that it had been a man? 'Martin! You must have noticed something.'

But my new acquaintance shook his head. 'The light from the lantern was shining in my eyes.'

'Nevertheless, there was someone there,' I insisted. 'Grizelda, let me come in and search.'

'No!' She blocked the doorway with her body, but her voice softened a little. 'Roger, I know you mean well and that you are concerned for my safety, but you have allowed your imagination to get the better of you, just as you did last night. Oh, it's not altogether your fault. I accept my share of the responsibility. I should never have encouraged you to inquire into this business in the first place, but I was angry and grief-stricken for my little innocents.'

'And now you are not?' My tone was icy.

'How can you ask such a question?' She reared her head. 'Do you think anything can ever assuage my grief? But I have come to accept that there is no mystery; that the simple explanation of how things happened is the right one.'

'This is a sudden conversion,' I flung at her angrily.

She sighed. 'Roger, I'm sorry. I suppose I always knew

where the truth lay, but it was an indulgence to unburden myself to a sympathetic ear, and one I was unable to resist. Forgive me. But the events of the past night have made me realize how fragile our hold upon our destiny is. I must put the past behind me. Forget it, and look towards the future. So must you. You have a child, and by your own admission, you have been absent from Bristol many weeks. Return to her.' Grizelda held out her free hand. The harshness had gone from her face and there was a rueful gleam in her eyes. 'I'm not the woman for you. No, don't deny that the thought has crossed your mind once or twice during these past three days, as, I must confess, it has crossed mine. But we should not suit. Now, go away, go home, and forget me. I'm sorry I cannot accommodate your friend and his companions, but if I am to find a place as housekeeper in this town, then I dare not let my good name be sullied by even the merest suspicion of disorderly conduct.'

I took her fingers in mine and pressed them against my lips. I was ashamed of myself, both for the way in which I had treated her earlier in the day, and for attributing vengeful motives to her.

'We'll be off,' I said, clapping Martin on the back, 'and trouble you no further.' But I could not help glancing over her shoulder, peering anxiously into the gloom of the passageway. Had I indeed seen someone lurking there? Or was Grizelda right, and was my imagination beginning to get the better of me? 'Take care,' I urged her, pressing her hand before releasing it.

She smiled. 'I promise.' She retreated from the threshold and closed the door.

Martin Fletcher turned curious eyes upon me, plainly sensing a story which he would dearly love to explore, but for the moment, his chief concern was for the safe bestowal of his wagon. Peter Coucheneed and Luke Hollis were equally dismayed with the failure of our mission.

'We must make haste and leave before the gates are closed,' Martin told them. 'There's nothing for it but to sleep in the Foregate. One of the cottagers will give us food and water for Clotilde.' And he tickled the mule affectionately behind the ears. 'Rogues and vagabonds like us can't be permitted to clutter up the streets of a respectable town.'

Meantime, Jacinta had emerged from the tavern to lure us back inside again, custom not being so brisk that she could afford to lose four young men set upon a convivial evening. When she knew of the mummers' predicament, she was angry, but could offer no remedy. The ale-house was hemmed in on all sides by houses and the outer walls of the castle. She turned to me.

'And you, lad, where will you be sleeping, now that you've lost your former lodging?' She eyed me up and down in a manner which made me most uneasy. 'You're welcome to find a bed here for the night, if you don't mind sharing a pallet with my son.'

I hurriedly declined the invitation, dismissing as unworthy the suspicion that the bed I would end up sharing might well be her own.

'I'll try the Priory guest-hall first,' I said, 'when I've seen my friends here safely beyond the walls.' And I set off down-hill once again, walking beside the wagonette.

We were within yards of the East Gate when there was a sudden commotion, and a party of horsemen rode through, showing a fine disregard for the gatekeeper and anyone else who happened to be in their path. The central figure was richly attired and mounted on a handsome black gelding, its jingling harness glinting in the torchlight. Half a dozen other men, in jackets of thick green frieze and helmets of boiled leather, were of only slightly less importance, in their own eyes at least, and one of them shouted for someone to run and fetch the Mayor. Behind these gentlemen, streamed a small cohort of servants. The lord Sheriff, having made all speed from Exeter, had arrived.

'I'll not get a bed in the Priory tonight,' I said to Martin, 'so I might as well come with you. I've acquaintances in the Foregate,' I added, thinking of Granny Praule, 'where I might find a welcome.'

He nodded and drove the wagon forward. Its tail had barely cleared the archway when the bell rang for curfew, and the town gates creaked shut behind us.

By the time a sheltered nook had been found for the wagon, food and water obtained for the mule and I had knocked on the door of Granny Praule's cottage, it was growing late and we were all tired and hungry. I refused Granny's pressing invitation for us to sup with her, guessing from her granddaughter's worried expression that they did not have sufficient food on the shelves for four extra people. I accepted with gratitude, however, the offer of Bridget's mattress for the night, while she shared her grandmother's.

'But we'll away to Matt's tavern for our victuals.'

'A pity, a pity,' Granny Praule mumbled. 'Four young men together under my roof, that's a chance I'm not likely to have again in a hurry.'

'We'll perform a special entertainment for you and Mistress Bridget tomorrow,' Martin Fletcher promised, kissing her wrinkled cheek. 'And no payment asked in return.'

Granny cackled delightedly and told me she would leave the cottage door on the latch.

'But don't be long, lad, and mind you push the bolts to, once you're inside.'

Matt's tavern was quiet and he was already thinking of locking up for the night as defence against any marauders, but the prospect of losing good money if he turned us away was not to be countenanced lightly. So he sat us down at a table, fetched us bread and cheese and ale and exhorted us to eat our fill, although it was plain that he hoped we wouldn't dally. After that, he left us to ourselves, disappearing down the cellar steps with his potman, to attend to his barrels.

I was grateful that sufficient time had by now elapsed to blunt Martin Fletcher's curiosity concerning my friendship with Grizelda, for I had no wish to discuss it. Instead, he and his friends kept me amused with tales of their life as wandering entertainers.

'The summer's the best time,' Martin said, and the other two nodded vigorous agreement. 'Going from village to village, town to town, the sun shining and the people running out to greet you, that's as great a reward sometimes as the money you can make. But best of all are the fairs, especially the big ones, like St Bartholomew's in London. Everyone's there. You meet up with all your old friends, hear all their gossip, find out how they fared during the winter, whether or not they had a roof over their heads, and so on.'

'I like the fine ladies,' Luke put in thickly, without bothering to clear his mouth of bread and cheese. 'There's always lots of them at fairs, looking for silks and velvets and ribbons to spend their money on. And in between, they stop to watch the jugglers and mummers. A lady threw me a gold coin once. A very beautiful lady. About three years ago, it would be, come Bartholomewtide. I've never forgotten because someone said she was the Duchess of Gloucester, come down from the north with her lord, for a visit. They hadn't long been wed; only a few months I reckon. Their son, little Prince Edward, hadn't been born then, at any rate. Whether it was true or not, I don't know for certain, but it's sure someone said it was Duchess Anne, and she gave me gold.'

In return for their confidences, I told some of my adventures since I took to the road, but nothing of any consequence. I kept the stories light and amusing. I was too tired, and the hour too advanced to give details of anything other. The landlord had emerged from the cellar and was hovering nearby, waiting on our going. We took the hint and paid what was due, then went out into the Foregate.

The threatened rain had come to nothing, the clouds moving away southwards, leaving the heavens clear and starry overhead. Moonlight showed us a path leading up from St Peter's Quay, ribbed by the shadows of tree trunks. The wagon stood on a patch of rough ground not far from Granny Praule's cottage, in the lee of a cluster of brambles. Martin Fletcher and his two companions climbed in beneath the canvas awning, and, without even bothering to remove their shoes, stretched themselves out on top of the muddle of bedding and costumes. I guessed they would soon be dead to the world, weariness and the ale we had consumed at Matt's tavern assuring them of a night's sleep, oblivious to all disturbance.

Granny Praule had left the cottage door unbolted, as she had promised, and, as I entered, I could hear her snoring. Bridget was nowhere to be seen, having decorously draped a much darned and patched sheet over a string, hung between two walls of the cottage. Her straw mattress, however, was plumped up invitingly and spread with clean linen. I carefully shot home the bolts, stowed my pack and cudgel close to the door, stripped down to shirt and hose and tumbled thankfully into bed. I, too, would sleep soundly.

Chapter Sixteen

I did not stir the whole night through, and awoke just after dawn to the distant crowing of a cock. There was a dull ache behind my eyes, which opened reluctantly upon the pallid daylight, only to shut themselves again as fast as possible. My mouth tasted as if I had swallowed pigswill, and when I moved, the stubble on my face scraped against the linen covering of the mattress. I had drunk more deeply the previous evening than I had realized at the time, and guessed that Martin Fletcher and his two friends must be sharing my discomfort. They, however, could afford to sleep a little longer in their wagon. I, on the other hand, must rouse myself at once, for I could already hear rustling sounds from the other side of the makeshift curtain; sounds which told me that Bridget was up and stirring. Granny Praule, also, for, a moment later, there was a familiar, if subdued, cackle of laughter.

I got up, trying to ignore the pain in my head, and pulled on my boots and tunic. I cleaned my teeth with willow bark, and taking one of the bone combs from my pack, ran it quickly through my hair. Until Bridget heated some water, I could not shave. Sometimes I wondered if it would not be less trouble to grow a beard. Needing to relieve myself, I unbolted the door and went outside, round to the back of the cottage.

It was raining a little; not the thick pall of dense drizzle which, yesterday afternoon, had blotted out the far horizon, but bright, white spears of springtime rain, which would soon give place to sunshine. Fragments of blue sky were already showing through the cloud, promising another fine, warm day. I returned to the cottage after a few minutes, to find Bridget and her grandmother both up and dressed, the former lighting a fire on the central hearthstone. Beside her, a leather bucket stood ready to fetch water from the well, farther up the hill.

'Let me do that,' I said, grasping the bucket's handle.

The words were hardly out of my mouth when there was a frantic knocking at the cottage door. A voice I recognized as that of Peter Coucheneed, shouted urgently, 'Roger! Roger Chapman! Are you there, man?'

'Come in!' I called. 'The door's unbolted.'

'My, my!' Granny Praule exulted. 'What a to-do! Whatever can be the matter?'

The door opened and Peter Coucheneed burst in, forgetting to stoop and cracking his high, domed forehead against the lintel. Such was his perturbation, however, that he scarcely seemed to notice. His face was ashen, what hair he possessed awry, his clothes crumpled from sleeping in them. There was a smear of blood on one of his cheeks and another dark patch on the breast of his tunic. His hands, too, were liberally stained. Granny Praule gave a horrified shriek and Bridget looked as though she were going to faint. I dropped the bucket and guided her to a stool. Then I turned back to Peter.

'What in God's name has happened? Where are you hurt? Who has attacked you?'

'Not me! Not me!' he gasped, once he had found his tongue.

'Martin and Luke, both murdered as they slept.' He lifted one bloodstained hand and made a sawing motion across his neck. 'Their throats are cut.'

Granny screamed again, but she was made of sterner stuff than her granddaughter, who gave a little moan, slid off the stool and sank, unconscious, to the ground.

'It's them wicked outlaws!' Granny Praule wailed, going to Bridget's assistance. She knelt down, gathering the girl into her arms. 'Wake up, child! Wake up! This is no time to be losing your senses. Someone has to run for the Sheriff. What a piece of good fortune he's here in the town.'

'I'll go,' I said, but Granny shook her head. She let Bridget's inert form slip back, unceremoniously, on to the beaten-earth floor, and scrambled with surprising agility to her feet.

'You go to the wagon with this poor lad,' she instructed, unhooking a rusty black cloak from a nail beside the door and draping it round her shoulders. 'Wait with him till I come.' She saw the worried glance I cast at Bridget, and added impatiently, 'Let the silly child be. We can't be bothering with the megrims at a time like this. She'll come to, if you pay her no attention.' And with this callous utterance, she was out of the door and off up the hill before I could stop her.

Peter Coucheneed was shaking from head to foot, so I found a pitcher of Granny's damson wine and poured us both a generous measure. It was a potent brew. A slight colour crept back into his cheeks, and the palsied movements of his hands steadied a little. By this time, Bridget was beginning to stir, and I was able, with his assistance, to see her comfortably laid down upon Granny's bed before we left the cottage.

The wagon stood a hundred yards or so to the south, not far from St Peter's Quay, in the lee of some bushes which hedged the Cherry Cross estate. It was still not full daylight and few people had as yet strayed very far from home. No word of this new disaster had reached them, so at present, the cart was of no interest. It stood silent, its shafts empty, the mule some way off, contentedly nibbling the grass. As we drew close, Peter Coucheneed stopped and gripped my arm.

'You must prepare yourself . . .' he began, but was unable to say more, his voice clogged with horror, his eyes bright with unshed tears.

I patted his arm. 'I understand,' I whispered, and braced myself for what I was about to see.

I stared into the open back of the wagon where the two sprawled figures lay. The canvas, stretched over the willow framework, cast a gloom which made it seem, at first, as though both men were still asleep, but the sickly-sweet smell of blood quickly dispelled any such notion. As I leaned nearer, I was able to see that the head of Martin Fletcher, who lay stretched out with his feet towards the front end of the cart, was at a peculiar angle to his body, and that his exposed throat looked almost black, as did the stiffened breast of his shirt and tunic. The bedding and pile of costumes beneath him were also darkly stained, and, at his side, the supine body of Luke Hollis showed similar signs of abnormality. I touched the neck of each man in turn, and my fingers came away sticky with congealing blood. I shuddered.

'Where did *you* sleep?' I asked Peter Coucheneed, although I could guess the answer.

'At the front, across their feet, from side to side of the wagon. Not so easily reached. It's probably what saved my life.'

I grunted, but made no other reply. It was certain that whoever had killed Martin Fletcher and Luke Hollis had been presented with an easy task. The back of the canvas hood was open to the elements, both men's heads towards the cart-tail, both deep in an ale-soused slumber from which very little would have roused them. And, because of this, both were probably sleeping on their backs in order to breathe the easier. The silent-footed murderer would have had no difficulty in lifting each man's head and cutting his throat with the minimum of fuss. Yet, having killed two, and with no danger of an alarm being raised, it would have been simple then to walk round to the side of the cart and dispatch the third. So, surely, if Peter Coucheneed had been spared, it was not because of his whereabouts in the wagon.

The next question to present itself was why had the two men been killed at all? I asked if anything had been stolen.

My companion shook his head. 'No, nothing. What do we have that's worth the taking? But do wolf-heads need a reason for what they do? They live by violence. The murder of innocent people is nothing more to them than sport.'

This was a point of view shared by most of the town's inhabitants as word of the killings spread rapidly amongst them. The Sheriff, busy assembling his *posse* in the Priory forecourt, was too hard pressed to come himself, but sent instead one of his sergeants, who had no hesitation in branding these latest murders the work of the outlaws. News had only just been received, within an hour or so of sunrise, of the looting of a farm and holdings in the parish of Berry Pomeroy. It was plain that the outlaws, returning to their lair, had come across the wagon, and slaked their blood-lust by murdering two of its sleeping inmates.

Such, at any rate, was the conclusion drawn by the sergeant, and eagerly taken up and repeated by all those who had gathered at Cherry Cross, attracted, as folk always are, by the smell of death and destruction. In half an hour, it would

215

be in every mouth, and quoted as Gospel truth, without any need for further thought or explanation. An atmosphere of hysteria pervaded the town and Foregate, for if the outlaws had not yet managed to breach the walls or stockade, it seemed as if they had come very close to doing so; far too close for peace of mind and comfort.

I left Peter Coucheneed to the ministrations of Granny Praule and Bridget, the former cock-a-hoop at thus finding herself the centre of attention, with a succession of visitors calling to inquire after herself and her guest. Four of the strongest Brothers from the Priory were summoned to take away the bodies, and I went with them, at Peter's request, walking beside the litters.

Inside the town, all was feverish activity. Seemingly, from the numbers thronging the streets, few people remained indoors, only the very old and very young children. News of this latest outrage had spurred many able-bodied men to swell the *posse*'s ranks who might otherwise have hesitated to spend long days in the saddle, riding over rough and uncharted terrain. I saw Thomas Cozin, mounted on a mettlesome bay, his wife and daughters hanging devotedly about his stirrups and trying their best to dissuade him from such a hazardous enterprise. The Sheriff was dividing his volunteers into groups and placing each one under the direction of a sergeant. Plans were drawn up as to the ground to be covered by the different companies, so that as much of the surrounding countryside as possible would be covered.

I saw the bodies of Martin Fletcher and Luke Hollis safely bestowed in the mortuary chapel, before leaving them to the ministrations of the Brothers. Pushing my way back across the crowded forecourt, I found myself unexpectedly accosted by Oliver Cozin. He was on foot and clearly not a member of the *posse*. He seemed irate.

216

'Master Chapman, I'm glad I fell in with you. You have some explaining to do, sir, have you not? Damage to my client's property.'

I was confused, there being no room in my mind at that instant for anything other than the deaths of my friends. For however short a time I had known them, I had grown to count them as such; and Martin Fletcher, because of his likeness to his brother, had quickly found a special place in my affections.

'Damage?' I asked stupidly. 'What damage?'

'Don't play the innocent with me, lad!' was the sharp rejoinder. 'I am talking about the gallery, which now lies in ruins, thanks to your heavy-footed carelessness. For Mistress Harbourne says you fell through its floor.'

'She told you so?' I demanded, feeling betrayed.

'She told Master Colet when he observed the damage for himself, rightly deciding that she should not be held responsible for something which was not her fault.'

'The wood was rotten,' I answered truculently, at the same time wondering what else Grizelda might have been tempted to disclose.

'Quite probably,' the lawyer replied austerely, 'but you should have informed me of the accident when I called yesterday morning, and not chosen Mistress Harbourne to confide in.'

I was in no mood for such a scolding. 'If Master Colet thinks I shall pay for the repairs, he may rid himself of any such notion. I did you and him a favour by sleeping in the house, only to be turned out unceremoniously when my services were no longer needed. Good-day, sir!' And I turned to walk away.

Oliver Cozin caught at my sleeve. His tone was still frosty, but his words slightly more conciliatory.

'I mentioned nothing about payment, Master Chapman. But my client and I would have appreciated a little honesty.' He took a breath and forced himself to unbend even further. 'I am distressed to hear about these terrible murders. I understand that you befriended the mummers when they arrived in the town yesterevening. One of them, I am told, leaves a brother who is a monk at Glastonbury Abbey, known to you when you yourself were a novice there?'

The last words ended on a rising note of query, as though he could not quite credit that I had ever had so respectable a calling. I inclined my head in assent, and the lawyer continued with sudden warmth, 'Then let us hope that the lord Sheriff and the goodmen of this town have successful hunting. Such foul deeds cannot be tolerated. Although for some of our number to be joining the *posse*,' he added, glancing with concern in his brother's direction, 'is inexcusable folly! Goodday to you, Master Chapman!' And he swung on his heel, elbowing his way through the crowd to Thomas's side.

I remained, wedged in a corner of the Priory forecourt, staring after him. It occurred to me that everything which had recently happened amiss in the good town of Totnes, was being laid at the door of the outlaws. No other explanation was even contemplated, so large did the wolf-heads' presence in the district loom in people's minds. Watching the swirl of feverish activity all about me, I sensed the underlying fear, which this morning's gruesome discovery had only excited still further. There was no gainsaying the fact that the robbers were evil men, and bore the stigma of murder as well as theft, but surely that did not make them guilty of every crime committed in the neighbourhood. Why should they have paused last night for wanton killing, without the possibility of gain? It made no sense. The killing, moreover, of two wandering mummers as poor and as homeless as the outlaws themselves, and for whom, if such men had feelings, they might have experienced a sneaking sympathy.

I thought of the burning of Grizelda's cottage. She had claimed it as an act of spite by the outlaws, and she could be right. Yet that same night, they had attacked the outlying homesteads of Dartington. Satisfied with their haul of plunder, why should they go out of their way to exact a petty revenge? Then there was the killing of Andrew and Mary Skelton. As recently as three days ago, when I first heard the story, there had been lingering doubts in a few people's minds as to the outlaws' guilt, but these suspicions were now forgotten, swept aside as unjust after the events of the past two nights. All the same, there were still too many unanswered questions about this particular crime for my liking. And whatever others might think, I knew that someone had tried to maim or even kill me; someone who could imitate the voice of a child; someone who was worried in case I stumbled on the truth.

But what was the truth? My thoughts came round full circle to be brought up short once more by the testimony of Bridget Praule, Agatha Tenter and Master Thomas Cozin that Eudo Colet had been out of the house when his stepchildren vanished. They had been there when he left, but had disappeared by the time he returned. He had had no opportunity to harm them.

Suddenly the Priory forecourt began to clear as the *posse*, with the Sheriff at its head, moved off. In moments, I was left with only the other onlookers for company, and I saw Oliver Cozin put a consoling arm around his sister-in-law's shoulders. The three girls huddled together for comfort as they and many others proceeded to the parish church to pray for their loved ones' safety. I went with them as far as the porch, but then walked on to High Street and turned left, downhill, towards the East Gate.

Granny Praule had water heating for me over the fire, and when I had shaved, she insisted that I sat down to breakfast.

'A shock like that needs feeding, lad,' she said, frying a lump of fat bacon in a skillet, and producing a slice of horse bread from a crock which stood in one corner. She cast a scornful, if affectionate, glance at her granddaughter, who was sitting on the bed beside Peter Coucheneed and holding his hand. 'I've no patience,' she went on, gnashing her tooth-less gums in irritation, 'with folk who fall over, like trees in a gale, every time there's a bit of trouble. If the good Lord had intended us to live in comfort on this earth, it stands to reason He'd not have needed to create the Hereafter. Bestir yourself, girl, and fetch that poor creature alongside you a cup more of my damson wine. He looks as if he needs it.'

To my protests that I was taking the food out of her and Bridget's mouths, Granny turned a deaf ear, and my offer of payment brought the vials of her wrath down about my head. When she was young, she informed me severely, travellers had a right to expect sustenance on their journeys from whomsoever had the means to provide it, especially those of them who had suffered misfortune. She plunged a knife into the sizzling lump of bacon and tossed it on to the plate I was holding on my knees, pressing it with the flat of the blade so that the fat ran out and soaked into the horse bread. For this small consideration I was grateful, always having found the coarseness of such bread, with its mixture of peas and beans and bits of chaff, unpalatable.

When I had finished eating, I took Peter Coucheneed gently

by the arm and urged him to his feet.

'Come outside,' I said. 'The air will do you good.'

He followed me, docilely, like someone who had lost the power to think for himself and would do whatever he was told.

'What will you do now?' I asked him gently. 'It has to be thought of, in spite of your grief, and the sooner the better. How long have the three of you been together?'

He roused himself a little, rubbing his forehead like a man awakening from a dream.

'A month,' he answered, 'perhaps six weeks at most. I fell in with them on the road from Southampton, where they'd spent the winter, and Martin suggested that I join them.'

'Ah!' I was surprised by this. 'I thought you had all three been friends for some long time.'

Peter shook his head. 'No. Martin and Luke had known each other since childhood, leaving their parents' company to set out on their own, flying the nest as we all must do sooner or later. But I was a stranger to them until we met in the shadow of Romsey Abbey. It was Martin who saw at once that with my height, my thinness, my baldness, I was the perfect foil for Luke, who, as you saw, was short and stout and blessed with more hair than any man has a need for.' He smiled wryly. ' "As a pair, you'll raise a laugh wherever we go," Martin said, and he was right, for people had only to see us side by side to begin to chuckle.' Peter's eyes filled with tears which overflowed and ran down his cheeks, his body racked with sobs. 'I thought I'd found a family to replace my own, who all died of the plague one summer. But now I'm alone again. Sweet Jesus! Why ever did we come to this accursed town? If only we'd known earlier about the outlaws.'

I put my arms around him and hugged him, but I am

ashamed to remember that the comfort I offered was absent-minded. I was deep in thought.

Was it simply chance which had decreed that the two men who had been friends since childhood, who had spent their lives in one another's company, should be the victims of this murderous attack, whilst the newcomer, a member of their band for only six weeks, should escape unharmed? Or was there some deeper, more sinister reason? Then I recalled the speech I had had, earlier, with Oliver Cozin and froze into stillness . . .

I became aware that Peter was asking me a question.

'What am I to do about the wagon? It belonged to Martin and Luke, yet it seems a shame to abandon it here to rot. Martin has family . . . a brother . . .'

'Nick won't lay any claim to it, you may be certain,' I answered, determinedly cheerful. 'And where the rest of Martin's kin are scattered, or Luke's for that matter, I have no more notion than you have. Take the cart, use it for yourself. I'm sure it's what both of them would wish, could we but ask them. And who around here knows enough to contest your right?'

He smiled gratefully, the advice being what he wanted to hear.

'I'll be on my way in a day or two, then, when I've seen Martin and Luke decently buried. Do you think Dame Praule would let me remain here for a while with her and Bridget? I have a little money. I could pay my way.'

'By all means ask her,' I said, glad that his thoughts were taking a positive turn. 'I don't doubt but she'll agree. Moreover, she'll help you cleanse the mattress and the pile of costumes. Women understand these mysteries. My mother, God rest her soul, had remedies for any kind of stain, although she always said blood was difficult.'

But the mere mention of the word 'blood' was sufficient to start him trembling all over again, so I accompanied him back to the cottage and did his pleading for him. Not that Granny Praule needed much persuasion. She was delighted with any diversion in her humdrum life, especially one which would give her such standing amongst her neighbours. And the prospect of a little extra money pleased Bridget.

'And we'll take the mattress and the clothes down to the river, to the ford, and hold them under the running water,' Granny said. 'There's nothing like cold, running water for dealing with blood.' She patted Peter Coucheneed's arm. 'There, there, lad. Don't take on so. We must be practical, and it would be a wicked shame to throw those good things away, or burn them. No, no! A little time, a little patience and we'll have them almost as good as new.'

Feeling that Peter was now in good hands, I picked up my pack and cudgel.

'I must be going,' I said. 'I have things to do.'

Granny sighed. 'You'll be away from here, I suppose. You've your living to earn.' She proffered me her wrinkled lips to kiss. 'Take care of yourself, lad. It's dangerous out there, on the roads. Where are you bound for?'

'London,' I answered. 'There's someone there I need to talk to. A woman.' Granny snorted derisively. 'You mistake,' I told her. 'Neither a sweetheart nor a leman. In truth, I've never set eyes on the lady. I shall be gone some weeks, but I'll be back. That, however, is for your ears only. If anyone should ask, *anyone at all*, you understand, I have left Totnes and resumed my travels.'

Granny Praule regarded me with bright, shrewd eyes.

'You can trust me,' she promised. 'But you're up to

something, and you can't tell me otherwise. Go on, get along with you, but remember what I said. Take care!'

Chapter Seventeen

Before leaving Totnes, I again made my way uphill to the East Gate. The gatekeeper assumed a resigned expression when he saw me.

'What is it this time?' he sighed. 'Or do I wrong you, and you've finished asking questions?'

'My mother always said I had the longest and most inquisitive nose in Christendom,' I apologized. 'One more answer, if you will, and then I'm done.'

He shrugged. 'If I know it. Very well.'

'When the Sheriff and his men arrived last night, the mummers and I were just leaving the town.' The gatekeeper nodded in agreement. 'I would have sworn we were the last ones out before the gates were shut, but I have to confess I didn't glance behind me. Did anyone else follow in our wake?'

'Now that I really couldn't say.' The man pursed his lips. 'I remember your departure, because a cart's a cumbersome thing, however small and light, and sticks in the memory. I closed the main gates after you, but someone could have slipped through the postern without me noticing. It was a good few minutes later I secured that door. Yes, it's possible someone might have gone out on foot without being seen.'

'Thank you.' I doffed my hat. 'I shall pray for you and

yours. And now I'm off on the road again to sell my wares.'

'Leaving us, are you?' The gatekeeper pulled down the corners of his mouth. 'Can't say I blame you. Things are growing too dangerous around here for those who don't have to stay, to linger. I'd not stop if I were a stranger. First, those two innocent children murdered, then Grizelda Harbourne's cottage burned down and some poor woodsman charred to a cinder, and now two lads with their throats cut while they slept! These are wild times, I grant you, with our betters squabbling like stray curs over who wears the crown, but this has always been a law-abiding township, and now three slayings in as many months, and the last right on our doorstep. Yes indeed, I'd be on my way if I were you. Let's pray that the lord Sheriff and his *posse* can track these wolf-heads to their lair and smoke them out!'

I heartily endorsed this sentiment, thanked the man once more for his patience and settled my pack on my back, shifting its weight a little from left to right. I then set out, taking the Exeter road, which I had travelled yesterday and which skirted the grounds of the Priory and the edges of the tidal marsh.

It was by now the middle of a morning which had fulfilled its promise of a sweet, warm day. All about me were signs that spring was blossoming into an early summer; but it would need only one sharp frost to blacken the burgeoning shoots and shrivel them into nothing. Too much sun too soon in the year could prove a mixed blessing.

As I walked, swinging along with an easy stride, the words of the gatekeeper went round and round in my head. 'Two innocent children murdered ... cottage burned down ... woodsman charred to a cinder ... throats cut while they slept ...' And all three crimes attributed, without hesitation, to the outlaws. Yet the first two were linked, however tenuously, in the person of Grizelda Harbourne, and each time she had suffered great loss and distress. She had been deprived of two people she loved, and then of her home and livelihood. The last murder, the wanton slaying of Martin Fletcher and Luke Hollis, seemed, at first sight, to be unconnected, and yet . . . and yet . . . Was I foolish to believe that I could see a link between it and the others? Well, foolish or not, that conviction had set my feet on the road to London. If I was right, I should return to Totnes in two or three weeks; if not, I would have to let things be and make my way home to Bristol.

In the latter case, it was unlikely that I should ever set eyes on Grizelda Harbourne again. I felt a tug of the heartstrings and a profound regret that we had not parted the best of friends; but at the same time, a sense of regained freedom surged through me. As I had told myself on several occasions, it was far too soon after Lillis's death to think seriously of another wife, and I did not believe that Grizelda would allow herself to be wantonly seduced. There was too much dignity, too much sense of destiny, about her to permit of her giving herself lightly to any man. She had been right when she said, last night, that she was not the woman for me; that we should not suit. Yet, on her own admission, she had considered the idea, and only dismissed it after much careful thought. She had felt, as I had, the pull of attraction between us: the older woman, the younger man – very often the recipe for a sound and settled marriage. (Had it not proved so in the King's case, when he wed the widowed Lady Grey, five years his senior?) But in the end, Grizelda had recognized, as I had, that I was not ready again for such a tie; that I needed to be my own man a while longer. If nothing else, my childish display of temper the previous day, my inability to be laughed at, must have dispelled any lingering doubts she might have harboured. She could not be doing with someone so immature. It was time we parted.

But supposing I *did* return to Totnes, that I was able to prove to her that her suspicions and her dislike of Eudo Colet were well-founded, what then? Might not some spark be rekindled between us? On the other hand, was that what either of us really wanted? How could I possibly tell, here and now, with the outcome of my pilgrimage still uncertain? Only God and time could give the answer.

The afternoon was already some way advanced when I heard the rumble of wagon wheels on the track behind me. The circumstance reminded me so forcibly of the previous day's events, that I hesitated for a moment to look over my shoulder, lest I should behold a phantom. But when a voice hailed me in familiar tones, I turned with a smile to greet Jack Carter.

'Leaving us, are you?' he asked, echoing the gatekeeper's words. 'Very wise, too. I'm off to Exeter myself with this load of wool bales. If you care to ride with me that far, I don't deny I'll be glad of the company. But don't let me prevent you from peddling your wares.'

'I'll be happy to join you,' I said. 'I shan't stop to do any selling today, and I'd be thankful to find myself in a safe haven by nightfall. Moreover, I need to replenish my stock, which I can do tomorrow, in Exeter market.' The cart drew to a halt beside me. I threw my pack and stick in among the bales of wool and clambered up beside Jack Carter. He jerked the reins and the grey mare resumed her plodding gait. 'You'll not be sorry to be away from Totnes yourself for a night or two, I daresay?'

'And that's the truth.' He touched the mare's rump lightly with his switch and she quickened her pace a little. 'It's a peaceful enough town in the normal way, but there's been too much excitement these past few months for my liking.'

'Since the outlaws came to this part of the country?' I suggested.

He nodded vigorously. 'Aye, that's the truth of it. Just after Michaelmastide, last year, we first heard of stealing and looting in one or two of the outlying villages, and it's been going from bad to worse ever since.'

There was silence for a few minutes while Jack forced his mare up a difficult incline, the poor beast labouring so desperately that I felt obliged to get down and walk. When, however, I was able once again to take my seat in the cart, I ventured, 'Of all the townspeople, Grizelda Harbourne seems to have suffered the most. She's lost her home, her living and her two young kinfolk, to whom she seems to have been devoted.'

'Oh, aye, she's been unlucky,' Jack conceded, 'but then misfortune's dogged her all her life. The stars were out of conjunction when that one was born, all right.'

'Indeed?' I murmured, leaning forward and clasping my hands loosely between my knees, my face turned inquiringly towards him.

The mare had settled down to a steady pace across a broad, flat, open stretch of country. Jack could afford to relax his concentration for a while, and, like most people who spend long hours with only their own company for solace, was pleased to have a gossip. And I was a willing audience.

'It's the truth,' he said. 'Her mother died when Grizelda was little more than a child, some nine or ten summers, at a time when girls most need a female hand to guide them. And although she's grown into a handsome woman, she was plain enough when she was younger. Almost a man's face she had, as I recall her, and a mannish way to go with it. No feminine wiles or graces. And then Sir Jasper, whose wife was distant cousin to Ralph Harbourne, took her to live with him as companion to his daughter.' Jack Carter laughed. 'Leastways, that's what he called it, but servant would be nearer the truth. If Mistress Rosamund had been of a different disposition, it might not have been so bad, but she had a spoilt, mean and vicious nature. And to make matters worse, she was as pretty and rich as Grizelda was poor and plain.'

'But Grizelda told me that she and her cousin were the best of friends,' I interrupted.

The carter snorted. 'She'd be too proud, poor soul, to have you, or anyone else, think otherwise. Pride and the ability to mask her true feelings were two of her greatest virtues. She never complained, however badly she was treated. You've no doubt noted that scar on her face? In some lights it shows more than in others.'

'She told me she fell out of a tree as a child.'

'Or was pushed by Rosamund. My Goody was a servant in the Crouchback household at that time, and she swore that she saw what happened; that Mistress Rosamund deliberately shoved her cousin from the branch on which the two of them were sitting. Grizelda caught her cheek on a lower branch and ripped it open, but she always maintained that it was her own fault; that she had grown dizzy and fallen. Oh, there was affection between those two, all right, but it was Grizelda's affection for Mistress Rosamund.'

'Are you so certain that the younger girl felt nothing in return?' I queried; although I could see that Grizelda's fierce pride would make her conceal the truth, perhaps even from herself. Perhaps most of all from herself. As a connection of a wealthy and well-born family, she would never be able to admit that her kin treated her with perhaps less respect than they would have shown a servant.

Jack Carter shrugged. 'I only tell you what my Goody told me at the time, and the evidence of my own eyes over the years. I'll cite you one piece of proof, if you want it. Grizelda never had many clothes. She'd wear the same dress, the same cloak year in, year out, until the things were almost threadbare. Now, granted, she and Mistress Rosamund were not of a size, but there was not that much difference between them, and Grizelda was always good with her needle. A seam let out here, a hem let down there, and she could have worn many of Mistress Rosamund's cast-offs. And the saints know that that spoilt madam had more shifts and gowns and coifs laid by in her coffers than she knew what to do with. Any mistress worth her salt would have passed one or two of them on to her maid, let alone a kinswoman. No, no! I tell you Grizelda was only valued in the Crouchback household as long as she could be useful.'

'And was she useful?'

Jack Carter's eyebrows mounted his forehead and nearly vanished into his thick, dark hair.

'Of course she was useful! When she was younger for taking the blame, and often the punishment, for pranks which her cousin had played; and, later on, as nurse to the two Skelton children. Children were too much trouble for Mistress Rosamund. She couldn't be bothered with them, and that's a fact, particularly when there was no husband to see that she performed a mother's duties. Grizelda doted on those little ones. They were more hers than their dam's; which was why, when they were murdered, her agony was so great. And before that, of course, she had found a new enemy in Eudo

Colet. Yes, I tell you, chapman, that woman has had more than her fair share of trials and tribulations.'

'What will become of her now?' I asked him. 'She talks of keeping house for some Totnes worthy.'

The carter grimaced. 'If she can find a place, though that may not be so easy. A pity she and Master Colet dislike one another so much, or she might have got her feet beneath his table, at this manor house of his, which common gossip has it he's obtained out Dartington way, where the succession's foundered. I recognize Lawyer Cozin's hand in that particular pie. A man with a great deal of influence, not only in this shire, but also in London. As it is, it seems Agatha Tenter will carry the keys at her girdle. Or so my Goody reports, and it's a brave man who'd contradict her, for she's rarely misinformed. She has a nose for other people's business that I'd back against all comers.'

I laughed, and would have been happy to be entertained by more of his prattle, but the track had dwindled to a narrow path between two belts of woodland, and he needed all his wits about him to make sure that the mare didn't stumble. Moreover, the sun was getting low in the sky, and we were both growing hungry. It was time to think of our night's lodging, and by mutual agreement, we pressed on to the Abbey at Buckfast, where we were given food and shelter.

The following day, we finished the journey to Exeter, and Jack Carter left me close to St Mary Steps Church, wishing me well.

'For I doubt our paths will cross again,' he added cheerfully.

I made no comment. 'The Lord be with you and yours,' was all I answered.

I reached London a week later, having been fortunate

enough, a few miles east of Shaftesbury, to fall in with a wagoner who was going all the way to the capital, and who was willing for me to ride with him to journey's end. Like Jack Carter, he was as glad of my company as I was of his, and of the shared conviviality of bed and board at the various religious houses we stopped at along the way. As we got closer to our destination, the traffic increased, for apart from the usual people to be met with at that time of year – pilgrims, friars, pardoners, lords and their ladies moving from one castle or manor to another, knights riding to Shire Day meetings with friends and tenants – the roads were clogged with the levies now being mustered for the invasion of France.

I finally alighted from the wagon close to the Chère Reine Cross and made my way along the Strand and Fleet Street to the Lud Gate. Here, the press became even thicker, with tradespeople swelling the throng passing in and out. The beggars, who congregate around the main entrances to any large city, rattled their cups and bowls, and those who were not maimed, and were nimble enough on their feet, shouldered a path between the crowds, laying greasy, imploring hands on sleeves and jackets. Some gave, and were blessed for their generosity, others threw them off with an imprecation and were roundly cursed for their pains. None of the beggars bothered me, however, sparing only a cursory glance before deciding that I was unlikely to have anything to give, being as poor and needy as themselves. Long years of practice had taught them not to waste their time if they wished to claim the lion's share of alms.

I had not been in London for a long while, and felt a sudden sense of exhilaration at all the hustle and bustle going on around me. For me today, now that I am an old man, settled in the quiet and peace of my native Somerset, the city holds no attractions; but then, I was young and vigorous, and London was like a tray full of sweetmeats, each tempting delight waiting to be sampled, my mouth watering as my fingers hovered, not knowing which to choose first. For the present, however, I had work to do; my time was not my own. But later, if this mission should prove abortive, or when, with God's help, it was successfully concluded, I promised myself that I would return to the capital and sample the many temptations it had to offer.

Pausing in the shadow of St Paul's, I cudgelled my brains to remember something Grizelda had told me over a week ago, when we were talking in her cottage. Three years since, Rosamund Skelton, by then a widow and living in Totnes, had come to London to visit an old friend who lived in Paternoster Row. 'A Ginèvre Napier and her husband, Gregory. Gregory Napier is a goldsmith with a shop in West Cheap, between Foster Lane and Gudrun Lane.' I thought carefully for a moment or two, satisfying myself that those had indeed been Grizelda's words, then asked directions of a fellow pedlar, who was selling his wares just inside the churchyard.

He eyed me suspiciously, and was inclined to be unhelpful, until I assured him that I had no intention of setting up a rival pitch anywhere near at hand. Then, he was pleased to assist me.

'Go along Old Dean's Lane, and to your right, on the opposite side of this churchyard, is Paternoster Row. At its other end, by the church of St Michael at Corn, you'll come into West Cheap. You'll find most of the goldsmiths there.'

I thanked him and followed his directions, walking slowly the length of Paternoster Row and wondering which of the gaily painted houses belonged to Gregory Napier. He must, I reflected, be a very wealthy man if he and his wife did not live behind the shop, but in a separate dwelling. But this was to my advantage, for if I could speak to Ginèvre Napier on her own, free of her husband's presence, I fancied she might talk more frankly. But first, I must make sure that Gregory Napier was busy at his work.

I accosted a small street urchin who, together with a flock of kites and ravens, was scavenging among the refuse piled up on the cobbles. Having watched him drive away several other boys who had ventured into this part of the Cheap, I judged it to be his patch, which he would defend against all comers. He would be sure to know which shop belonged to which craftsman, just as the owners, in their turn, would know him, by sight, if not by name.

I opened my palm to disclose half a groat and at once a dirty hand reached out to snatch it.

'Not so fast,' I protested, caging the money within my fingers. 'Does one of these goldsmiths' shops belong to Gregory Napier?'

The blue eyes narrowed with suspicion: the urchin was protective of his benefactors, who no doubt left him tit-bits from time to time, among the festering rubbish. I thought at first that he would refuse to answer, and that I should have to ask elsewhere; but the thought of the half-groat concealed in my palm proved to be too great a lure. He nodded towards a shop in front of whose booth no less than three capped apprentices called and toted their master's wares.

'That's Master Napier's,' he grunted, and shot out his hand again for the money.

But I still clenched my fist. 'And is he working there, inside?'

This time, the eyes widened and the gaze became malevolent.

'What's that to you, pedlar?'

'What's my business to you?' I retorted. I relented a little. 'I give you my solemn promise that I mean Master Napier no harm.'

The urchin hesitated, then decided I was honest.

''E's there,' he said. 'You can see the smoke comin' out the chimney. Workin' on a very delicate piece for my lord 'Astings, or so I 'eard, an' 'e won't trust anyone but 'imself to work the bellows.' The boy nodded knowingly. 'Right temp'rature's everythink in such cases.'

I laughed and released the coin into his eagerly waiting palm, before reaching into my pouch for a second. I held it up between finger and thumb, and the lad's eyes sparkled. A whole groat in one day was unlooked-for beneficence. He could scarcely believe his luck, and was by now ready to tell me anything I wanted to know without further quibble.

'Master Napier doesn't live behind the shop, I understand, but has a house in Paternoster Row. Can you tell me which it is?'

''Course I can!' he answered scornfully. ''Ere! Follow me!'

He led me back past the church of St Michael at Corn, where it stood at the junction with the Shambles, into the narrow, cobbled Row, made gloomy by its dozens of over-hanging roofs. My lad pointed a grimy forefinger, indicating a house some four storeys high, the carved timbers of its gable picked out in scarlet, blue and gold. The windows of the lower two floors had wooden shutters, at present standing open to the warmth of the afternoon, but the upper ones were made of glass, a sure sign of riches, the top three showing a leaded trefoil, the lower three circles within a triangle, both signs of the Trinity of God.

'Tha's it. Tha's the one.' The urchin once more extended his open hand and I placed the half-groat in it.

'Will Mistress Napier be within, do you think?' I asked, and heard the boy suck in his breath on a respectful whistle.

'Like that, is it then?' His teeth showed suddenly white in his dirty face. 'I'll keep a watch on the shop for you, if you want,' he offered.

I cuffed his ear. 'You'll keep a civil tongue in your head and put a curb on those lecherous thoughts of yours!' I told him severely. 'I know nothing of Mistress Napier, but have no doubt that she's a virtuous lady. And she certainly has nothing to fear from me.'

The urchin sent me a sidelong glance, full of meaning.

'You might 'ave nothin' to say in the matter, chapman.' He chuckled. 'I've 'eard stories about 'er as ud make your 'air curl.' He nudged my ribs. 'Eats the likes of you fer 'er brekfust.'

I sent him on his way with another box on the ear, but as he was accustomed to such treatment, I doubt it had any effect. He looked over his shoulder, grinning cheekily, as he made off, back to the Cheap to resume his scavenging. I, in the meantime, hesitated to knock on the door of the Napiers' house, wondering if there was any other entrance. While I did so, I became aware of someone watching me from behind one of the open, lower windows. A moment later, the door opened and a young maidservant made her appearance.

'My mistress bids you enter, chapman, if you're selling your wares. She has need of some new silk ribbons.'

Chapter Eighteen

I followed the young girl into one of the downstairs parlours, where such light as there was came through the unshuttered window from the street outside. It was a richly furnished room, with fresh, sweet-smelling rushes covering the floor, three finely carved armchairs, the ceiling beams newly painted in glowing reds and gold, the walls hung with splendid tapestries, whose colours had a pristine glow, a corner cupboard, displaying bowls and cups and plates crafted in gold and silver-gilt, and a large table, fashioned from the finest oak. From the middle of the ceiling was suspended a candelabra of latten tin, its many filigree pendants tinkling in the slightest breeze. It was the room of a man of wealth, of a man who knew what was due to himself and to his standing within the community he served.

'Ah, chapman, empty the contents of your pack on the table there, so that I can examine them at my leisure. I'm looking for some silk ribbons to adorn the sleeves of a new velvet gown.'

The woman who thus addressed me, was seated in one of the armchairs, her feet, elegantly shod in pale blue leather, resting on a low stool of carved elm. At first glance, it was difficult to guess her age, but I suspected her to be older than she would have had people think. There were lines around the grey-green eyes which seemed to grow more numerous the longer I observed them, and the slender, beringed hands already showed one or two brownish spots. Her eyebrows had been plucked and her forehead shaved to create the smooth, domed, mask-like appearance so prevalent in those days amongst women of fashion. A few stray hairs, which had escaped the razor, were auburn in colour, but the rest of the mane was tucked out of sight beneath a brocade cap and wired, gauze veil. Her full-sleeved gown was made of pale green sarcinet, embroidered with tiny blue flowers on thin, gold stems, and her girdle, studded with semi-precious stones, was of the same blue leather as her shoes. A gold and coral rosary was wrapped about one slender wrist, and a beautifully wrought gold pendant, on a thick gold chain, dangled from her neck. Her many rings were also of gold, as was the brooch, in the shape of a peacock, pinned to one shoulder of her gown. Master Gregory Napier made certain that his wife was a walking showpiece for his wares.

I emptied my pack as I was bid, spreading out its contents across the table, thankful that I had restocked in Exeter last Friday morning. I had managed to obtain several lengths of very fine silk ribbon from a Portuguese ship which had only just then tied up at the city quay. But even as I displayed them for her approval, I was conscious that Ginèvre Napier was far more interested in me. Her eyes kept straying from the ribbon to my face, and at every opportunity, her hand brushed one of mine. At length, she bade me draw up a stool.

'For I can't make up my mind which ribbon to choose,' she said. 'They are all so beautiful.' After a few more minutes, however, she abandoned all pretence of interest, leaned back in her chair and asked, 'Why were you watching this house? No, don't deny it. I saw you.'

I recollected the shadowy figure at the open casement, and decided that I must be honest with her.

'I've come to London from Devon,' I said, 'from the township of Totnes, on purpose to seek you out.' She raised the faint, plucked line of her eyebrows in puzzlement, and I continued, 'It concerns Lady Skelton and her second husband; the man she married here in London, Eudo Colet.'

A momentary wariness flickered into the grey-green eyes, and the heavy, almond-shaped lids closed over them, briefly. Then the narrow shoulders were hunched with a ripple of pale green silk.

'Now, why does a pedlar want to know about Master Eudo Colet?' she demanded.

'If you've the patience to listen,' I said, 'I'll tell you. If not, you have only to say the word and I'll take my leave at once.' But I sent up an urgent prayer to heaven that she would hear me out.

Ginèvre clasped her hands together and regarded me thoughtfully across the bony knuckles.

'Oh, I've the patience to listen.' She added candidly, 'I can always find time for a lad as good-looking as you.'

I ignored this last remark as best I could and plunged without further ado into the events which had occupied my mind, waking and sometimes sleeping, for the past twelve days: those surrounding the disappearance and subsequent murder of the two Skelton children; as yet, I mentioned nothing about the burning of Grizelda's cottage and the death of Innes Woodsman, nor of the killing of Martin Fletcher and Luke Hollis. When, at last, I had finished, my companion pursed her lips.

'I pleaded with her not to marry that man,' she said after a pause, 'but Rosamund was always headstrong. Headstrong and wilful. That father of hers could never curb her fits and starts. Not that he ever tried to, as far as I could tell. A foolish, over-indulgent man, who thought his precious only child could do no wrong. As for her husband, Sir Henry Skelton . . . well! A man concerned more with his own advancement than trying to please his wife. A cold man, uninterested in the pleasures of the flesh.' She stole a sidelong glance at me to see if she had caused embarrassment with such plain speaking, but I gave her no satisfaction, keeping my features under control. Ginèvre continued, 'But then, as you may know, he was killed after only two years of marriage, and Rosamund went home to Sir Jasper, in Devon.'

I nodded. 'And her cousin with her.'

'Her cousin?' Once again, Ginèvre was puzzled. Then comprehension dawned. 'Oh, you mean Grizelda Harbourne. That poor creature!' She was dismissive. 'I'd forgotten she was kin to Rosamund, as anyone might, considering the way she was treated.'

'And how was that?' I ventured.

'She was nurse to young Andrew after he was born, but before that, no better than a servant. If she led you to believe otherwise, she's lying.'

'I begin to think so,' I agreed, and my heart went out to Grizelda for her proud and painful deception. 'She wasn't asked to accompany her kinswoman, when Lady Skelton came to stay here, with you, three years ago?'

Ginèvre Napier laughed. 'No, indeed! For the first time in her life, Rosamund was her own mistress. No husband, no father. She was free to do as she pleased. She brought only her maid, a young, biddable girl who would protest at nothing, and do exactly as she was told.'

'And it was during that visit,' I said, 'that Lady Skelton met Eudo Colet when you both visited St Bartholomew's fair.'

Mistress Napier's eyes opened very wide and fixed them-selves on my face. 'Now, how do you know that?' she asked softly.

I made no attempt to answer the question. 'He was a mummer,' I hazarded. 'A singer who could also play the flute a little. And he travelled the roads in summer, going from fair to fair.'

My companion nodded slowly, a frown creasing her fore-head. 'He was with a troupe of mummers and *jongleurs* who had a sideshow at the fair. But I ask again, how do you know? For I'd stake my life that Rosamund would have told no one, and nor would he. I'd have been willing to swear that Gregory and I were the only two people who were party to the truth.'

Once more, I did not answer, posing instead a question of my own.

'Would you be willing to tell me how it all came about? Now that you find I know as much as I do.'

Her frown deepened. 'You're the strangest chapman I've ever met,' she said. 'Who are you? And what can possibly be your interest in Rosamund's affairs?'

'My interest is in Eudo Colet. I believe him to be an evil man who may have done murder. As for who I am, I'm what I appear to be, a pedlar by trade; a man who was once a novice of the Benedictine Order, but who abandoned the religious life for the freedom of the open road.'

'Ah!' Ginèvre Napier continued to regard me, absent-mindedly biting the nail of one finger while she considered my words. 'That explains much,' she went on at last. 'A pedlar with book learning, and handsome, too! You could do as well for yourself, chapman, as Eudo Colet, for his looks, though pleasing to the female eye, are as nothing compared with yours.' She sighed. 'If only I weren't so happily married . . .'

'I am more than content with my life,' I interrupted hastily. 'And I have a little daughter at home, in Bristol.'

She drew down the corners of her thin, painted mouth in mock despair.

'You're married! And faithful to your wife! Alas! The best men always are.' I did not enlighten her and she continued, 'You asked me about Rosamund and Eudo Colet. Very well. I see no reason, now that she's dead, and you, as you say, know so much, why I should not tell you the truth. Indeed, there's little to tell, I should imagine, that you haven't understood for yourself already. It was St Bartholomewtide and Rosamund and I visited the fair. Our maids were with us, of course. We were not unchaperoned. Eudo was there, performing with a troupe of mummers and singers, and for some reason, he immediately caught her eye. She was bewitched by him from the very first moment that she saw him. Don't ask me why.' Ginèvre spread her hands, a stray shaft of sunlight catching her rings and making them glitter. 'These things happen, I know, although I have never experienced such a *coup de foudre* myself.'

'Did you ever know the names of any of the others in the mummers' troupe?' I asked her.

My hostess looked affronted. 'No, nor did I wish to. I was only acquainted with Eudo Colet because of Rosamund's foolish infatuation and her determination to marry him. Folly! She could have taken him as her lover, enjoyed his body and then paid him to go away. These things are better arranged so.'

I had no doubt that they were, and I suspected that she knew from experience just how it was done. She caught my eye and smiled.

'You disapprove, chapman, I can see it in your face. But

when there is too little to do, servants to run one's every bidding and pander to one's every whim, a woman grows bored. A handsome man is a pleasant diversion.' She crowed with laughter. 'And now I've truly shocked you.'

I murmured a protest, but without much conviction, and asked, 'But in this instance, Lady Skelton was determined on marriage?'

'I've said so. And so, of course, was he, once he saw which way the wind was blowing. Not that I blame him, you understand. What man with any sense would not exchange poverty for riches; a wandering, tumbling, mummer's life for a roof above his head and a soft bed with a pretty woman in it? I tried to dissuade her from such a course, and so did Gregory, but to no avail. Her mind was set on making Eudo her husband. She had married to please her father the first time, she said, and now she would marry to please herself. There was no one to prevent her. She argued that Eudo provided her with everything she had ever wanted in a man; everything that she had looked for in Sir Henry Skelton – and been disappointed!' Ginèvre smiled lasciviously, the eyes momentarily veiled before being opened wide. 'They spent most of their time in bed. The house reeked of the farmyard.'

I was beginning to dislike Ginèvre Napier: she made me uncomfortable. Under the guise of moral outrage, her thoughts and desires were salacious.

'And you and Master Napier were the only people who knew of Eudo Colet's origins. What of Lady Skelton's maid?'

'Rosamund rid herself of the girl. She found her a place with a noble family whose home was in the north, well away from any probing tongues. Which was just as well, for a month or so after Rosamund returned to Devon, two men arrived at our door, asking questions. It turned out that they had been sent by Sir Jasper's partner.'

I nodded. 'Master Thomas Cozin, a highly respected burgher of Totnes. And you and your husband told them nothing?' But I already knew the answer.

Ginèvre's thin lips curled in a sneer. 'Why should we? What business was it of anyone but Rosamund herself? And Gregory is not the man to allow himself to be interrogated by servants. If this Thomas Cozin wanted the truth, he should have come to London himself, not sent menials to do his work for him.'

'And what of Eudo Colet's fellow mummers? Did they have no idea of his good fortune?'

'Of course not!' Ginèvre was scathing. 'Eudo wasn't such a fool as to tell any one of them! What! Lay himself open to some chance meeting in the future? To have it revealed that he was nothing but a poor *jongleur*? To be claimed as friend by a parcel of vagabonds, when he had risen so high in the world? You must be mad even to ask such a question! He crept away in the middle of the night and came here, to Rosamund. They never knew what had happened to him nor where he had gone. As far as they were concerned, he had simply vanished.'

'And you sheltered him? Willingly?'

Ginèvre Napier's eyes snapped with sudden anger. She sat forward in her chair.

'I'm growing tired of these questions, chapman! Consider yourself lucky that I have not asked you to leave, or had you thrown out, ere this.'

'I'm sorry,' I said, rising quickly, and realizing that once again, as so often in the past, I had overstepped the bounds of familiarity in my insatiable eagerness to get at the truth. 'I'll go.' And I began to refill my pack.

Breathing heavily, Mistress Napier sank back in her chair, the anger dying out of her face.

'No, no!' she exclaimed irritably. 'Sit down.' She began to bite on another of her fingernails. After a few moments, she asked, 'You truly think Eudo Colet guilty of the murder of Rosamund's two children? What of these outlaws who are preying on the countryside around Totnes? You told me most people believe them to be the murderers. Why don't you?'

I resumed my seat at the table, trying to assume a more respectful expression.

'I believe they may have been the killers, if we are talking of wielding the knife. But I think it more than likely that Master Colet could have been in league with the wolf-heads, and paid them to do the deed.'

Ginèvre raised one eyebrow, or what there was left of it after the razor had taken its toll.

'But you told me that Eudo was out of the house when the children disappeared, and did not return until after they had vanished. So what do you accuse him of? Witchcraft?'

I drew a deep breath. 'There are those who, until recently, thought him capable of that.'

'And you?' The lips curled into a contemptuous smile. 'Do you think him in league with the Devil, able to perform the black arts?' When I hesitated, she laughed; but I saw her, nevertheless, make a sign to ward off evil.

I said defiantly, 'I am convinced that he had a hand in those children's deaths. I confess to having no idea how he got them out of the house during his absence, but I believe him to be a very wicked man. I believe him to be the murderer of two mummers who arrived in Totnes last week. Their throats were cut as they lay asleep in their wagon.'

'Mummers?' I had her attention now, her eyes wide with

painful anxiety. 'You mentioned nothing of this before.'

'No. I wished to assure myself first that I was right in my assumptions about Master Colet. I had already learned that he could sing and play the flute, information which only had significance for me after the death of these two mummers. Furthermore, I recollected Grizelda telling me that Lady Skelton had visited you around St Bartholomewtide. It seemed possible to me then that she had met her husband at the fair. That he was in fact himself a *jongleur*. For all those who knew him, swore he was of peasant stock.'

Ginèvre gave a crow of delight. 'Of course they did! I told the pair of them that fine clothes and a scented beard wouldn't fool people into thinking that Eudo Colet was a gentleman. That everyone was bound to recognize him for what he really was. But Rosamund was so besotted with him, and he was so set up in his own conceit, that they refused to believe me or heed my words. "Give me a month or so to teach him how to behave," she said, "and no one will know he's not as well born as you and me." The fool! Did she truly think she could make gold from dross? That no one would know the difference?' She looked at me with a new respect. 'And you were able, from these slender facts, to draw so accurate a conclusion?'

'With God's help. And I was given one more hint. There was a third man belonging to the little troupe, who was also sleeping in the wagon. He had known the other two for only five or six weeks, and he was left unharmed. It seemed unlikely to me that outlaws, killing for pleasure, would have spared him. All the same, I have no proof that Eudo Colet murdered either Martin Fletcher or Luke Hollis.'

My companion shook her head. 'The names have no meaning for me, chapman. I told you earlier that I know nothing of Eudo's companions. But I do recall one who was very short and fat. A tumbler, surprisingly agile.'

'Luke,' I said. 'So Eudo Colet would have known him, and therefore would also have known Martin Fletcher.'

The silk gown whispered faintly as Ginèvre shifted in her chair.

'But surely they, too, would have recognized him had they met? Even if Eudo still wears the beard he grew while he was in this house, a man's voice and the manner in which he walks never alter.'

'But they did not meet, not face to face,' I responded eagerly, forgetting myself once more and leaning forward to close one hand over her wrist, giving it a little shake. I told her, as briefly as I could, the circumstances in which Martin and I had gone to call on Grizelda Harbourne. 'While we were talking at the door, I thought I saw someone move in the passageway behind her. Grizelda was holding a lantern, and its light was shining directly on me and on Martin Fletcher. Both our faces would have been plainly visible to anyone standing in the shadows.'

'And you believe that person to have been Eudo Colet?' The fingers of Ginèvre's other hand crept up to cover mine, but I was too wrapt up in what I was saying to notice.

'I'm sure it was, although, again, I cannot prove it.' I frowned. 'But why Grizelda denied that there was anyone there, I cannot fathom.'

'A lover's tryst, perhaps?' My hostess gave a slow, lecherous smile and passed the tip of her tongue between her lips. 'Eudo always had an eye for a handsome woman; and my recollection of Grizelda Harbourne is that she was passably well-looking.'

'She hated him,' I retorted angrily, at the same time

becoming aware that our hands were linked, and withdrawing mine hurriedly. 'And he disliked her as much as she disliked him. No, if he were indeed there . . .'

I broke off, realizing that Eudo must have been there that night, for what other chance would he have had to observe for himself the damage my fall had done to the gallery? He had been able to inform Oliver Cozin of it the following morning, for the lawyer had been in possession of the facts by the time of the muster in the Priory courtyard. Here was sure proof of my suspicions, if only to myself. But why, oh why, had Grizelda denied his presence?

Ginèvre Napier pouted and sat back in the chair, resentful of my abrupt rejection of her.

'A jealous lover, is that it?' she sneered. 'Or would-be lover. Yes, now I begin to read the signs. You would have liked to bed Mistress Harbourne yourself.'

I rose stiffly to my feet and gave a cursory bow.

'Madam, I thank you for your courtesy in receiving me, and for answering my questions, but now I must take my leave. There is nothing more to be said between us.'

Ginèvre made no answer, but watched with smouldering eyes as I returned my wares to my pack and closed it. As I would have taken my leave, she said quietly, but with venomous spite, 'A weak man, Eudo Colet, easily led. If he and Grizelda Harbourne are lovers, then you must accept that it is by her wish more than by his.'

I replied, trying to suppress my anger, 'I have told you, she hates him. She believes him guilty of a pact with the outlaws to get rid of Andrew and Mary Skelton. For some reason that I don't understand, you are trying to turn me against her. You won't succeed.'

It was Ginèvre's turn to rise to her feet, trembling from

head to foot, her eyes mere slits in the painted mask of her face.

'I've a good mind to complain of you to my husband. He'd soon see to it that you were whipped at the cart's tail and put in the stocks. But it would be a shame to mark that splendid hide of yours, so get out now, before I change my mind!'

I needed no second bidding, and found myself in the street without having any idea of how I got there. I shouldered my pack and set off blindly along Paternoster Row. I had almost reached the Cheap, when I heard the patter of footsteps behind me. The next moment, a hand was laid on my sleeve, and I turned to find Ginèvre's little maid at my elbow.

'My mistress begs that you'll return with me, sir,' she panted. 'There's something, she says, she has to tell you.'

'Then why did she not tell me earlier?' I demanded. 'No, no! She takes me for a bigger fool than she already thinks me, if she believes I'll go back there.'

The girl tightened her grip imploringly. 'Please come with me, sir.' She added confidingly. 'My mistress would never harm a man such as you. Take my word for it! I know her! It would go against her nature. She means what she says. She really does have something to tell you.'

I was unconvinced, but suspected that the girl would suffer if I did not do as I was bidden. For her sake, therefore, I retraced my steps, but not without great misgivings.

My fears, however, proved to be unfounded. Ginèvre had regained her composure and faced me calmly across the table.

'I have been thinking,' she said, 'that the murder of two innocent children is not a thing to be lightly dismissed. There is something, therefore, that you should know about Eudo Colet. Perhaps, after all, he *is* in league with the Devil, for

251

he possesses a fiendishly clever talent. Sit down for a moment more, and I'll tell you what it is.'

Chapter Nineteen

I made my way to St Lawrence's Lane, to Blossom's Inn – so known locally because its sign showed St Lawrence Deacon surrounded by a wreath of flowers – and called for ale. Then I found a cosy corner and withdrew into the shadows, remote from the press of bodies all about me and the clatter of tongues, speaking in an alien brogue. For in those days, and maybe now, for all I know, that particular tavern was journey's end for carters and carriers from the eastern counties. I had chosen it deliberately, needing to think, and not wanting, however remote the chance, to meet anyone I knew from my own part of the world, who might wish to engage me in conversation.

I managed to secure the end of a high-backed bench, where a party of carriers from the fens were renewing acquaintance with much good-humoured chaff, brimming mazers and plates of steaming mutton broth. They had no interest in anyone but themselves, and once I was able to shut my ears to their talk – not difficult considering the thickness of their speech – I focused my thoughts on the events of the previous hour, and more especially on Ginèvre Napier's final disclosure.

'Eudo Colet,' she had told me, 'has the gift of being able to speak without moving his lips. And when I say "speak" I mean with clarity, not in the imperfect, muffled way that you or I might, if we tried to do the same. I have seen him, at the fairground, invite an onlooker to stand at his side and make it sound exactly as though that person were talking. I watched him perform this trick many times during the three days that Rosamund and I visited St Bartholomew's fair; for she was so infatuated, from the very first moment of clapping eyes on Eudo, that we returned again and again to gawp amongst the crowds around the mummers' pitch. Until I tired, that is, and grew bored and went off to view the rest of the sights.'

'I have myself seen this sort of trick performed,' I said, 'but not, I fancy, with such skill as you describe.'

'Wait!' Ginèvre had raised one pale hand, its tracery of knotted veins showing up cruelly in the pallid sunlight. 'There's more. Eudo could also mimic other people's voices. In fact, if you closed your eyes and listened, you could imagine him to be an old man or even an old woman, a crying baby or a young child. It was remarkable – and frightening.'

'A child,' I said, and the roof of my mouth felt dry with excitement. 'You say he could mimic a young child?'

'I tell you, he was able to copy anyone.' Ginèvre brought her hand down hard on the table-top, her many rings making a dull thud as they struck the wood. 'But neither was that the greatest of his talents.' She had reached out and laid her hand on mine, although I do not think, on this occasion, she was altogether aware of what she was doing. 'He could make his voice sound as though it were coming from a distance. Once, during the months he stayed here, while Rosamund did her best to turn him into a gentleman – an impossible task, as we have both agreed – I was in this room with him, when I heard my husband speak, behind me. I whirled about, expecting to see Gregory at my shoulder, but he wasn't there.

And when I turned back to Eudo Colet, he was laughing. I was so furious, he never practised the trick on me again, in spite of Rosamund encouraging him to do so. She thought it amusing and very clever, until I warned her that if Eudo fooled people in such a manner when she was home, in Devon, his fairground origins might soon be guessed at. I think the force of this argument must have struck her, for after that, Eudo ceased to exercise his peculiar talents. But take it from me, chapman! I have never met anyone, either before or since, who possessed one tithe of his ability. A gift from God – or from the Devil!'

Her words were still ringing in my ears as I sipped my ale. The mutton broth smelled good, but for once in my life, I wasn't hungry, in spite of not having eaten for many hours. I was too excited, and needed to make sense of what I had learned. First and foremost, I now knew, beyond all doubt, that the childish voice which had lured me from my bed, belonged not to the earth-bound spirit of either Andrew or Mary Skelton, but to Eudo Colet. Secondly, that being the case, his knowledge of the damage to his property stemmed from that night, and not from anything he might have seen on a later occasion. And that, in its turn, led me to the conclusion that I was mistaken in believing he had paid Grizelda a visit the night of the second murder. Eudo could have spied Martin Fletcher and Luke Hollis anywhere within the walls of Totnes, or indeed outside them, without our noticing him. I had imagined the shadowy figure in the passageway, behind Grizelda. It had been a trick of the darkness. She had not deceived me into thinking that she was there alone.

I heaved a great sight of relief, and found that my hand was trembling so much I was in danger of spilling my ale.

Carefully replacing the beaker on the table, I leaned back in my corner and closed my eyes for a moment, overcome by the realization that my feelings for her ran deeper than I had so far admitted to myself. She held a fascination, an attraction for me which, if it was not yet strong enough to be called love, was nevertheless something closely akin. It was difficult to say exactly where the enchantment lay, for I had met many younger and more beautiful women without succumbing to their charms; although, if I were honest with myself, I knew that I was susceptible to sudden infatuations, quite often for women who felt nothing in return for me.

I opened my eyes again, drank some more ale and considered how Ginèvre Napier's disclosures weighted the evidence in favour of Eudo Colet's guilt concerning the killing of his stepchildren. But as the afternoon waxed and waned, as my table companions paid their shot and left, to be replaced by yet a second gathering of carters, this time from around Norwich, I was still left with the same dilemma which had dogged me from the outset of this case.

My newfound knowledge concerning Eudo made it possible to believe that he himself had killed the children sometime between Grizelda's departure and his visit to Thomas Cozin. Casting my mind back as well as I could, I felt sure that neither Bridget Praule nor Agatha Tenter actually claimed to have seen Mary or Andrew Skelton during that time, but had only heard their voices from the upper floor. Eudo playing his tricks! Even when he had stood at the foot of the stairs and shouted up to them, 'God be with you,' and Mary had been heard to answer, 'And with you, too!' it could have been nothing but an illusion that the child was still alive. A clever man. A very clever man, who had used his talents for his own evil ends. And yet ... When he returned to the house, it was Bridget who had been sent to look for the children and summon them to his presence, but, according to her, they could not be found. Alive or dead, they had vanished.

It was a warm night, the April air untouched by chill, the sky soft, deep, and luminous, lit by a thousand twinkling stars, and I slept snugly enough in the hayloft of a barn on the outskirts of Paddington village. My appetite had sufficiently recovered, before I left Blossom's Inn, for me to consume two steaming platefuls of their mutton broth, together with the heel of a loaf and another generous stoup of ale. By the time I awoke the following morning, I was thoroughly refreshed and determined to return to Totnes as soon as possible. I washed and shaved in the stream which watered the surrounding meadows, begged some bread and cheese from the farmer's wife, in exchange for a pack of needles, and set off along the dusty highway which led westwards, trusting that, before long, I should fall in with a carter travelling in the same direction.

Once again, my luck held; and in spite of two days when I had only my legs to carry me, less than a week later I found myself approaching Exeter. The carter who had let me ride in the back of his wagon for the past two days, was anxious to be home and had therefore kept up a good pace, with small regard for the bumps and other obstacles of the road, not caring to talk or to stop more than was necessary; with the result that on Friday afternoon, he drew up close to St Catherine's Chapel and the adjacent almshouses, with an hour or so to spare before Compline. As I slid from the back of the cart, from between the bales of linen destined for a local mercer, I thanked him and asked if he knew where the lawyer, Oliver Cozin, dwelt. The man nodded dourly.

'Oh, aye,' he said, 'there's few that don't know Master Cozin in this city.' He eyed me sharply. 'Why would the likes of you wish to speak to a lawyer? Not in trouble with the law, are you?'

I hastened to reassure him that his wagon had not been harbouring a wanted criminal, and was directed to a handsome, half-timbered house near to the West Gate, in Stepcote Hill. My knock was answered by a thin, hawk-like woman, who was plainly the housekeeper, and who would have sent me about my business had I not had the foresight to put my foot between the door and its jamb as soon as it was opened.

'If you will but mention to your master that Roger the chapman desires a word with him, I feel certain that he will see me,' I wheedled. I smiled at her, hopefully.

'Lawyer Cozin's at supper,' she retorted, but I could tell that she was beginning to waver. I smiled again. 'Oh, very well!' she snapped. 'Wait there. But you're not to cross the threshold until I return.'

I gave my word, and she disappeared through a door to her left. I heard the low murmur of voices, followed by an exclamation of annoyance, then a testy, 'What brings him here?' But a moment later, the woman reappeared and gave a jerk of her head.

'In there. The master will see you, but you're to be quick. He's an engagement before curfew in another part of the town.'

I nodded submissively and entered the lawyer's diningparlour where the remains of his supper stood on the long, oaken table. It was a room boasting few concessions to comfort, except for one or two faded tapestries on the walls and a single armchair. It was a room typical of its owner, and just how I had imagined the home of Oliver Cozin would be.

'Well?' he demanded abruptly, and without formal greeting. 'What do you want, chapman? When did you leave Totnes?'

'A fortnight since,' I answered, easing my pack from my shoulders and placing it on the floor. 'A day or so before Your Honour was due to return home to Exeter. In the meantime, I have been to London and back.'

'London, eh?' He raised his eyebrows, his attention quickening a little. 'I assume that fact has some significance, or you would otherwise not have mentioned it. Therefore, enlighten me. I haven't all night to spare.'

So I told him all that I had discovered from Ginèvre Napier, the reasoning which had led me to seek her out in the first place and the conclusions I had drawn from what I had learned. Master Cozin heard me out in complete, but attentive, silence, a frown creasing his brow as I talked, and growing deeper by the minute. When, at last, I had finished, he said nothing for a while, staring at the table and gnawing his lower lip. Finally, however, he raised his head and looked at me.

'So!' he said. 'You have been able to discover Master Colet's origins where my brother, Thomas, failed. Understandably, I suppose, when one considers the source of the information. This Mistress Napier, judging by your description of her, is the kind of woman who could be persuaded to part with secrets by a good-looking youth, where an older man would be spurned.'

Somewhat to my surprise, I found myself warmly defending Ginèvre.

'Pardon me, sir, but I think you do the lady an injustice. Firstly, Master Thomas did not go to London himself, but sent a servant to do his business for him. Secondly, Rosamund Colet is now dead, and can no longer be hurt by her secret becoming generally known. But more than that, her two children have been murdered. No friend worth her salt would keep quiet in such circumstances, not if she thought her knowledge could perhaps aid the truth.'

'But does it?' The lawyer drummed his fingers irritably on the table-top, fixing me with an accusing stare. 'I grant you *may* have proved that Master Colet *could* have murdered his stepchildren, and then disguised the fact by imitating their voices as though they were still upstairs. Furthermore, I accept your argument that neither Andrew nor Mary Skelton went down to breakfast; that neither was actually seen by either Bridget Praule or Agatha Tenter between the time they arose and the time they disappeared. But you still have not proved to my satisfaction how Master Colet was able to remove the bodies from the house.'

'He must have done it somehow,' I pleaded desperately. 'Their deaths would make him even richer than he was already. And surely, sir, you must agree that he also had a sounder reason than the outlaws to kill both Martin Fletcher and Luke Hollis, before they recognized him and gave away his secret.'

'Ye-es.' Oliver Cozin pursed his lips. 'Of course, you will not be aware that the outlaws were smoked out of their lair three days after the Sheriff's arrival, and are now securely under lock and key in the county gaol here, awaiting trial. Nor will you know that amongst the crimes for which they have vigorously denied responsibility, are the murder of your mummer friends and the Skelton children.'

'There you are then!' I exclaimed excitedly. 'It *must* have been Eudo Colet, the one person in each case who had something to gain by the murders.'

The lawyer heaved himself to his feet.

'Then prove to me how he removed the children's bodies from that house to the banks of the Harbourne! For he certainly had no opportunity before he left to visit my brother, and none, either, after he returned. Dead bodies weigh heavily, Master Chapman, even children's; and from the time that Bridget found them missing, Master Colet remained, or so I understand, within sight not only of her and Agatha Tenter, but of everyone else called in to aid in the search.'

My elation died and I suddenly felt very tired. Defeat stared me in the face. Yet there had to be an answer! I could no longer believe Eudo Colet innocent of the crimes. Somehow or another, he had had a hand in his stepchildren's deaths. Master Cozin must have thought so too, for, to my astonishment, he came round the table, pushed me down on to a stool and poured me a cup of wine.

'Here, drink this,' he said. He went to the parlour door and called his housekeeper, instructing her, when she came, to fetch me some food. 'And make the chapman a bed for the night by the kitchen fire. After that, send Tom to the livery stable and say I shall need my wagon and horses soon after breakfast tomorrow.' When the surprised and curious house-keeper had departed to do his bidding, the lawyer turned back to me. 'I shall come with you,' he said, 'back to Totnes.' He added, as one granting an unheard-of concession, 'You may ride with me, in my carriage.'

The painted wagon, with its seats upholstered in dark red velvet and its side-curtains of matching leather was one of the finest equipages I had seen; astonishing it should be that of a lawyer, a profession which, pleading constant poverty, normally travels, then as now, on horseback.

Both Oliver Cozin and his brother, beneath their crusty exteriors, were warmer-hearted men than Oliver, at least, cared to be thought, except, perhaps, by members of his family. I could imagine no other man of his standing giving a common pedlar a place in his carriage, nor permitting me to sit at his table in the roadside tavern where we stopped to eat dinner. He did, of course, insist that I left my pack and cudgel inside the wagon, and frowned a little over my threadbare attire, but otherwise offered no indication that I was an embarrassment to him.

During the first part of our journey, he made me repeat all that I had learned from Ginèvre Napier, nodding at some parts of the narration, shaking his head dubiously over others, but making no comment that was worth the having, other than, when at last I had finished, 'There is still the matter of the disposal of the children's bodies.' After a moment's silence, he added, 'If we cannot prove Eudo Colet guilty of the children's murder, I doubt we shall prove him guilty of the mummers', for I know that the lord Sheriff, like everyone else, is ill-disposed to believe the outlaws' protestations of innocence on that head.' He gave a barely perceptible smile. 'No one will be anxious to accuse a seemingly honest citizen when there is a bunch of rogues at hand on whom to pin the blame.'

I began to feel almost an affection for Master Cozin, an emotion I would previously have deemed it impossible for a lawyer to excite. Most of his breed would have been very reluctant to believe ill of a man who was their client, and one, moreover, who was a source of wealth, particularly when the accusations came from so lowly a person as myself. But Oliver Cozin, I realized, was that rare thing, a lawyer who loved justice for its own sake.

After we had dined, and the sun was climbing slowly towards its zenith, the warmth increasing as midday approached, our conversation dwindled and sleep overtook us both. Master Cozin's man, Tom, who had made it plain, to me at least, that he resented my presence in the carriage, vented his annoyance by jolting us over every bump and irregularity of the road's surface that he could find, without laying himself open to his master's reproaches. In spite of this, however, the lawyer and I, each in our own corner of the velvet-covered bench, began to doze, Master Cozin rather more quickly than I; for by the time I finally lapsed into unconsciousness, the carriage was filled with the sound of his gentle snoring.

I would have sworn that my mind was too preoccupied with the murders of Andrew and Mary Skelton, and the mysterious means by which their bodies had been disposed of, for me to sleep. But I had reckoned without the effects of a good dinner, which, together with the motion of the carriage, however erratic, lulled me like a baby in its mother's arms. It was not, however, a peaceful slumber: the lentil stew, followed by pike in galentyne sauce and then honey cakes with pine nuts, lay heavily on my stomach. I began to dream . . .

I was in woods of intense and pillared blackness, being lured forward by the singing of a child. Sometimes the voice was close to me and sometimes farther off, but always in the distance, the singer unseen. The roots of trees snaked across my path and I often stumbled, scratching my hands and grazing my knees, until suddenly, the track, absurdly, gave way beneath me, just as the gallery had done, and I began to fall . . .

I came to my senses literally with a jolt, as the carriage traversed a series of bumps worse than anything we had so far encountered. I could hear Tom whistling to himself as he drove the poor horses forward with a sting of the whip. I glanced at Oliver Cozin, but he still slept on, blissfully unaware of his man's disapproval. I settled myself again in my corner and stared out at the passing countryside, the leather curtains having been drawn back to give us more air. It would soon be May Day, and the young, green leaves of early summer bedecked the trees. Deep pink flowers of campion starred the tall grasses.

I thought of the night that I had heard the singing; how at times it had seemed to be close at hand, at others far away. I shivered. Eudo Colet must have been as near to me in the darkness as I was now to Master Cozin, yet always keeping just sufficiently ahead to be out of sight. He had stolen out of Thomas Cozin's house without disturbing the inmates, leaving the door unlocked against his return. Then he let himself into his own house, probably into the outer courtyard, made his way through the kitchen to the inner one, where he loosened, with knife and saw, the middle strut of the gallery. Returning to the kitchen, he climbed to the lofts and tiptoed gently across the walkway, no doubt taking great care not to tread too heavily on the weakened centre. He had then entered the bedchamber, traversed the landing and let himself into the upstairs parlour, where he could see me asleep, below. Using his talent for mimicry, he had begun to sing . . .

Yet again, I shivered. He had enticed me forward as he retraced his footsteps, at times falling silent, in order to rest his throat. Once he knew me awake and following, he must have retreated across the gallery, giving himself time to step with caution, and leaving the far door open to attract my attention. The rest had fallen out exactly as he had trusted it might – with the exception that my midnight experiences had not quenched my burning desire to get at the truth. Eudo Colet had not rid himself, as he had hoped, of my inquiring presence.

I must have dozed again, without even being aware of that moment when I crossed the borderline of sleep. For suddenly, although I was still jolting along rough roads, I was sitting beside Jack Carter in the front of his wagon. He was talking to me; I knew because I could see his lips moving, but most of what he was saying, I was unable to hear. It was just a jumble of low-pitched sound. Only now and then, did any words make sense.

'She was pushed . . . she was pushed . . . she was pushed . . .' 'The same cloak, the same dress, year in, year out . . .' 'Pride and the ability to mask her true feelings . . .'

Then, in the unpredictable manner of dreams, Jack Carter and I were no longer in the wagon, but sitting at a table in Matt's tavern. I could sense that he was about to tell me something of great importance; something which would unlock the key to this mystery of the Skelton children and how their bodies were removed from Eudo Colet's house. He opened his lips to speak, but as he did so, his face seemed to melt and reform, becoming that of Innes Woodsman. He leaned forward until his face was close to mine, and shouted, 'You leave 'er be.'

I was wide awake, to find Master Cozin regarding me with concern.

'You cried out in your sleep,' he said. 'I couldn't quite make out what you were saying, but you seemed to be disturbed. You're very pale. Are you feeling unwell?'

I shook my head. 'No, not unwell. Just sick that I have allowed myself to be so blind and foolish.' I slewed round on the seat to face him. 'For I know now how the bodies were removed from the house, to be found, weeks later, on the banks of the Harbourne.'

Chapter Twenty

'You!' Grizelda exclaimed, staring at me in astonishment. 'I thought you'd left Totnes.'

She had taken a minute or two to answer the door, and I had begun to fear that she had gone from the old Crouchback house near the West Gate. I had redoubled my knocking and also shouted her name.

'Fate brought me back this way again,' I replied, 'and I had to see you once more before taking my final farewell. At our last meeting there were many things left unspoken between us. Won't you invite me in?'

She hesitated, then shrugged and stood aside to let me enter.

'I'm in the kitchen,' she said, 'preparing my supper. You can come and watch me if you wish. Whatever you have to say can be heard as well there, I imagine, as anywhere else.'

I offered to bolt the door behind us, then followed her along the passage and across the inner courtyard to the kitchen, where the appetizing smell of rabbit stew made my mouth water. Grizelda went over to the table and continued chopping herbs, an occupation I had obviously interrupted.

'Well?' she asked discouragingly. 'What is it?' She eyed me sharply. 'What have you done with your pack?'

'I left it where I'm lodging for the night.' I had no wish to tell her that this was with Master Thomas Cozin, a circumstance demanding explanation, so I hurried on. 'I confess I'm somewhat surprised to find you still here. I thought Master Colet might have turned you out by now.'

Grizelda finished her chopping and wiped the knife clean on a piece of cloth. Then she tipped the herbs into the iron pot hanging over the fire before replying.

'Master Colet and I,' she said, carefully avoiding my eyes, 'have come to an understanding. I have acknowledged that I did him a grave injustice when I accused him of being a party to the children's disappearance and subsequent murder, and he' – she took a deep breath – 'has been gracious enough to accept that I might have had good reason for my suspicions. We have, in short, made up our differences.' She returned to the table and began to knead a mound of dough, which was resting on a marble slab. And still she did not look at me. 'But I shall,' she continued, 'be leaving this house very shortly. Master Colet has asked me to be his housekeeper in his new home.' Here, she gave me a brief glance from beneath her lashes, before lowering her eyes once again. 'Don't judge me too harshly, Roger. I am sincere when I say that I no longer think him guilty of having had any hand in Mary and Andrew's deaths. And as for the other, what else am I to do? I need a roof over my head and money in my purse quickly, before he finds either a tenant or a purchaser for this house. And it could be many months, if at all, before I find such employment elsewhere.' Her voice softened. 'Tell me you understand.'

I was leaning against the wall, just inside the door, one foot hooked behind my other ankle, and there was a pause while I shifted my weight to my opposite leg.

'Is it important that I should think well of you?' I inquired eventually. 'Do you care?'

Now she smiled directly at me. 'Yes, I *do* care. Don't ask me why, for I don't know myself. But your good opinion matters to me.'

Again, I did not answer immediately. Instead, I stared thoughtfully at her; at the strong hands which continued their kneading, at the strong forearms, revealed by the rolled-up sleeves of her shabby blue gown, at the strong, dark features with the faint white scar running from eyebrow to cheek. Strength, I realized now, was the one word which best summed up Grizelda Harbourne; strength of body and also strength of will. I recalled her self-proclaimed ability to haul heavy buckets of water up the steep banks of the river to her cottage. I remembered Jack Carter's description of her as a woman who had shown fortitude in the face of an adversity which had dogged her all her life; a woman who did not waste time and energy bemoaning her fate, but who bided her time and who, I believed, had seized her opportunity when it was finally offered to her in the shape of Eudo Colet. A woman who allowed neither the natural ties of affection nor the milk of human kindness nor Christian teaching to stand in the way of what she wanted. An evil woman, Innes Woodsman had called her. And it was for that, and for what else he had known, that he had been burned alive ...

'I hear the outlaws have been taken,' I said, breaking my silence, 'but that they deny the murder of Andrew and Mary Skelton.'

Grizelda snorted. 'So I, too, have been told. That and the death of the mummers. The two most heinous crimes they have been charged with and which have people baying for their blood.'

I said, giving careful weight to my words, 'I have discovered that Martin Fletcher and Luke Hollis were not mummers, but *jongleurs*. As well as playing instruments, they also sang. At least, one of their number, a former member of their troupe, who left them some years ago, did so. And very sweetly, if the porter of this town's East Gate is to be believed.'

Grizelda paused in her kneading and glanced up in perplexity.

'You twist and turn too much for me, Roger. I've lost the thread of your discourse. What has one of the Totnes gatekeepers to do with these mummers? And with one in particular, who, you say, left the company some time since.'

'*Jongleurs*,' I insisted for a second time. 'The porter knows this man, and has supped with him, on occasions, at Matt's tavern, in the Foregate. A man who also has a very special talent' – I recollected Ginèvre's words and added – 'either from God or from the Devil.'

There was a moment's utter stillness. The evening shadows lengthened across the inner courtyard and crept in through the kitchen doorway. Grizelda seemed briefly turned to stone, like someone who had looked upon the head of Medusa. Then, with a little laugh, she once more resumed her kneading.

'You mean that this man – this mummer or *jongleur*, whatever you choose to call him – has settled here, in Totnes?' She sounded incredulous.

I nodded. 'I do. And I note that you do not ask the nature of his peculiar talent. But then perhaps you already know it.' I raised my eyebrows in inquiry, but Grizelda did not answer. I went on, 'This man has the strange gift of being able to speak without moving his lips. Not only that, but he can also make his voice sound as though it is coming from some way off; from the mouth of another person; from above, below, beside or behind him. I saw this art practised once, when I was a child, in the market place in Wells, and I have never forgotten it. It was like magic; although that man's skill was not so great I fancy as that of Eudo Colet, who can also mimic other people's voices.'

Once again, there was complete silence in the kitchen, except for the bubbling of the stew in the pot. Grizelda reached for the cloth and wiped her hands, carefully peeling the clinging dough from between her fingers. At last, she asked in an expressionless voice, 'Are you saying that Eudo Colet is this man?'

'Yes. And you see what this means.' She did not answer, but looked at me with eyes as flat and opaque as pebbles. 'It means that he could well have murdered both Andrew and Mary Skelton before he left the house to visit Master Thomas Cozin. The children's voices which Bridget Praule and Agatha Tenter heard belonged to *him*. Even when, according to Bridget, Eudo Colet stood at the foot of the stairs and called up to them, and Mary answered, it was all illusion. Mary was dead by then, and so was her brother.'

Grizelda continued to stare at me as though she were in a trance, then, with a sudden movement which made me jump, hunched her shoulders.

'You seem very well informed,' she snapped. 'Who told you all this?'

'I've been to London and back during the past two weeks. I went to see Mistress Napier.'

'Ah! Ginèvre!' Grizelda's eyes went blank again, making it impossible to tell what she was thinking. After a moment, however, she said, 'But when Eudo Colet returned from

271

Master Cozin's, the children had vanished. How did he dispose of their bodies?'

I drew myself away from the wall and stood upright, easing my shoulders.

'On the face of it,' I acknowledged, 'that appears to be a difficulty not easily resolved.' I walked towards the table and, leaning across it, plucked at Grizelda's sleeve. 'This blue gown,' I said 'is very well-worn. I've never seen you wear another, not even for the hocking. Jack Carter, who let me ride in his wagon as far as Exeter, told me that you had never had many clothes; that you were treated scurvily by your cousin, who rarely gave you any of her cast-off gowns.'

'So?' The colour flared in Grizelda's cheeks. I had touched her pride; the pride which had so often been ripped to tatters by her treatment in the Crouchback household. 'Finery has never meant much to me. I was content with the little I had.'

'Yet when you quit this house, you left two gowns behind, in that chest in the room that you shared with the children. Don't deny it, because I saw them.'

'Poking and prying, were you? That appears to be one of your less pleasant habits.' The dark eyes had lost their blank look and burned with anger, but almost immediately their fire was dimmed, as Grizelda took herself once more in hand. 'I was very upset that morning, after my quarrel with Master Colet. It was hardly surprising that I failed to take everything with me. By the time I discovered my omission, it was too late, and I was not going to go cap in hand to Eudo Colet and ask his permission to retrieve them. Well? Are you satisfied?'

Slowly, I shook my head. I leaned forward once more, the palms of my hands pressed against the top of the table.

'Then why,' I demanded, 'if you had so few garments, and if two of those had been left behind, was your box so heavy?

Why was Jack Carter, having dragged it downstairs, forced to call for the stableman to help him load it on to his wagon?' She did not answer my question, but I saw her eyes suddenly dilate with fear. 'I'll tell you why, shall I?' I persisted, leaning even closer, until my face was within an inch of hers. 'Your box was so heavy because it contained the bodies of Andrew and Mary Skelton.'

The rabbit stew, so long untended, bubbled over and quenched the flames of the fire with a boiling hiss, but neither of us heeded the clouds of steam nor the stench of burning meat. I doubt if we even noticed them at the time. It was only afterwards that I was aware of having heard the one and smelled the other.

It seemed an eternity before Grizelda spoke, although I suppose it was no more than moments.

'So!' she said; and, quite unexpectedly, she smiled. 'Now, how have you reached that conclusion, Roger?'

I straightened my back and folded my arms across my chest.

'There is,' I said, 'no other explanation. You didn't hate Eudo Colet, nor he you. From the first moment of seeing each other, you felt a mutual attraction, although I suspect his passion for you was not as great as that of yours for him. He was, after all, quite content with his position as Rosamund's husband. Her determination to marry him must have seemed like the consummation of all his dreams; the very summit of good fortune. He was not anxious to endanger that position by responding too keenly to your advances. Indeed, for his sake, it was better that the two of you should not appear too friendly. More than likely, Rosamund was jealous of him. But he liked women, had a reputation for it, and in secret, your friendship blossomed. He confided to you the history of his life before he met your cousin; and no doubt, he also entertained you with examples of his strange, but fascinating talent.'

A tic appeared in one side of Grizelda's face, the side where she had the scar.

'Go on,' she ordered.

'You hated your cousin,' I said. 'Perhaps not without good reason. She and Sir Jasper treated you from the beginning like a servant. You were their kinswoman, of their blood, but in their eyes, your poverty outweighed any such consideration. Your pride, however, would not let you complain. You could not admit your grievances to the outside world, so you pretended that all was well; that Rosamund and you were as close as sisters. Even when she deliberately pushed you out of a tree and your face was scarred for life, you told everyone it was an accident and that you fell. Am I not right?'

Grizelda reached for a stool and sat down before replying.

'Maybe. Maybe not. Go on, tell me more. Tell me about my part in the children's murder.'

I took a deep breath. 'Eudo Colet is a weak man, easily influenced for good or ill by minds stronger than his own. It was his misfortune that fate cast him in the path of a woman with a bent for evil, and whose resentment of her cousin and her cousin's children had turned, over the years, first to dislike and then to loathing. You. For I would be prepared to wager that Andrew and Mary Skelton, like most children, were influenced by their mother and aped her treatment of you. Moreover, they were children who had learned early to dissemble their true nature in front of adults, and who were not the saintly little beings – two little holy innocents as Mistress Cozin once described them to me – that older people thought them.'

Grizelda curled her lip and suddenly spat among the rushes. But, 'Go on,' she said once more.

I did so.

'To repeat myself, you fell passionately in love with Eudo Colet, but although he returned your affection, he would not jeopardize his marriage by abandoning Rosamund. Not, I think, that you really desired him to do so, for you wanted your cousin's wealth as well as her husband, and in order for that to happen, Eudo must inherit after her death. No doubt your fertile imagination was already busy with plans of murder, when fate stepped in and relieved you of the necessity. Rosamund died giving birth to Eudo Colet's child. Now all both of you had to do was wait until a respectable time had elapsed. But then you, or perhaps he, realized that you could be even richer if her children were to die. By the terms of Sir Henry Skelton's will, which you knew well, Eudo, as Rosamund's next of kin, would also inherit the money left to them by their father. Plainly they had to be disposed of, but in such circumstances that neither you nor he would be implicated. A difficult task, considering that Eudo was the one person who benefited by their deaths.'

Grizelda smiled a slow, secret smile. 'So?' she persisted, after a moment.

'So, you – and I have little doubt from which of you two the idea originally came – suddenly saw how his strange, fairground talent could be put to good use. You formed a plan; a plan which most likely owed its conception to the sudden presence of outlaws in the district. But first, during the two months following Rosamund's death, you carefully fostered the idea of two people growing daily more at odds with one another. For the benefit of Agatha Tenter and Bridget Praule, you quarrelled unceasingly over the children and the running of the household. The pair of you had never admitted to the liking you felt for one another; a precaution necessary, doubtless, for you to keep your place in your cousin's house, and which now stood you in excellent stead.'

'You seem to know everything, chapman,' Grizelda remarked with composure. 'But I interrupt. Pray continue.'

'The morning of the murders, you went to church. Shortly before he knew you due to return, Eudo picked a violent quarrel with Andrew and Mary; a quarrel which was still in progress as you crossed the threshold. As arranged, you rushed upstairs, leaving Agatha and Bridget cowering down below. The shouting persisted, but now it was between you and Master Colet. Bridget recalls that you called him a wicked, hard-hearted man to bedevil two innocent children so. He replied that you were a harpy who should be tied to a ducking-stool. So it proceeded.' I caught and held her eyes, refusing to let her glance escape mine. 'And it was during that time, that noisy quarrel, that you murdered those two children. I believe that you strangled them. You dared not risk blood, so no knife could be used. To suffocate them might take too long and be unsuccessful. But a ligature or hands around the neck of unsuspecting persons could not fail, particularly if those persons were smaller and more fragile than their attackers. The bodies were loaded into your travelling box, leaving little room for anything else. After that, you ordered Bridget to summon Jack Carter. You were leaving, you said, going home to your holding above Bow Creek.'

'And how did I dispose of the bodies?' Grizelda wanted to know.

'You're a very strong woman. At some time during the following weeks, you carried the bodies, by stages and probably at night, down through the woods and some miles along the river bank, where you left them to be discovered by a passing stranger or a woodsman. But first, you mutilated them in order to conceal the marks of strangulation. You were, however, seen at some time or another by a man who had a grudge against you; a man who had been dispossessed of the roof over his head by your sudden return to your cottage. It was when Innes Woodsman called you an evil woman that you began to see him as a possible danger. Once again, you used the depradations of the outlaws, and the fact that they had robbed your own holding, as a cover for your murderous intent. You let Innes Woodsman use your cottage, telling him that you were sleeping with your friends in the village. You probably left him some of your potent ale, knowing that he would drink himself into a stupor. And while he slept, you set fire to the cottage with him inside it.'

I waited for an expression of guilt or a denial, but Grizelda merely shrugged. 'I'm still listening,' was all she said.

'Very well, but my tale is almost at an end. I've digressed. I'll return to the morning of the murder. When you had departed with Jack Carter and your box – your heavy box containing the children's bodies – Eudo had to play his part. He had to go downstairs and break his fast, while all the while pretending that Mary and her brother were alive and well upstairs. Bridget Praule made no mention of hearing them during the meal, but when Master Colet went to fetch his cloak and hat, he was once more able to mimic Andrew's voice and carry on a "conversation" with him. He banged and rattled the bedchamber door to make it appear that his stepson was still in a temper. And, as I have said before, when he returned downstairs, Eudo Colet once again exercised his peculiar gift to persuade his listeners that Mary spoke to him. He then departed for Thomas Cozin's house, instructing the servants to let the children be, saying that they might be in a better mood by the time he came home again. And when he did so, he sent Bridget to look for them. But of course, they were nowhere to be found.'

Silence descended on the kitchen. The fire was extinguished. The stench of burned meat hung bitter on the air. Then, after a while, Grizelda nodded.

'Yes,' she said slowly. 'Everything happened exactly as you have described it. You're a clever man.'

'But why did you encourage me to inquire into the matter for you?' I asked. 'What did you hope to gain by that?'

She laughed. 'I wanted to scare Eudo into making a push to leave Dame Tenter's cottage. He was too settled there and growing too close to Agatha. I needed to remind him that he was in my hands; that I could stir up trouble for him if I wished. Unfortunately, what I did not foresee was that the fool would try to scare you off with his silly antics.' She spoke with fond contempt. 'Eudo's no judge of character. He couldn't understand, as I did, that trying to frighten you, would only strengthen your determination to get at the truth.' She got up off her stool and shook out her skirts. 'So, now that you, and doubtless others – for I cannot believe you came here without confiding your suspicions to others – know of my complicity in the crime, what is there left for me, if I do not wish to burn at the stake?' Before I realized what she intended to do, she reached out and seized the knife with which she had been chopping the herbs. 'Only death by my own hand. But I don't mean to die alone.'

She came swiftly round the table, the point of the blade turned towards me and pointing straight at my heart. I backed away, not daring to take my eyes from her in order to search for a weapon. I cursed myself for not bringing my cudgel. Once again, she laughed, a high-pitched, mirthless sound.

'You won't escape me, Roger. I'm as strong as you are, and you yourself bolted the outer door.'

'You are mistaken, Mistress Harbourne,' Oliver Cozin said, stepping into the kitchen, a sergeant and two of his men from the castle garrison at his back. The knife fell with a clatter from Grizelda's suddenly nerveless fingers. 'The chapman here only pretended to lock the door. Master Colet is already in custody and has confessed to everything. You stand condemned out of your own mouth. These men and I are witnesses to all that has passed between you and the chapman, for we followed him in and crossed the courtyard while he engaged you in conversation and distracted your attention. We have been standing outside the kitchen door this past half-hour.' He turned to the sergeant. 'Arrest this woman, if so depraved and evil a creature deserves to be called so, and take her away.' Grizelda, white-faced and with staring eyes, was hustled unceremoniously past me as Oliver Cozin held out his hand. 'Master Chapman, the cause of justice owes you a debt which it can never repay. If I can ever do anything for you, you have only to call on me. My name,' he added with simple dignity, 'means something, I flatter myself, both in Devon and beyond. You will not find it unknown, even in London.'

I thanked him, and in answer to his inquiry as to my immediate plans, replied that I was returning to the capital. My conscience told me that I should go to Bristol and see my baby daughter, but it was overpowered by the desire I had to lose myself for a while in London pleasures. I felt strangely sullied by the affection – the more than affection – I had felt for so evil a creature as Grizelda Harbourne, and it frightened me that my judgement could be so led awry. I did not want to be alone too long with my thoughts. I needed distraction, and the sooner the better.

'Your brother has kindly offered me the shelter of his roof for the night,' I told Oliver Cozin, 'but I shall be gone soon after daybreak. For reasons of my own, I shall be glad to leave Totnes.'

And I followed him across the inner courtyard, along the passage, out of the door, and shook the dust of that accursed house from my feet for the very last time.